Red River

By Kelly Van Hull

Edited by Denise Gottshalk

Cover design by Laura Wilson

For Troy,
I couldn't do this without you.

Chapter 1

It's happening. It's really happening. I look down at Brody's neck and the marking almost seems to be pulsating. It's a circle so perfect, it almost looks fake. I touch the pads of my fingers to it, but they're shaking so I snatch them back. How could I have not seen this? I smooth the curls back down, hoping no one has noticed. I can't believe it. How could this be? Everyone has stopped their four-wheelers and they are slowly dismounting, curious.

I can't speak. I feel a stifled panic squeezing my throat, caught between the laryngeal rings. My heart feels like a hummingbird has lodged itself between my right and left ventricle and is trapped, scratching to get out. I force myself to take a deep breath and I look back up at the river.

There's no way around it. It's red. Not only is it swirling in blood curdled waves, dead fish are popping up and staring out with menacing eyes. My worst fears are coming true. If the river is red, it's means Burke is no longer a religious lunatic gone wild on the world. It means he's right. It means the man who is responsible for my brother's death will be vindicated and given even more power now that the waters have turned. It's the first plague in the Bible. And now it's actually happening. How could I have been so foolish to believe that if the plagues weren't in the right order, they weren't really plagues?

My mind is scrambling to put together all of the plagues that have happened. Locusts, check. Rabid animals, check.

Red river, check. If this is true, it means it's only going to get worse. My mind is still racing, trying to figure out the rest of the plagues.

I feel lightheaded and sick. My mouth is starting to water and I try to walk away. I only get about ten feet when the briny yellow bile shoots out of my body. It's instantaneous and when it's over, I feel a split second of relief, even though my teeth now cringe in the acidic aftermath. But then I remember what's happening.

"What's going on?" Bentley asks. His overgrown blonde hair hangs in his inquisitive, green eyes and he tucks it behind his ears. "Are you okay?"

I continue to stare at the river and finally he looks over.

"Holy shit," he whispers.

"Literally. There's no way we can cross that," I say, as I stare, mesmerized by the crimson tides. I'm aware of every breath I take: raspy, foreign even to me. Deep in the distance at the far end of the river, I can barely make out something moving by the riverside. It doesn't look human.

My mom and dad walk up to me and I see the color has drained from Mom's face. Dad keeps his usual calm posture and asks me what I want to do. I find that question almost as startling as the red river. Why is he asking me? He's the adult. He should figure this out. Quiet anger grows inside me. How could he put this on me again? I don't answer.

"Jonah?" My dad asks.

Jonah seems to be in awe as he watches the thick blood travel downstream carrying a carpet of hundreds of dead fish. I find myself looking past the river again, searching for Brody's wolf that has now disappeared. Hungry birds that appear to be vultures lurk above us. Every so often, they dip down into the water and scoop out a floating fish. I've never seen one in real life before, but surely that's what they are.

"We have to find cover, now!" Jonah responds. "Plan still the same?"

"Um . . . yeah, I think so. I don't have a better one. We need to get back to that Tent City of yours. We gotta get out of here, especially now," Dad says.

"Go around?" Jonah glances quickly at his wife, Jessica, as she holds their baby. She's weeping quietly. Clouds roll in and cast a shadow across her face.

"No. We cross," Dad says.

"What? You've got to be kidding," I finally say. "How could we? You can't expect—"

"It's the only way. We're losing time," he shoots back, and then almost scurries to his four-wheeler, eager to continue the journey. He looks back to me, "I'd like to carry the children across in case the wheelers tip. I'll take Bro—"

"I've got him," I say, as my hand instinctively goes out to keep Brody by my side.

"Dani, it'll be fine," Bentley says. "It's only water. Just tell yourself that. It's only water." He tries to convince me as he lightly touches my forearm. I look back down the river to find the moving creature gone.

I consent only because I can see my dad isn't going to budge. I look around at our group and everyone seems to be shell-shocked. We've already been through so much and now this.

"Okay, Brody." I lean down and fasten a handkerchief over his eyes and behind his ears, careful not to reveal his marking. "We are playing another game. While your eyes are covered, I want you to count. See if you can get to a hundred. If you do, start over and do it again." I do the same for Avery. Her grin spreads across her face as I tie the cloth and she's already counting.

How can we expect five-year-olds to comprehend this? It feels kind of stupid to cover their eyes when they have already seen the full spectacle, but any kind of distraction feels better than nothing.

The river looks to be about the same depth as last time we crossed. Some of us are driving the wheelers over the scarlet water and some of us are walking. I carry Brody and Callie carries Avery.

The most shocking thing about the water besides the smell is the temperature. I fully expected it to feel warm and sticky, but this feels alive. The river's heat crawls up my legs and almost chews to get inside my skin. I try to avoid the fish, but they get caught up in my jeans and between my legs. I want to swat them away, but I can't because Brody has claimed my arms.

The smell is calling up more vomit, but I swallow it down. It smells like dirty carp that get left on the beachy sand to rot, mixed with the metallic scent of blood. I can't get through it fast enough. I'm careful not to let Brody's feet dangle in the blood. He's counted up to 79. I need to move faster.

I look back again. The others are not going through as fast as we are on foot, but the wheelers look steady. I glance back down river to be sure we're alone when I see it again. It's the creature, only there are three of them now, and whatever they are, they're coming our way. I am hustling through the water, careful not to lose my footing while still trying to see what is barreling towards us. It can't be. These things are bears and they're charging at us. They should be slow and lethargic given their size, but they are covering what feels like a quarter mile in seconds. They all keep their heads down as they plow down the river. It feels like they're never going to stop. Riding the bear train. So fast. I'm feeling a combination of fear and awe. It's made me shaky. I squeeze Brody in closer, as if it will keep him safe.

I lose my footing on a sludgy rock pile by the shore and I fall down to my elbows. I try to absorb the blow in my funny bone and shake it like crazy, almost losing my grasp on Brody. For the first time, I realize it's not the victim who the bone was named for; it's for whoever is watching. I look down to Brody and notice the impact of our fall has pushed the blood into his hair and splashed all over my face.

"I'm so sorry, Brody," I choke out as I scramble up as fast as I can. Feeling the blood in my fingers brings a new sensation. It's slimy.

"Bentley!" I shout, just as I finally free myself of the river. I'm relieved to be safely out, but the others are not.

My voice seems to bring the bears to a stop. One of them, the largest, stands on its hind legs and sniffs the air before letting out a deafening roar. This buys a few seconds. It's almost as if he is demonstrating his size, protecting his turf.

Bentley finally sees what I see and doesn't hesitate. His face focuses and he speeds his wheeler through the river, kicking up blood on those around him. My dad shoots a glare at him as he wipes blood from his mouth, but stops dead cold when he sees what's coming our way.

Bentley doesn't waste any time. He gets out his shotgun and fires a warning shot into the air. I help Callie and Avery out of the water and I think about running to the forest, but I don't know what's out there so I line us up behind Bentley.

The bears pause, but don't look nervous—not that I know what nervous bears look like. The biggest bear that is the closest to us looks around before licking his lips and some of the blood from his fur. Gross, he's eating the blood. He seems to be contemplating his next move when Bentley fires another shot. This time it's not a warning. The bear is so close that I can see the BBs impact the bear's fur and its entire body recoils in pain. The bear appears to give Bentley a look of "why did you do that?" before he looks back to his friends. He looks to Bentley one last time before he trots away, leaving his own trail of blood.

I lean down to remove Brody's blindfold only to find he has been watching the whole time. He doesn't look frightened, more like amused. He and Avery ask to go play and Mom and I both answer. She looks at me curiously before shrugging it off. Looks like I'm not ready to hand him over yet. He's still mine.

When we're back far enough in the woods not to be seen, I gather leaves to scrape the crud off my body. I've already located another outfit and changed. Most of the grime is off, but there's no removing the smell. It's putrid and provoking my gag reflex.

Everyone is cleaning up and trying to figure out what to do. I can't help but wonder if it's a trap.

"Is it real?" I ask Jonah. He seems to be the one who knows the most about the plagues since he came from the religious compounds.

He's silent for a while before he answers. "I think so. I'm not sure what it all means, but it appears real."

“Could Burke have put the blood in the water himself? He was just here . . . getting Jack.”

“The thought crossed my mind, but I think the time for disbelief is over,” he answers.

“So what does it all mean?” Tears are slipping out of my eyes, but at this point I don’t care. Bentley tries to comfort me, but I shake him off.

“I think that’s something we all have to figure out.” Jonah says as he walks away.

Chapter 2

It took two long days to get back to Sylvan Lake, but I didn't care once I saw blue water instead of red. It could've taken a week and I wouldn't have cared. The entire ride, all I could think about was Sylvan Lake and what I was going to do if it was red. We passed a couple more streams on the way here and they were clear as well.

Everything here is exactly as we left it, and I suppose it should be, as it was less than a week ago we left this place. Bentley thinks there are deserted cabins further up in the Black Hills away from Sylvan Lake. Cabins will be necessary as we are about to head into winter. I still haven't told my parents I plan to leave again as soon as they're settled. Bentley and I occasionally make silent eye contact reaffirming our vow to leave. Imagining facing Burke again gives me butterflies in my stomach, but then again, so does the thought of seeing Jack.

We spend our first night around a fire at Sylvan Lake while Bentley is still out hunting for a cabin. As I set up the kids on sleeping bags inside the tourist shop, I notice the shop is untouched. There are still loads of t-shirts hanging, most stating "I've climbed Harney Peak!" and I take some time to dump all my old clothes that even have one drop of stenchy fish guts and blood and replace them with the cheesy t-shirts. I needed a wardrobe change anyway. I swipe all the children's t-shirts too.

Back in the kitchen area, I find coffee, oysters in a can, and a bunch of SPAM. Since I'm not sure they ever actually served SPAM, it makes me believe that this was a shelter after the locusts. Where are the people now?

Kit and Grant have set up a tent of their own further up into the rolling Black Hills. I take a look around at all the pines and I'm still not used to their massiveness. They are huge and intimidating, but inviting at the same time. But their invitation feels dark, like they want to swallow me up. An icy breeze whistles through the trees sending a chill down my spine. The mood is somber, as even the moon seems depressed tonight. I would like to have Jonah to myself for my questions, but it doesn't look like I'll get that.

I encourage the fire with more twigs and take my seat beside Jonah. Callie is on the other side and my parents sit across from us. Dad is staring in awe at the majesty in the hills that surround us. I try to look to the hills with the same wonderment, but all I can sense is them eavesdropping.

"So . . . what's going to happen?" I ask Jonah.

He stays silent, so I ask again.

"I mean with the plagues . . . what's next?"

"I don't know, Dani. The plagues happen because God's people aren't listening. I imagine it's about time we started."

"What does He want?" I ask back. Everyone else is quiet and listening to our conversation. I hesitate on the word He. It feels like lead on my tongue.

"I know you don't believe all of this," he answers, "but I believe that the Golden Child will tell us."

I stiffen up and nervously glance at the cabin. This confirms that he doesn't know what I know. I can't explain why, but I don't want *anyone* knowing about Brody. It seems ridiculous not to tell my parents, but I'm not sure they would keep it a secret and for now, I know it needs to be.

"So . . . when will the Golden Child be born then?" I ask Jonah.

"Not sure. Burke has been tracking all the new births for a while . . . but if you ask me, I think he's already been born."

My pulse quickens. "Why do you say that?"

"It's time." He drops the subject as he gets up and bids us all goodnight. That's actually what he says, "I bid you good-night," and then finished with a fake tipping of his hat. Everyone is acting so strangely tonight.

Mom and Dad both seem happy and I'm contemplating if I should talk to them about leaving for the capital while Bentley is away, since it's more than likely going to turn into an argument. Callie's still sitting around the campfire and maybe that helps. I haven't talked to her yet, but I assume she's coming with us. That won't be awkward.

"I'm leaving," I blurt out.

Dad focuses his attention on me. "What do ya mean, sweetheart?"

"I'm leaving. As soon as Bentley comes back. We're going to find Jack. Me, Bentley and Callie," I say.

"Count me out," Callie says as she gets up to leave.

"What do you mean? You're not coming?" I ask. This is shocking to me. I assumed she would follow Bentley anywhere.

"Three's a crowd?" She's fidgeting with a stick and poking it around in the fire.

"It's not like that . . . you know that." I say.

"Do I? You guys haven't even acknowledged me all day. How do you think that makes me feel?" Hurt flashes across her face, but then turns to an angry scowl.

"Callie, it's not like that," I repeat. "You have to come."

"Why?"

"Now just hold on a minute," Dad interrupts. "No one's going anywhere. Not when we just got ya back."

I look over at Mom. She looks confused and her eyes are watery again. Will that woman ever stop crying?

"You can't tell me what to do!" I'm standing now, fully indignant.

"Oh yes, I can. I'm still your father." He's standing now too. Callie has quietly slipped away.

"All you have done is send me away and fill me full of lies. Some father you are." Adrenaline is pumping and I think that's why I said it. I mean to sound more grown up, but I just feel young and immature. But I can't help it; I'm burning with anger.

"I've explained all that," he says, a little calmer as he walks towards me. I back up, but I'm ready for a fight, almost welcome it.

"You knew he was murdered and you let me believe it was the flu!" My tears have sprung free and I feel a rush of guilt as I see that my mother is sobbing now too.

"What else could I do?" he asks.

"Tell me the truth. Isn't that what you always tell *me* to do?" I fire back, still seething. I have visions of slapping him across the face and it scares me.

I sit back down in my chair and the full weight of the grief sets in. I have been foolish enough to believe that I'd accepted my brother Drake's death. And maybe I had. Maybe I could have accepted that he got sick and died. But being lied to by my own parents leaves wounds almost as deep as the death itself. How can I ever accept that my brother was murdered? How could I ever move on knowing that the one responsible is alive and still walks around a free man? I've lost myself in my own vengeful thoughts.

"I want to kill him." The thought was in my head, but I realize it slipped out in words.

"Who?" Dad asks.

"Burke," my mother whispers.

I walk away.

Chapter 3

Bentley returns the next morning. His hair is tousled and it appears as if he hasn't slept, but he's more excited than I've ever seen him.

"You're never going to believe what I've found," he says smiling, the grin devouring his face.

I didn't sleep well the night before and I'm irritated at everything. Even seeing Bentley happy doesn't lift the dark cloud that lingers around me and catches me like a disease. It doesn't seem to have caught for everyone else and I watch from the outside as Bentley explains what he's found.

"It's huge and I'm sure it's been abandoned. It's got at least six rooms in it and it will easily hold all of you. There's enough dust to build the Badlands, so it needs some cleaning, but that's a good sign. It looks like no one has touched the place in years," he says, rubbing his hands together for warmth. "And here's the best part . . . the solar start box is still intact."

"You said 'hold all of you'," my dad says to Bentley with a wary glare.

"Well . . . all of us," Bentley stammers.

"She already told us, Bentley. So you can drop the act. Who do you think you are? We just got her back and you want to take off?" Dad has advanced so that he is now face to face with Bentley, noses an inch apart.

"Seems to me she's old enough to make her own decisions . . . no offense," Bentley replies back with an almost smirk on his face and his hands raised as if to say *hey, don't look at me*.

"We're still her parents and we're in charge here."

"Since when?" Bentley challenges back. When I look at Bentley, I feel shame . . . and pride.

"Let's just get settled into this new place," Mom interrupts, "it's freezing and we need to get to a shelter."

"Fine. Whatever," Bentley says as he leaves to go pack. Dad shoots me a look of warning before he does the same.

Everyone is busy packing and I don't have the energy to get up. I'm still thinking about the red river. I'm trying to figure out a way it could be a ploy. If it's not, which plague is next? I'm so lost in thought that I barely notice him.

It's Brody's wolf and I've stopped being startled by it. I see him all the time. I can't believe no one else has noticed. Brody does, of course, but we don't talk about it. The wolf is around so much that I've decided to name it. I've given him the name for what he does best: Waite.

He only lets me look at him for a few seconds, and when he knows I have spotted him, he trots off, and I always wonder if that will be the last time I see him.

It doesn't take long to get to the cabin on the four-wheelers. I find myself curious about how Bentley found the place. It's so hidden in dense woods; it's hard to spot even when coming right on it. The trees seem to have grown over the roof, hugging the cabin in a protective embrace. It does need a lot of work, but I'm glad for the distraction.

We spend the entire day making it livable. I avoid Mom and Dad whenever possible. If they work in the kitchen, I go outside. If they come outside, I go in and clean the bedrooms with Kit.

The cabin is so picturesque it could be taken from a textbook on "How to Build Cabins." The sheer size of it would even impress Paul Bunyan. I walk inside to be met with huge vaulted ceilings with a single hanging chandelier dripping with glass ice droplets. Pictures adorn every wall, each wall featuring a different animal. Already, I'm drawn to the wall with wolves. I avoid the wall of stuffed deer heads, as one of them is frozen in a permanent wink, some kind of sick joke by the taxidermist.

There are six rooms total. The largest one goes to Jonah and Jess's family. The room across from them goes to Mom and Dad. Kit and Grant have claimed a room upstairs. I could sense my mother's disapproval, but she has not forbidden it. Callie and I take the room across from Kit. I don't really care where they put me. I'm not staying. Avery and Brody settle in the room right next to Mom and Dad since it already has bunk beds in it. The last room remains unclaimed, as Bentley states he won't be sticking around. He throws his bag on the couch in the living room.

The cabin is fully stocked with propane for now. Mom starts cooking meat and potatoes and the aroma of the gravy saturates the cabin. My stomach growls in appreciation. The cabin's dining room is enormous and more than accommodates the twelve of us. Callie and my mom have formed some sort of bond. I can see they love to cook together and Callie's already teaching Mom how to cook pancakes over a fire by thickening the batter and placing it in strips on a suspended stick. Mom looks impressed.

Everyone is busy shoveling food into their mouths and not saying much. Brody and Avery giggle at private jokes.

Jess and Jonah's baby, DJ, is gurgling happily. I don't know why, but their joy isn't catching.

"Hello? Earth to Dani? Anyone in there?" I look up to find everyone staring at me. "Everything okay?" Dad asks again.

"What?"

"I asked when are you leaving" Dad replies.

"You're letting me go?" I ask back.

"Do I have a choice?" he asks.

I look over at Bentley who has stopped chewing to watch for my reply.

"I guess you don't . . . I don't know. Bentley?" I ask.

"Couple days," he says with food in his mouth before he realizes we're all watching him. He pauses to swallow and says, "I want to show your dad some hot spots for hunting and I was hoping to get into contact with Randy before we left."

Randy. Will he be the one to save us again? He's the one who made it possible for me and Brody to escape last time. Maybe we don't need him now that my parents are here.

"Have you spoken to him?" I ask.

"No," he replies. "He has been hard to get a hold of. I'm not sure what his position is now. It'd be nice though. Give us more to work with. I'm not even sure how to find Jack."

"I sure would've liked to meet this young man, Jack." My mother says. "He sounds like he must really be something." She winks.

"Mom!" My face is flushing.

"So, I heard about something kind of interesting," Kit says, as she changes the subject. I shoot her a look of appreciation.

"Oh yeah, what's that?" my dad asks. "Pass the bread."

She hands him the bread and says, "Grant was telling me about advancements. Of course, I think it's a bunch of bull, but it is interesting." We all look to Grant, but he keeps his eyes planted on Kit, saving his secret smile only for her.

"Advancements?" Dad asks. Bentley is blushing now.

"It's just a theory," Bentley says.

"Well, I'd love to hear this theory," Dad says.

"It's nothing," Bentley replies, as he gets up and scrapes his pheasant bones into the garbage and leaves the room.

"Callie knows," Kit says, and she is holding back a giggle. She's so annoying sometimes. I consider following Bentley out.

"Well?" Dad asks Callie.

Callie explains the same version she gave to me right before I left the last time. She explains that since the locusts first happened, some people are developing advancements. Sort of like superpowers, but not really. Just enhancements of abilities we already have. I fear she is going to bring me into it as I see she has already explained Jack and Bentley: Jack's ability to heal and Bentley's unusual speed and strength.

"So have you guessed Dani's?" Callie asks Dad with a false smile.

"Dani? My daughter, a superhero?" he asks with amused sarcasm.

"See, now you're mixing the story up, John," she smiles now with warmth. "Not superpowers, just advancements. Dani's isn't obvious, but it's there. I'm certain of it now."

"Why do you say that?" he asks with full attention. He has put down his fork and he is staring at Callie. The whole table is, even Brody and Avery. I imagine Brody finds superheroes worthy of his attention.

"Wasn't it just yesterday you said Dani wasn't going anywhere and now here we are . . . you are practically wishing her well on her way," Callie says as she clears her throat.

"What else was I gonna do?"

"See? That's her advancement. If she wants something, it will happen."

"That's not a superpower," he says back as he suppresses a chuckle.

"If you say so," she replies, and she turns to look at me again, almost challenging me.

I'm about ready to announce how ludicrous it all is when a gunshot booms outside. I knock my chair over as I run to open the front door.

Bentley is standing out front, shotgun still smoking.

"What are you shooting at?" I ask, breathless.

"I thought I saw an animal out there—a coyote, or wolf, or something."

"What are you doing shooting at it! Are you crazy? Did you hit it?"

"Nah, it scattered. Why do you care? It's not the first time I've shot an animal," he says as he secures the safety on the gun and sets it down.

"You can't shoot that one. Don't ask why, but don't shoot that wolf."

"You think it was the same one?"

"What same one?" I never told him the story about the dandelions when Brody and Avery were lost and I found them nestled safely with the wild wolf I've come to know as Waite.

"The 'guardian'," he says with sarcasm.

"That's not what it is . . . just leave it alone will you?" I stalk back inside and slam the door.

Bentley says we'll leave in the morning. I spend the night talking with Kit and packing only what I absolutely need. I'm avoiding Mom because I don't have the energy for her tears . . . or the conscience.

"You seem different," Kit says as I lay on her bed and she inspects her skin, picking at invisible blemishes.

"How so?" I ask, only mildly interested.

"I don't know . . . it's like you're angry ALL the time."

"So what if I am?" I scowl.

"See what I mean?" She turns around and looks at me with her eyebrows raised, her hair now in her hands, at the mercy of her teasing. I don't answer her and she changes the subject.

"So what do you think about all this Golden Child crap?" she asks.

"I don't know. Why?" The image of Brody giggling plays in my head.

"You don't buy any of it do ya, Superwoman?" she asks as she sits down on the bed now, giving up on her current hair project.

"Definitely not about the superpowers, at least the one they think I have anyway . . . but, I'm not sure about the Golden Child. I wish I knew more."

"Yeah, it's weird how Jonah doesn't want to talk about it. I thought that religious freaks were supposed to spread the word."

"He doesn't want to prophesize stuff he doesn't know," I say as I sit up now. I feel a little protective about Jonah, even if he is half crazy.

"Is that a real word?" she scoffs sarcastically.

"Why would you care? You're the queen of making up words." I finally smile back at her.

"Well, Grant says that as soon as Burke finds the Golden Child, he's going to kill it."

"What!" I stand up abruptly and ask again. "What did you say?"

"He's going to kill it."

"It?" I'm annoyed that she's calling my brother "It", but she doesn't know.

"Why would he do that?"

"Who knows? Why does he do anything that he does? Because he can. Probably to make sure he can keep his throne. Why do you . . ."

I don't let her finish. I'm flying out the door to find Bentley. I find him in the living room talking with my dad about how to set some kind of trap.

"Bentley, I need to talk to you."

"What's up?" he says smiling, but stops when he sees the look on my face.

"Privately."

Bentley and I go to the front porch and I ask him what he knows about the Golden Child. He tells me all the stuff I've already been told and I'm impatient for the truth.

"Does he plan to kill the Golden Child?" I finally ask.

"Maybe."

"Why?"

"Isn't it obvious?"

"No, actually it isn't. That's why I'm asking." I'm pissed that he doesn't seem to be alarmed by this. After all, shouldn't he have *some* emotion? It is his dad we are talking about—his dad, killing a child.

"There's really only one reason . . . If there really is a Golden Child, it would expose him for the fraud he is."

Chapter 4

I go back to the room I share with Callie. She's lying on the bed reading one of my books.

"*Into the Wild*," she says, waving the book. "You mind?"

"No, not at all."

"Is it any good?"

"Yeah, it's good. They made a movie out of it, but the book is better. My mom got it for me because the guy spends some time in South Dakota. It's a true story."

"What happened to him?"

"He died."

"Well, that's not a very happy ending."

"No, but it's still good. I like the way he looked at things. He was this rich kid who decided he was done with it all. He gave away all his money and burned what was left in his wallet. Then he hitchhiked all the way to Alaska. He was a free spirit. He just wanted to live off the land."

"So, how did he die?"

"You'll just have to read the book." I smile at her. "So, you're really not going with Bentley?"

"Like I said, three's kind of a crowd. Besides, he's not exactly thrilled with me right now."

"Well, I'm not going either."

"Why?"

"I'm just not. Why's he mad at you anyway?"

"Because I lied to him when I helped you escape to go save your parents."

"He lies all the time," I respond. Surely, he can't be terribly offended by lying.

"He thinks I put your life in danger."

"Knight in shining armor." I can't help but roll my eyes. She almost smiles, but sadness sneaks in.

"Does Bentley know you're not leaving?" she asks. "What about Jack? I thought you two were madly in love?" She smirks and I don't answer. She softens and says, "hey, I was only kidding. Seriously, why aren't you going?"

"I'm just not," I say again, and I leave the room as she picks the book up and continues reading.

I'm not sure what I'm going to tell Bentley, but if Burke's true goal is to kill the Golden Child, I can't go anywhere. I'm wrestling with the idea of telling Mom and Dad about Brody. I really wouldn't even have to say anything. All I would have to do is lift his hair and let the marking that I've come to think of as The Sign do all the talking. Something inside me tells me to be quiet.

I find Bentley outside on the porch sharpening his knife on a small stone.

"Whaz up?" he says as I sit down beside him.

"When are you leaving?"

"What do you mean?"

"For the capital."

"What do you mean, when am *I* leaving? Having cold feet?" He doesn't seem too upset at this point. Swipe, swipe, swipe.

"I can't go."

"Parents?"

"No."

"Then what is it?"

"I don't want to talk about it."

"Are we back to this?" he asks as he stops moving the knife. I want him to keep going. I find the sound of the blade swiping soothing. He tests the blade on his fingernail and then begins again.

"Back to what?" I ask.

"Back to where you shut down," he says as he concentrates on the smooth strokes.

"I'm not shut down. I just can't go. That's all!" I go back inside, but not before slamming the door. That's twice now. What's wrong with me?

I spend the night tossing and turning. I can't imagine anyone is getting any sleep around here. Jess's baby, DJ, has been crying all night. She's walking the halls trying to soothe him, but nothing is helping.

It's finally morning and I drag myself out of bed, led only by the promise of coffee.

"What's wrong with DJ?" I ask Mom.

"He's sick . . . Be nice to have a doctor around," she says as she wipes down the counter. Yeah, it would be.

I don't even bother to drink the coffee and I bound back up the stairs to see Jess on her bed trying to soothe her agitated infant. She looks exhausted. Her hair is unwashed and oily and she has dark circles under her eyes. The room is rank with the smell of dirty diapers and unwashed bodies.

"Let me have him," I say, as I hold out my arms. "You need rest."

"I got him. He's sick and he won't eat. I'm the only one who can feed him," she says as she tries to shove her exposed nipple into his mouth, but he jerks his red face away, almost in disgust. I look away, embarrassed for both me and baby DJ.

"Jess, you need help. I can take him for five minutes so you can get some air."

"Fine, but it won't work. I've tried everything." She hands him over to me and the first thing I notice is that he's burning up.

"Have you given him anything? Medicine?" I ask as I look him over. His body is in a tight ball as he screams. This is truly a miserable child.

"No. I've been praying. God will take care of him."

"Jess," I start, and as I'm rocking him he goes quiet. We both look at him to see why.

"That's not possible," she gasps.

"He needs medicine," I say. "At least Tylenol."

"I can't believe it. He's been crying for ten hours straight and now he's stopped. Unbelievable. Hand him back to me." I do, and the wailing starts again.

"I give up! He hates me," she cries as she hands him back over and flees the room. She runs out the front door. I peek out the window and I see her enter the forest. That should give me some time.

I go to my room and search my bag. I know she said she would leave it up to God, but I need to get some medicine in him before she gets back. I find the children's acetaminophen and fill the dropper half full. After about five minutes, his eyes get droopy and he falls asleep.

I come down to the kitchen and hand DJ to Mom. She takes him to the living room to rock him.

"The whole house is held hostage all night and you couldn't bring yourself to do that earlier?" Callie asks, as she sweeps the kitchen from breakfast's mess.

"What?" I ask.

"You're so dense sometimes. Let me guess, you went up to Jessica's room and I bet you really wanted that baby to stop crying didn't you? Think about it. What were you thinking when you entered the room?" she asks. I don't reply.

"Thought so," she says.

"He just needed a change of scenery." Or maybe some medicine. Not treating a child and leaving it up to God just seems irresponsible.

I search for Bentley and find him sleeping in the empty room on the floor, head propped up on his old army canvas bag. I realize I've never seen him sleep before. When we were in Tent City, he was always on the move, always on a raid, which is why I wanted to talk to him. I turn around to leave when he stirs.

"Hey," he says in a hoarse voice.

"I can come back."

"No. I'm up. What's going on?" he asks, rubbing the sleep from his eyes.

"So are you going or staying?" I ask.

"I don't want to leave you," he says, and then looks to the floor.

"What about Jack?" I feel sick about this. I can still picture his tormented face as he boarded the helicopter with Burke. When Jack left with his psycho dad, I sort of promised myself I would find him since I knew he would do the same for me.

"I don't know. That's why this whole thing sucks. I was sure we were doing the right thing before when I thought you were coming with . . . but now, I just don't know. All I know is that I want to be where you are. Is that so wrong?"

"I know what you guys think. I heard you guys talking back at Tent City." My pulse is racing. I had also promised myself that I wouldn't talk about this. But all of this advancement crap is really starting to irritate me. "I have no special powers. And if I do, well then . . . I release you Bentley. You are free to go."

"That's what you think this is?" He's sitting now, fully awake.

"You can't really believe all that stuff do you? Advancements, persuasion advancement. If you think . . ."

"Come with me," he says, as he's up on his feet and dragging me by the arm.

"Bentley, wait. Let go. What are you doing?"

"Just come with me." I do, feeling as though he's the Pied Piper and feeling distracted by what that makes me.

We spend about an hour getting through the woods until we come to a clearing, which is a gravel road. It winds up a hill to what looks like a house at the top.

"What are we doing?" I finally ask.

"You ready for this?" He smirks.

"Get on with it. I'm kinda over all the mystery."

"Okay, okay. You wait here. Just watch. If I start here, how far do you think it is up this hill?"

"I don't know, maybe a half mile?"

"Good. That's what I thought. How long do you think it will take me to get to the top?"

"At full speed?"

"Yeah," he responds with an impish grin.

"Two minutes minimum."

"That's a good guess. You ready for this?" His energy is so amped up, it's practically vibrating. I look at him expectantly, only mildly curious.

"All right, on your mark, get set, go!"

Okay, here's the weird part. I play it over and over again in my head—over and over to make sure I've seen what I've seen. I'm still confused, so I make him do it again.

It's not humanly possible what he's just done. I'm not exaggerating when I say that he sprinted so fast, he actually looked blurry. He does it a third time before I stop him.

"How is this possible?" I ask.

"I'm not sure."

"When did this happen? That couldn't have taken more than 30 seconds. How is this possible?" I repeat.

"I don't know, but it's pretty rad. Wanna see it again?"

"No. I'm good. Have you told anyone else?" I ask.

"Not yet. I wanted to show you first. Now you try."

"Try what? I can't do that. It's official. You are the fastest and there is no way I'm going to be able to beat that."

"No. That's not what I mean. Let's try yours."

"How?" I ask.

"Come here," he says and I follow him. "See there." He points at a couple of squirrels that are at the top of a tree. "See if you can get them to approach you. Wish for it. Hard."

"Okay." I'm definitely curious now and honestly, a little jealous. If this is what superpowers gives you, then sign me up, but the most I can get out of them is a sideways glance before they scatter away.

"You weren't trying," he says, almost disappointed.

"I swear, I was. I never wished for anything so bad in my life. They just wouldn't come. Face it, I don't have a superpower. But I will say, yours is pretty awesome."

"I am awesome, huh? Could have used that a few months ago though, when we went on all those raids," he says.

"That reminds me of what I wanted to talk to you about."

"Yeah?"

"First off, you hafta swear you won't tell anyone."

"Scouts honor," he says, with his pinky clipped down by his thumb and three fingers raised.

I explain to him what I'm up to, and like I expected, he has no problem with it, not even a little. I think he's relieved to have a little excitement back in his life.

"Where should we start then?" I ask.

He nods up towards the top of the hill. "Why not there?" he asks.

"Which one? The white house, or brown?"

"Brown," he says, as if picking the answer out of thin air.

"It's as good a place as any," I reply, finally feeling the beginnings of a good mood.

He matches me, "wanna race?"

Chapter 5

When we get to the top, there are two houses only about 100 feet apart. It has me wondering if they liked being such close neighbors, or if they were enemies. My imagination has gotten away from me as I imagine them in their end of the world scenario. I picture them holding each other at gunpoint, demanding each other's leftover supplies. More realistic though, they were probably both well stocked. I've come to notice the people of the Black Hills were generally prepared, whether by knowing how to live off the land, or by being great hoarders.

We step to the front of the porch and suddenly I have a very bad feeling. I don't know if it's from the fact that we are raiding, or the smell that seems to be seeping from inside the door that is cracked open. Why would it make me feel better to break in?

"Are you sure about this?" Bentley asks, as he seems to be having the same apprehension I do.

"Why is the door open?" I ask.

"I don't know . . . lucky break?"

"What about the smell? What is that?" My throat catches in fear. I see him instinctively check his back holster for his pistol.

"Might as well find out. Stay behind me."

He opens the door and there's nothing . . . nothing that could have prepared me. I almost yelp out a scream, but I'm paralyzed.

"What's going on here?" I finally whisper. He says nothing.

The entire first floor is devoid of any furniture. The only thing in the oversized living room and dining room is what looks like a stone altar. The walls are covered with red lettering, presumably blood.

THE END IS NEAR SINNERS REPENT THE END IS NEAR SINNERS REPENT

The same two phrases are smeared all over every open wall and even on the wooden floor. There is rotten flesh and flies swarming the meat. It looks to be pieces of a goat or maybe even a cow, as one of the skulls looks too large to be anything smaller. Animal carcasses encased in flies and maggots litter most of the floor, but that's not what has my attention. The altar has something too small on it to be a cow, or even a goat, and my heart is at my throat when I realize what it is. When I form the words in my mind . . . human . . . baby . . . I'm about to vomit, but I keep it down. I have to know what it is.

"We have to leave!" Bentley whisper-shouts, which carries more weight than if he'd yelled out loud. I look over to him and he looks like he might be sick too.

"No, I have to know." I don't know if I'm asking his permission, or convincing myself. I take a few steps forward before my feet have bumped into pieces of what looks like maybe a dog.

"This is crazy," he says a little softer. "They could still be here. We need to get out of here now." He grabs me by the arm but I yank it back and continue.

It only takes another couple of steps and I'm careful where I step now. Flies are buzzing around my face and it occurs to me that they are cased in animal blood as they land on my lips and near my eyes. One tries to lodge itself in my ear. It's almost as if they are attacking me. I swat them as I make my way to the front of the altar.

I can put the questions to rest. It's a dead baby. I see it's a little boy. Most of him is intact, and he looks as if maybe he has been sitting here only a couple of days. Unable to help myself, I reach out to touch his hand and that's when I see it.

On the inside of his forearm is a birthmark. I remember this from something. It was a long time ago, but right now it doesn't feel like it. Mom was teaching me history, and I was bored out of my mind when I found a picture of some other country's past presidents, Russia I think, and he had this same birthmark on his head. Even as a child, I was fascinated that someone with such great power could have such a disfigurement. I admired him. My mom called it a port-wine stain. She said it was a birthmark some babies are born with. This is the same birthmark. Was this why the child was killed? Or was he just another sacrifice? Did they think he was the Golden Child? Who are these people?

I can faintly hear Bentley begging me to leave, but he must have run out of patience because before I know it, he has slung me over his shoulders. He hops around avoiding body parts and we are out the front door. He runs a good twenty feet away from the house before he drops me. I collapse on the ground, stunned.

"That was someone's baby," I say, still in trance. I almost can't believe what I've seen. The only reminder that it was real is the lingering flies that are still swarming around my face.

"We have to get out of here," Bentley pleads. He is standing and pacing, stealing glances towards the front door.

"We're going back in," I say as I stare towards the door, expecting someone's ghost to come out at any minute.

"It's official. You've lost your mind. There's nothing we need in there." He almost laughs in disbelief.

"We're going to bury that little boy," I say, and I expect him to fight me some more about the dangers of going back in, but all he does is nod.

We argue a little about whether to bring him back to have a proper funeral at our cabin with the entire family, but realizing Brody and Avery would be a part of it, we decide to just do it ourselves.

Bentley takes care of the actual grave. I don't see him spooked very often, but he clearly is now. He keeps a safe distance from me when I'm holding the infant. I want to hold the baby every second I can, if only to prove to him someone still cares.

I wrap the baby in my sweatshirt after I clean the blood from his skin. I'm on autopilot. Using the sink inside the house takes all the willpower I have, but I don't want him buried with all the blood on him.

I keep the baby cradled in my arm as I search for some sticks to make a grave marker. I accept that I'm losing my mind as I realize I'm talking to him as we walk around. I tell him about my own little brother, about the beautiful trees and the peaceful resting place we are going to give him. I ask him his name. He doesn't answer, so I scratch "baby boy" on the sticks as he sits in my lap.

"It's ready," Bentley says as he wipes the sweat from his brow. I wait for him to step away as I move forward with the baby and he surprises me by holding his arms out.

I pass him the baby and he clears his throat. "I'm sorry, little guy." He tucks the arms of the shirt around the baby tighter into a proper swaddle and places him in the dirt and that's when the finality of it hits me. I start to sob. Bentley finishes the job and sits down beside me and waits for me to get myself together.

"You ready to go back?" he finally asks.

"We haven't got what we came for. I need that medicine for DJ."

"It can wait. I'm never going back in there . . . ever. I don't know exactly what that was, but I ain't never going back," he repeats, and I look back to him. He really is spooked.

"Not there. Let's try the white one."

"Fine." He's pulling himself together and I can see he's decided to put his game face on. This is his take-charge self. I don't know how he does it. Is it something he was born to do, or has it become some kind of survival mechanism?

We reach the white house and I know we're both nervous because we're holding hands. He squeezes tighter as we get to the steps and checks his gun one more time before we take our steps in unison and give each other one more look, maybe in a question as *last chance to back out.*

"What are we looking for anyway?" he asks, as he finally drops my hands and begins to pry the house door open with a crowbar he found in the open garage. I don't know why, but the house being locked has me feeling better.

Breaking into a house feels a little stranger than a cabin. Cabins always feel like someone's home away from home. I usually tell myself that it's okay because the people are living peacefully at their other residence and I'm just borrowing something they don't need anyway. If the people aren't here, what has happened to them? Or maybe they are the same kind of people their neighbors were.

"Antibiotics. DJ's sick."

"Anything else?" he asks as the door snaps open. It's not a clean break-in. Shards of wood now litter the porch.

"As much as we can carry. Let's make sure no one's here," I say as I start to look around the abandoned house. We both let out a sigh of relief at the sight of a normal home. Normal couches, normal tables, normal TV. No altars.

"Pretty sure whoever lived here is long gone," he says as he kicks around some old trash covering the stained carpet.

"Check anyway."

"I'm kinda surprised you want to start raiding again. I thought those days were behind you . . . So tell me again, why can't we tell anyone?"

"Do you have to ask?"

"I see. I forget what's it's like to have parents. It's been too . . ."

"Shhh . . . I hear something," I say placing my finger to my lips.

"Let me go first," he says in a whisper, as his hand goes down again to the pistol that I've come to know as an extension of him. He removes it and releases the safety.

"I'm coming with."

"Okay, but stay close."

It sounds like it's coming from upstairs, so we try to move slowly, but it's not doing much good as each winding stair announces us with a loud creak.

Bentley opens the door to what looks like a bedroom and then we see the source of all the noise. It's a dog and it's not friendly. It's growling and baring its teeth. I quickly scan it looking for the signs of rabies. For some reason, I can't help but think every animal could be infected. It looks to be healthy, just protecting its domain. Bentley slams the door shut before it can attack us. The dog scratches and bites at the door. The sight of its toenails clawing under the door almost brings a giggle to my lips. I really am losing my mind.

"What do we do?" I ask, breathless.

"Stay out of this room, for starters," he says as he laughs.

"Good plan. Where do you wanna start?" The thought occurs to me that I might be kind of sick in the head. A little excitement from a crazy dog has me feeling at ease again. Maybe it's because now I'm thinking about his vicious teeth instead of the baby we just buried.

"Did you hear that?" he asks. I strain towards the door, listening for the dog. It's not a St. Bernard, but it reminds me a lot of Cujo, the star of my mom's favorite book. It has stopped barking. Then I hear it. It's the soft murmuring of a human. Before I can stop him, Bentley has opened the door again.

"Don't come any closer," she says. It's a girl, maybe in her early 20s. She is dirty and thin. Her hair is in one lump and gives dreadlocks a bad name.

"It's okay," Bentley says as he lowers the gun. "We're not going to hurt you. Do you live here?"

"Get out! Both of you get out!" she screams as she holds the collar of the dog. "I'll let him go. He's a killer. I'm warning you." I take a better look at her. She's trying to maintain a brave front, but really, she's just scared.

"Go downstairs. Let me talk to her," I whisper to Bentley.

"Are you crazy? That thing is dangerous. You've got to be kidding."

"Trust me," I say, as I put my hand to his chest. His heartbeat is steady. He gives me an awkward embrace, hiding the fact that he has just shoved his pistol in the back of my pants.

"Call me if you need me," he says. "I can be back up in a flash."

He leaves and when I hear he has reached the bottom of the stairs, she visibly relaxes.

"Duke, quiet," she commands and the dog stops snarling.

"That's some dog you got there," I start. "What breed is he?"

"German Shepherd," she replies, "and he's a she."

"Duke?" I ask.

"Long story," she says.

"So . . . you live here all by yourself?"

"No. I live with my boyfriend. He'll be back any minute." Her eyes shift to the ground and I know she's lying.

"Okay, we'd love to meet him too. We don't mean any harm. We just came for supplies. We thought this place was abandoned."

"Well, it's not," she shoots back, almost with too much force for it to be sincere. Her hands are trembling and she has started to sweat. For the first time, I notice dozens of empty pill bottles around her.

"Are you okay?" I ask. I expect her to shout at me and tell me to leave, but she says nothing at all. "We can help you."

Then she hides her face in the crook of her elbow and starts to cry. I take a step in to see if she will let me come in further. The dog that was terrifying a minute ago is still following her command and not coming after me. She allows me to come in a little further. She is cowered in the corner. She can't be more than 100 pounds. Her cheeks are sunken in and I wonder about the last time she's eaten.

I know I shouldn't, but I ask her if she wants to come with us. It takes me fifteen minutes to convince her that she's safe and she tells me she will come for one meal. She's terrified, but I can also tell she's lonely. On closer inspection, I see her wrists have deep wounds from an old request to leave the world.

We come down the stairs and Bentley is visibly relieved. I hand him back the pistol and he looks curiously at me.

"She's coming with us," I say.

"Are you sure?" he asks. The girl backs away from him and Duke, the German Shepherd, growls in warning at Bentley.

That crazy dog keeps an eye on us as we enter the kitchen. Bentley looks to the girl and she gives a nod of approval. He works mechanically, scanning what's good and what's not. I watch him in appreciation as his skills are obvious from so many past raids. He doesn't just look at the dates. He picks up the item shakes it, even smells it and taps on the top before deciding to keep or toss to the side. He pauses after he tosses an old can of prunes to the ground. He looks back up at her before he scoops it up and places it neatly back on the shelf. I can't get over the fact that the cupboards are full of food, barely touched. Is she *trying* to starve herself?

"Take whatever you want," she says.

We can't get her to say much more than her name, which is Hannah. When she walks out the front door, she cowers, blinded by the light.

"It's going to be okay," I tell her and offer to take her bag. It's heavy and overloaded and looks to weigh more than her.

"No. I got it. Let's just get this over with," she says and Bentley leads the way. I stay back and walk with her, as she seems more comfortable with me near and my mind races with why she's living in those conditions.

It takes us twice as long to get back. Hannah gets winded after only a few steps. Right before we enter the clearing to our cabin, I see movement in the trees and see Waite sauntering off. Before he leaves, he takes a sniff in the air, obviously smelling Duke, the German Shepherd.

Mom sees us first and without explanation she takes over with Hannah. Mom doesn't let Duke come inside, but the dog seems content to stand guard on the porch. Mom instructs me to get the bath ready and Hannah looks down embarrassed.

"It's okay, honey," Mom starts, "we'll take good care of you. Looks like you could use a meal."

Hannah's eyes water up, and the mystery of her takes my attention away from worrying about Brody and Jack, and even that baby. She doesn't let the bag out of her sight, but she does accept some clean clothes from Mom.

She emerges from the bathroom looking like a different person. I had previously thought she had brown hair, but it's actually dark blonde and falls into curls around her face. She has huge blue, doe eyes. She looks around nervously, fidgeting with the clothes that hang off her.

"Who's hungry?" Mom yells and everyone starts piling around the table. She loves this part— the big announcement right before the crash of hungry bodies piling in, eager to be fed. I've actually studied her before as she prepares food. Her face lights up in anticipation right after the last burner gets turned off, but right before you hear the clank of the plates. Food is love to her.

Mom saves a spot by her for Hannah and the girl sits down shyly. She seems overwhelmed and I wonder how long she's been living alone.

For being so skinny, she only picks at her food, which surprises me because Mom has outdone herself for our guest. No one else seems to notice and they shovel their food in, Bentley most of all. He's a big fan of Mom's cooking. Kit has convinced Hannah to let her give her a makeover when the meal is over. I wonder if she'll regret that.

After lunch, I go to find Jess up in her room. DJ seems to be fussing again and I offer to take him. She finally breaks down.

"I'm worried, Dani. I don't know what I'll do if something happens to him." That reminds me, I have to get back out again. With the chaos of finding Hannah and

Duke, I never did find those antibiotics, if that's even what he needs.

"It's going to be okay. Babies get sick all the time. It's what they do," I say, feeling lame.

"Will you pray for him?"

"Sure," I say. But honestly the thought of it makes me a little ill. If having a God means sacrificing babies and animals on an altar, then count me out. Every time I picture that little boy, it makes me ashamed to be a human. Why does Jessica put everything she has into her God? Why not do something about it yourself?

"Pray hard. Maybe if you pray hard enough . . . maybe He'll spare him. I have a bad feeling something terrible is going to happen," she begs. *Whatever you say, Jessica.*

I put my lips to his forehead and it's still burning, but he has quieted since I took him and I take that as a good sign. He just needs some rest.

Jess is sobbing now. "He won't eat. How can I help him if he won't eat?"

I feel a stab of fear and longing for Jack. He could fix this. It's been a week now. If Bentley and I had left when we said we would, we would be to the capital by now. Maybe closer to getting Jack back. I wish Bentley would just leave without me and get him. Maybe Jack will find a way back on his own.

DJ is finally dozing in my arms and I hand him back. Seeing him so peaceful makes the memory of the dead baby even more painful. How could someone do such a thing to something so innocent? I can't figure out any scenario for it to make sense.

Jessica senses something is bothering me and asks me what's wrong. I struggle with whether to tell her or not, but my mind is begging me to let it go, so I tell her everything. When I'm finished confessing, I collapse down on the bed, the last of my energy seeping out of me.

"Why would they do that, Jess? Did they say anything about that at the compounds? Did those people think that little baby was the Golden Child?"

"Probably."

"Why do they want to kill the Golden Child?"

"Couple of reasons . . . Either they wanted to remove the child's power, or take it."

"Take it? How can they do that?"

"Well some of the whack-a-doodles at the compounds believe that if you kill the Golden Child during a full moon, the power transfers to the person who kills the Golden Child."

"That's insane. How could you have ever been a part of that?" I accuse. I know I shouldn't, but I also know she willingly went to the compounds after her spiritual revolution. It feels like a betrayal that she was *ever* a part of it.

"We didn't know. When Jonah and I first went there, we thought it was just a place to be with other believers, normal believers. We're not all like that, Dani. All these plagues . . . they're bringing out the good with the bad. Unfortunately, the bad . . . is pretty bad."

"I don't see much good. Where's the good?"

"You just have to look a little harder," she says as she stifles a yawn.

"I'm sorry, Jess. I didn't mean what I said. I know you could never do something like that."

"I know."

I get up to leave as DJ finally finds a deep sleep. Jessica falls asleep herself, nestled in with her baby boy. I watch their chests heave in unison and quietly close the door.

Hannah takes the spare room and Bentley continues to sleep on the couch. I don't know how, but Mom has convinced Hannah to stay with us so we've become a baker's dozen.

I'm exhausted so it doesn't take me long to fall asleep, but I am restless. I find myself waking every hour with a new nightmare about Drake. The first one started as usual with us being kids and him waking me, crying that he was sick. In the second one, he was already dead and talking to me at his funeral. In the third one, his face was caved in and rotting, the effects of being dead. He's choking and crying for me to help him. I run to help him, but I pass a mirror and it's not my reflection I see. It's Burke's, and when I reach Drake, instead of saving him, I am shoving more poison down his throat. When I wake at last, my sheets are soaked and my overgrown hair is sticking to my exposed skin. The room is closing in on me and I scramble to my feet. I'm about to the door when I hear a scream.

At first I think it's me and I'm still dreaming, but it's coming from downstairs. I race down to find out what's wrong. It's Jessica and she's hysterical. I race to the entrance of her room and I can't believe what I see.

Chapter 6

"Leave the room. I have to be alone!" Hannah screams. She's standing over the baby, her hands hovering above DJ's face.

"Get away from my baby!" Jessica screams and Jonah stands motionless, unsure of what to do.

"I'm not going to hurt your baby." Hannah looks crazed and I curse myself for bringing her here. What was I thinking? DJ is wailing and it's adding tension to the room. Is Hannah the one who sacrificed the boy with the birthmark? What does she plan to do with DJ?

Everyone is up by now and Duke comes barreling in. The dog now stands between Hannah and the others. Her teeth are bared and she's growling in warning. Brody has woken and stumbles sleepily down the hall to see what's going on.

"Brody, go back to bed," I say, careful not to shout.

"What's going on?" he asks as he surveys the room.

"Oh," he says, looking at Hannah standing over the baby, "you need to leave them alone. She will help him."

It becomes clear to me as soon as he says it. No one knows what I do, but I hope I can pull this off. This will be the biggest gamble I've ever taken.

"Everyone, clear out," I say with as much authority I can muster.

Jessica looks at me as if I have betrayed her. Her sobs are very close to matching DJ's.

"You heard her," Bentley finally chimes in. "Give Hannah some room."

Jonah ushers Jessica out and once Brody sees it has been resolved, he scampers back to his room with Avery close behind. Two minutes ago, he was an authority figure I was obeying and now he looks like the child he is.

We wait outside for at least ten minutes, but it feels like an hour. I fight every urge to go in there. DJ has stopped screaming, but now it's Hannah who wails. Finally, she comes out. She looks worse than she did the day we found her. She hands the baby to Jessica who crumples in relief. Hannah remains silent. She drags herself to her room and passes out.

When I go to check on her the next morning, I find her in a pile of her own vomit. She is burning with fever and I ask her if there is anything I can do for her. Kit helps me clean up. Hannah finally responds and points to her bag.

"You want your bag?" I ask, as I pick it up and hand it to her. She's too weak to open it. I open it for her and gasp.

It's filled to the brim with prescription medications. I scan the labels and from the looks of it, they are almost all narcotics.

"What do you have all this for?"

She doesn't answer. I open one of the bottles and she holds four fingers up.

"You want four?" I ask, and she nods. I get her some water and she swallows them down. Within five minutes, she is out. Kit and I finish cleaning the room. It only vaguely smells like puke.

"What was *that* all about?" Kit asks as soon as we are outside.

We walk toward the nearby stream where we do the washing. The water is freezing cold and I'm reminded that it will snow soon.

"I don't know. Want to know what's even weirder?" I ask.

"Uh, yeah. I'm all about the weird," she says with a grin.

"DJ's better . . . It's like she took his sickness. You didn't see it, but when she was standing over him . . . it was like she was possessed. It's all just too bizarre. And now, she's sick. She always seemed a little sick, but now she's really sick."

"Maybe it's better not to look too deep into it. DJ's better," she says, as she swats the sheets out, trying to remove the last chunks of Hannah's supper. She dry heaves in disgust at the mushy substance she is unable to scrape off.

"Here, let me have it," I say as I take it from her. "You're not getting sick too, are you?"

"No, it's just that smell. I can't take it."

"Since when do you shy away from a little puke? Isn't that a specialty of camp mother?"

"Not when it smells like that," she says as she scurries off holding her mouth.

***

Hannah sleeps for days. She doesn't eat and barely drinks. If I thought she was thin before, it's nothing compared to what she is now. The only person she allows into her room is me and the only thing she allows from me is her pills and fresh water.

On the fourth day, she has started to come around and I see just a trace of light in her eyes. I breathe a sigh of relief and ask her if she wants something to eat.

"Just soup . . . if you've got it," she responds.

I call down for Mom to bring me some soup and it's as if she already had it waiting for Hannah because it has taken her only 48 seconds to bring it up. I help Hannah sit up as Mom leaves the room and the full effect of how ill she is demonstrates itself in her inability to even sit.

I watch her carefully as she removes the pieces of noodles and drinks only the broth.

"You don't want that? You need your strength," I say, encouraging her.

"Trust me, you don't want me to eat that," she says with a half smile. "You would just have to clean it up. I've done this before."

"Done what?"

"Been sick. It's what I'm good at."

"You know I have to ask."

"Yeah."

"How is that possible?"

"It's what I do. I saw Bentley outside my window that day you guys found me. I can feel what you can do and I know about Brody."

Goosebumps flash up my arm, spreading like dominoes. "You can't tell anyone."

"Secrets can make you sicker than any illness," she says as she sips the steaming broth.

"So what exactly is your advancement?" I ask. I have trouble even saying the word advancement because it sounds thick and heavy on my tongue. Of all the things I've had trouble swallowing about this new world, it's the advancements that I find the strangest, even though I've seen Bentley's, and there is no doubt he's changed.

"Advancement?" She considers this. "I guess I didn't really have a name for it, but that makes sense . . . I can take other people's sickness. I know, I know," she laughs quietly and says, "Won the lottery on that one."

"Doesn't seem fair," I say, as I take her bowl from her. She rubs her stomach as if the few ounces of broth were too much for her.

"Are you better now?" I ask.

"Yeah, a little. The baby's sickness wasn't so bad. I'll get over it. How is he?"

"Much better . . . thanks to you. How does it work?"

She's silent for a long time, spending most of her time catching her breath.

"It's hard to explain, and well . . ." she stammers, "it's kind of odd."

"Is that why you are so sick right now? Why do you need all these pills?"

"I haven't been well for a long time. I can't seem to say no. And the pills just make it easier," she says. "But do me a favor, don't tell anyone okay? I don't need anyone feeling sorry for me."

"I promise." I want to ask her again not to tell my secrets, but I don't have to.

We are bonded. In the short time I've known her, we've developed something even stronger than Kit and I have. I can't talk to Kit about advancements because she thinks it's crazy, and besides, she's more or less just obsessed with Grant. She wouldn't understand any of this and when I think about telling her about Brody, I feel oddly protective. I don't want her to know.

I don't even feel comfortable talking about this stuff with Bentley. He seems to confuse the intimacy of secrets as something else. I can't help but feel like Bentley is just after my affections because his brother is too. Or was. I just realized I haven't worried about Jack in days. If anything, I've almost grown angry with him. It was his decision to leave. I could have handled Burke myself. He gets so single-minded that he doesn't think about the consequences. He could have just let me deal with it myself. He didn't need to sacrifice himself to Burke. Every step he took towards the helicopter was a step he was taking away from me.

I remember back to the time when I first met Jack. He said something about "maybe the safety camps aren't so bad." What was he thinking anyway? I try to stop myself from thinking about him because I can see where this is going. I'm starting to doubt his motives and the cynical part of my mind is making up stories that this was Jack's plan all along. Maybe he and Burke are in on something together. But he can't be. He knows about Brody and he didn't tell Burke.

"Can you open my window?" Hannah asks, interrupting my confused daydreams.

"Sure." I see why she wants her window open. It's snowing.

"It's beautiful," she whispers. "Can you help me up?"

I ease her up and help her to the window. It's as if she's seeing snow for the first time. It comes down in dainty flakes and she puts her hand outside the window to catch them. They melt in her hand the instant they touch down.

She doesn't last long and she asks me to help her back to bed. I promise to check on her in a couple hours, but her eyes close before I even shut the door.

I go down to the living room where Bentley is fiddling with the TV set. He's trying to attach some sort of antennae with what looks to be tin foil. I forgot tin foil even existed.

"Whatcha doing?" I ask, as I plop myself down on the oversized brown couch and watch as the dust motes mingle around searching for another place to land. I trace the imprint of Bentley's slumber from the night before.

I watch him as he moves skillfully over the TV. He has popped off the back and is fiddling with things unknown to me. He's lost in his work. He is concentrating so hard he barely notices I'm in the room. His face contorts in a lovely way as he struggles in frustration. This is more entertaining than anything he could find on a station.

"Need any help?" I ask, almost giggling. Seeing Hannah get better has put me in a good mood.

He senses my change in attitude and looks up to give me his most killer smile.

"What could you possibly know about TVs?" He teases.

"Oh, I know tons. Like for example . . . the TV is on." I smirk.

"Huh?" He darts out from behind the TV to see the TV has in fact turned on. "Hmmm . . . must have been a loose wire. Let's see . . ." he says, as he adjusts the tinfoil and places the back cover back on.

There's static on the screen at first, but then the picture comes in clearly. It looks like some sort of newscast. It's just like any other I've seen over the years since Burke took over, but seeing him, now that I've actually met him, startles me. It almost has me forgetting the fact that Bentley is watching his father. The playful mood of just minutes ago has disappeared.

He sees him. I see him. No one says a word.

Chapter 7

Burke is talking, but all I can see is Jack. He is sitting there, inches from the enemy. He looks slightly uncomfortable, but he's definitely a willing participant. How could he? I mean, I know he was going with his dad, but to be by his side like this?

The camera is focused on Burke as he stands at a podium, but there Jack sits in the corner of the screen. He watches his father speak to the country and ask for assistance.

Burke is asking for help to find the Golden Child! I slump down to the floor folded on top of my legs, seated directly in front of the screen, my hand wanting to touch the corner of the screen where Jack sits. I think I hear Bentley talking, but all I can see is Jack.

The bulletin on the bottom of the screen reads: Calling all American Citizens – Your country needs you. The Golden Child has been born. Please call this number if you have any information. It is imperative that he be found. He's in danger. Calls may be confidential. Any baby born with any sort of markings is to be examined by The Council. Repeat . . .

My skin is prickly with panic. Sweat gathers in the small of my back. My breathing has become erratic. The bulletin goes on repeat at the bottom, but I look back up at Jack. Just before the screen goes blank, I see him glance at the camera and it's as if it's actually him I see. I can feel him. My gut aches at the mixed emotions I have. I back up, stunned.

"He's got a lot of nerve!" Bentley shouts as he throws the remote at the TV. It cracks as the back falls off, spilling the batteries on the floor.

"What's he doing?" I match Bentley's rage.

"And to think, I was going back for him," he says quietly as he slumps down on the couch and withdraws into himself.

Everyone else has gathered in the living room to see what's going on. I see Brody watching from the corner and he looks confused.

"Was that Jack?" Brody asks.

"Hey, Brody," I say, as I walk over to the TV to turn it off, "I found a great tree out back. Want to see if you can get to the top?" He brightens and forgets about Jack.

We spend a half an hour, just the two of us, as Brody gets even higher than I predicted he would. He makes it look easy as he maneuvers carefully through the Black Hills spruce, dropping cones as he skips up the branches. Almost too easy. I think he has gotten bored with trees and is just humoring me. He gets all the way back to the bottom branch and jumps into my arms.

"You hungry? I think lunch is almost ready," I say.

"You know him," he replies.

"What did you say?" I ask. I look at him, studying him. He looks so grown up, as he wipes the dirt away from his jeans, a move reminiscent of Jack.

"You know him." That's all he says. He walks back into the cabin with the posture of a grown man. I can't get over the changes in him. People say when you live with a person, you don't actually notice them grow or change until it's already happened. I find myself wishing it were true with Brody.

Mom has created quite the spread again. She found hoards of these prepackaged meals with government labels on them. Tonight's choice is "Fortified Rice-Soy Casserole" with the package reading "The Council Against Hunger. Feeding families around the country, and around the corner." Puh-leeze, like they didn't create this problem in the first place. Reading the package sours my appetite.

I take up a small portion for Hannah and she's looking much better. She devours it along with her four pills and she says she's ready to get out of this room.

Hannah and I spend the rest of the day exploring the area around our cabin. She shares with me about her childhood and how she got to be in the Black Hills.

"I followed my loser boyfriend," she says.

"I have to hear this story," I say with a smile.

We decide to rest by the stream because Hannah has gotten winded. The early snow we got has all melted now, unable to keep up with the hungry sun.

"I'm still so mad about it. I'm not sure I want to talk about it."

"Secrets make you sick, remember?" I prod.

"That's not what made me sick," she says. She has gathered a pile of pebbles and is now tossing them into the stream.

"We came out here because he got word his mom was sick. We weren't supposed to leave California because The Council was forbidding travel, but we snuck out anyway."

"California? I've always wanted to go there," I say.

"Yeah, we had a couple of close calls, but we did make it. When we got here, his mom was in pretty bad shape. We stayed for a couple of weeks and she just seemed to be getting worse. He got pretty impatient with me. We were fighting a lot and finally I asked him what his deal was. We got into *The* Fight. He accused me of being selfish, and that's when I realized why he brought me to South Dakota."

"*The* Fight?"

"The one that changed everything." She is crying quietly, not bothering to wipe the tears off her face. Her face is wet with shiny tears that illuminate the pain she's trying to hide.

"He only wanted me so I could heal his mother."

"No," I gasp. "What did you do?"

"What do you think I did?" she says, as she finally tosses in a rock that seems to weigh more than her.

"You actually did it? After what he did to you?"

"What choice did I have? I loved him. And she was really sick. Back then, I didn't know the full effects of what would happen. When I had done it before, I healed the person, and it just wiped me out for a couple of weeks. But this was a bad one. I never got better."

"What was it?"

"You mean what *is* it? I don't know for sure, but it's probably the big C."

"The big C?"

"Cancer."

My heart breaks for her. If she has this ability to heal others, but it only makes her sick, what good is it anyway? How could healing an old lady benefit anyone if the price is a young girl's life?

"So what happened? Where are they?"

"Oh," she laughs bitterly, "that's the best part. As soon as his mother was better, they left. They didn't even tell me. I just woke up and they were gone. That's actually her house I was living in. If I ever get better, I'm going back home. I've got a brother. I'm not even sure that he's still alive. That's the worst thing Jamie stole from me. My brother asked me not to leave, begged me not to go, but I did anyway and now I'll never see him again."

I don't realize it until I feel a breeze roll across my cheek, but I'm crying too. My damp skin is attracting the chill and I'm now aware I better get Hannah inside.

"Promise me one more thing?" she asks, as I help her to her feet.

"Anything." I say.

"Please, don't pity me."

"I don't pity you. I'm pissed. I'd like to find that D-bag and give him what's coming to him."

"D-bag?"

"You know, douchebag?" I cough out choked laughter as her eyes go wide in mild horror.

"Oh." She laughs in return and I put my arm around her as we walk back up to the house, her dog, Duke, never far behind.

We walk into the oversized dining room where Mom's got a cup of water, a comb and scissors set up on the table as Brody squirms in his seat.

"What are you doing!" Without thinking, I run over to Brody and scoop him up into my arms, knocking over the glass of water.

"What's the matter with you, Dani?" she says, her face contorted in confusion.

"You can't cut his hair," I say.

"Why not?"

"Because you just can't . . ."

"What's going on here?" Dad asks, as he comes from upstairs.

"Nothing," I respond. "Mom wants to cut Brody's hair."

"What's wrong with that? He needs one. He can barely see out of that mop," Dad says, as he runs his fingers through the front of Brody's hair. I back away.

Brody squirms out of my arms and chases Avery who is headed out the front door.

"Brody!" Mom calls after him.

"It's okay, honey, let him go play," Dad says to Mom. She sighs and shakes her head and starts to clean up the mess.

"Don't cut his hair Mom. Okay?" I take the dishcloth from her and clean the mess myself.

"Kids," she mutters under her breath and heads back into the kitchen.

That was a close one. I didn't see it coming. What am I going to do when they find out? It's only a matter of time.

***

It's been a long day and Hannah has been asleep for hours. I go to find Kit to hang out with, and of course, she's busy with Grant. All they do is stay holed up in their room. Everyone has gone to sleep, so I head out to the porch to find Bentley reading by a lantern.

"Where did you get that?" I ask, referring to his book, *The Hatchet*.

"I found it, under the couch, of all places."

"When you were looking for the batteries you lost in your temper tantrum?" I tease.

"I guess you could say that." He earmarks the page and puts the book down.

"Have you read it?" he asks.

"Yeah, it's been a long time though. I think Mom made me read it."

"Imagine if his mom hadn't given him that hatchet. His story would have ended a lot differently."

"I always thought that was kind of weird. Kid gets on a plane with a hatchet nestled in his belt and no one thinks anything of it."

"The kid's a fighter though. He never gives up. I think that's what I like about it."

"You picking up survival tips, or what?" I smile.

He laughs and the mood for the evening is light, but I can tell something is bothering him.

"So what's the plan?" he asks.

"What plan?" I've got my feet propped up on the banister of the porch and I consider sleeping out here for the night.

"How long are we gonna be here?"

"Ready to move on already?" I shiver, rethinking my idea about sleeping out here. He tosses his blanket to me.

"Thanks. Where else are we gonna go?"

"Your dad doesn't want to alarm anyone, but the propane is almost out."

"Propane?"

"We kinda need it for things like cooking, heat, you know the things that keep us alive in the winter?"

"Can't we get some more?"

"A truck would have to come out. Should we just call up The Council and see if they can make a delivery."

"We can't go on a raid for that?"

He stays quiet for a while.

"Maybe . . . but I've never done anything like that before. And I can't get a hold of your uncle."

"Why do you need him anyway? What are you up to?" I snuggle into the blanket, but it's not helping much as the last of Bentley's borrowed body heat evaporates.

"Nothing. I'd just like to know what's going on. Let's go in. You're freezing."

I don't fight him about it and we find ourselves on the couch he uses for his bed. I nestle in because I'm just not ready to go to bed. Callie has been sulking and only seems to want to be alone. We talk late into the night and not about The Council, plagues, or any of the other stuff that leads our lives.

"Movie?"

"Why not?" I smile.

"I've been saving this one for you," he says, as he tosses me a very worn looking DVD. I look at the title and can hardly believe it. "Bonnie and Clyde? I used to be obsessed with her."

"Bonnie?"

"Yeah . . . weird?" I can feel his smirk as I look down towards the floor.

"No, it fits you." He nudges my shoulder so I look at him. "But why?"

"Oh, I don't know, I found it kinda romantic. Sick, I know." I finish, but he's already laughing.

"What?"

"Most gals pick Sleeping Beauty or Cinderella."

"Did you really just say gals?" Now I'm laughing.

We don't talk during the movie. I try to start a couple of light conversations, but Bentley is silent, almost brooding. When the credits roll, he walks over to the TV, shuts it off and goes out to the porch. Curious, I follow him out there. The porch boards squeak as I make my way out into the chilly air.

"Did I do something wrong?"

He paces the porch for a while before he finally sits down on the rusted chair. He's looking out into the forest for an uncomfortable two minutes before looking up to me.

"We could do it, you know."

"Do what?" I ask as I take a seat on the rail of the porch and let my legs sling over. I have an urge to get up and take his hands because he looks anguished, but I stay put.

"We could take off. They don't need us. This place is making me crazy."

"I can't do tha—"

"No, think about it. Like Bonnie and Clyde. Just take off on our own, do as we please. Renegades."

"You did see the ending, right?" I say, as I give him a small smile.

"We could rewrite the ending. Bonnie and Clyde part two, alternate ending."

"You don't have to stay you know . . . if this place is driving you bananas."

"Ahh, forget I said anything. Another movie? I think I saw Night of the Living Dead in there somewhere."

"Sounds perfect."

I probably don't make ten minutes of the movie, because my dreams that night are filled with Tommy guns and outlaws, and not flesh eating monsters. I wake up confused because my mother is yelling at me.

"What do you think you're doing?"

I look around, unsure of my surroundings and the pieces are starting to fit together. Bentley is sleeping sitting up with my legs strewn across him as I lay on the length of the couch. She whips the blanket off us.

"Mom! What are you doing?" I ask, my voice hoarse from sleep or maybe lack of sleep. I could use a few more hours.

Bentley hops up looking guilty. "It's not what it looks like."

"It doesn't matter what it looks like. No daughter of mine is going to be sharing her bed with a boy under my roof." She is steaming. In a way, it's kind of nice to see her do something besides cry.

My face is blushing hot, but not from embarrassment. I'm pissed. I turn 18 in less than a month, and had been living on my own for five months, and she has the audacity to do this?

"It's a couch and you have no right," I say before I walk away.

"Just because Kit does it, doesn't mean you can!" she calls after me, as I try to ignore her. But then I stop.

I turn around and look her straight in the eye. "When is yours and Dad's anniversary again?"

"You know that," she mumbles.

"Just tell me again, humor me," I say with ice in my voice. There's a little bit of warning in me about not speaking to her this way, but I'm grumpy from lack of sleep and my fuse feels dangerously short.

“You know it’s February 2nd.”

“How many years again?”

“Dani, that’s hardly the point.”

“How many years, Mom?”

She doesn’t say anything.

“How many?” I persist.

“Eighteen this February, you know that.”

“Why don’t you think about that the next time you want to give me lectures on morality,” I say, as walk out the front door. I could use some air.

Chapter 8

The next morning, there is a quiet knock on my door. I expect it to be Hannah since we spend most of our free time together, but it's Bentley.

"Hey," he whispers.

"What's going on? What time is it?"

"It's early. Get dressed. I have an idea."

I do as he says. My fingers tingle in anticipation. This is something I've missed about Tent City. As good as it is to have my whole family together again, I wouldn't mind a little more excitement.

As soon as we get outside, he fires up one of the four-wheelers.

"I thought we were low on gas?" I ask.

"I found a dealership last week," he says as he smiles with mischief.

"You promised you'd teach me how to siphon. That's what you did right?"

"Next time." He promises.

"How dangerous can it be?" I look towards him, but he stalls with his answer.

"You'd know if you ever got a mouthful of gas. I told you I'd teach you. Isn't that enough?"

"Where we going?" I ask, ignoring his question. He ignores me back and I get on.

I have a feeling Mom wouldn't approve of our little outing, but I don't really care now that I think about it. The only thing I'm regretting is not leaving a note. What would it say anyway? "Hey Mom, Getting on a four-wheeler with a boy you don't want me hanging out with, to a place I don't know. It's more than likely going to be dangerous. Bye, love you lots!"

We drive for about an hour when we come up on a big building with the word PROPANE in large lettering. Now I know what we're doing. He shuts the wheeler off and we sneak up to see if the store is occupied. We're hiding within the trees.

"Bentley, we can't just go in there."

"I know. I just want to try and figure out a plan. Maybe we could come back at night."

"You need a truck don't you? For refill?"

"I thought maybe we could just get a couple of tanks to get us by. And look, there is a phone there. I bet it still works," he says.

"It's too dangerous right now," I whisper, as I see a worker exit the building and get into one of the propane trucks. My heart is beating so fast I can feel it in my ears. "I don't know why I'm so surprised to see people."

"I know, it's weird. But I'd really like to use that phone, try and call Randy."

"What are you gonna do, just walk right up to it?"

"I could. I look old enough."

"I've had enough of this. We need to get back. I didn't even tell anyone where we were going."

"Oh, come on, don't be such a baby. Where's that fearless girl I fell in lo—" He stops and catches himself.

My face probably drains. The almost thing he just said makes my heart skip. I don't want him to say it.

"Wait a minute," he says. "I might as well tell you. It's not like it isn't true."

"Just drop it Bentley." I'm walking away back to the wheeler as fast as I can.

"Will you just give me a chance to explain? It doesn't have to happen now. I think you know how I feel. I don't have to give it a label. It's okay. We can go."

"Good. Let's get out of here before they see us."

On the ride back it eats at me what Bentley was about to say. The thing that is irritating me is that he has no reason to. How could he think he loves me? The entire beginning of our relationship was built around fighting and me discovering what a liar he was. There is also something else itching in the back of my mind that bothers me. He seems to think he is drawn to me by my advancement. If he really believes that, then is that why he thinks he loves me? So when we get back I ask him.

"So . . . what were you going to say back there?" I ask, as soon as I jump off the back of the wheeler.

He turns the engine off and looks at me. "Come again?"

"You heard me," I say, holding my ground. I'm spinning around any number of possibilities of things he's going to say. I've got everything in my mind from him saying something like, "I don't know, I just do." To something wonderfully romantic like, "I love the way your hair moves in the wind. I love your bravery, your speed, your ability to put all others above you."

"No, really. What did you say?" he asks again.

"Back at the propane store." I'm blushing now and seriously regretting my impulse to ask.

"Oh, I see," he says in understanding. "I want to tell you a couple of things, but you have to promise not to freak out and become postal."

"Become postal?" I smile.

"You know . . . crazy?"

And then I can't help myself. "Do you know what that means? I think you meant to say 'go postal.' It's an expression that came out after a bunch of postal workers went crazy and shot a bunch of people. It happened in the 1980s I think." The memory of my mother's lesson is as fresh in my mind as it would be if it had happened yesterday. For being so smart, Bentley sure says some dumb things.

Despite the fact that I'm aware how much of a know-it-all I must sound like, I continue, "Maybe that's how the kids who started doing school shootings got the idea."

We're both quiet in thought. There was a time long before the locusts that we all went to public schools. From time to time, we would hear about school shootings and the country would mourn. But here in the Midwest we felt safe, untouched, especially in South Dakota. But then the shootings started happening in every state. Sometimes it was just a few children and then sometimes the numbers would be in the 20s and 30s. After a particularly bad one that took the lives of almost 50 preschoolers, our president had had enough. He mandated the closure of all public schools. Those who attended private school still had the option for school with teachers and fellow students. But the rest of us were forced into homeschooling. I didn't mind. I was already being home-schooled. The school shootings had Mom spooked way before the president.

"No, the first mass shooting was in 1764 in Pennsylvania," Bentley finally says. It shuts me up for a minute.

"I don't get you. You're like a walking encyclopedia," I say. He's always surprising me. *Now who's the dumb one?*

"You're one to talk . . . That's actually what I love about you. Yeah, I said it. So what? You don't have to act like it's a big deal. I'm not *in love* with you. I just love you. You're one cool chick. So smart," he says, almost challenging me.

"My cousin died in a school shooting," I blurt out, hoping to change the subject, but regretting it as soon as I say it. I've never really talked about it before and it has my insides swirling around.

"I'm sorry."

"Why? It's not like you were the one with the gun."

"Were you close?" he asks, still soft and not deterred by my sharp tongue.

"I guess so. As close as little kids can be. He was Drake's age. It was actually Randy's only son. His wife died in childbirth. He was all he had left."

"I didn't think people died in childbirth anymore."

"She wanted to have him at home, all natural like . . ."

"I never knew that about him . . . Randy, I mean. I've always looked at him as, well, almost not human. All business, ya know?"

I don't say anymore. He leaves me to think, but not before adding "I meant what I said," as he walks in the door. So much for changing the subject.

Chapter 9

It's late at night and I can't sleep again. I'm tossing and turning, counting sheep even though this has never worked. Instead of counting numbers, all I can hear is the bleating calls that start out timid and end up deafening. I look over to Callie who has fallen asleep, book still open on her chest. I'm grasping for my sanity.

I go to check on Hannah who's still sleeping. I wake her to make sure she's still alive. She opens her eyes and asks for more pills. I give them to her and go downstairs. Bentley's not on the couch. I can't imagine where he would be at this hour.

I don't like being alone. In the solitude, I find myself thinking about one of two things. The first and most common thought that repeats in my head is that I'm burning with hatred for Burke and it makes my insides feel gross. I find myself fantasizing about leaving Mom and Dad and going out and killing him. The time I spent in Tent City has desensitized me to death and instead of being afraid of it, I long to bring it to Burke, gift-wrapped with the prettiest ribbon. He's the one responsible for Drake's death. I don't feel like I can be right again until I even the score.

The second thing I think about is Jack. If I'm honest, I don't spend a lot of time on this. Being with Bentley pushes Jack out of my mind. Sick, I know. How could I have felt so strongly about Jack just weeks ago, but not even miss him today? And since I'm on the subject of sick, what on earth am I doing daydreaming about guys when the world is practically crumbling and my baby brother is supposed to be the one to change it? You'd think the subject might get pushed to the front of my mind. If this is a curse of being a teenager, I'm ready to grow up.

I'm desperate for something—something to put me at ease. I search around for a headlamp so that I can get out and run to burn off some of this negative energy. I find it so fast that it almost appears to have been waiting for me, eager for fresh air itself.

It's the middle of November now so it's pretty cold and it has the feel of snow coming in as huge gusts of wind blow past my face and take my breath away. I stick to the roads so I don't get lost. I've gone a couple of miles now and even the rhythmic crunching of gravel and fallen leaves under my feet doesn't bring me the relief I'm hungry for. I'm drenched in sweat despite the chill. Normally, I would be feeling better by now, but nothing is helping. I'm consumed with bad vibes and I can't seem to shake them.

I come back after only a few miles since it's not working anyway. I take a hot bath despite Mom's warning that the propane supply is low. I can't bring myself to care. I would do anything to feel better. But this doesn't work either.

I go down to the kitchen. Maybe it's food I want. I spend about ten minutes cooking some rice and potatoes, cutting it short as my guilt from using propane for the bath catches up with me. By the time it's done, I don't feel like eating it. I put it in a dish and place it back in the fridge. I'm sure Bentley will love the convenience food when he comes back from wherever he is.

I'm surprised when I see Kit coming downstairs, actually by herself for once. Her face looks puffy from lack of sleep.

"You're up early," I say, as I start some coffee. Looks like she could use it.

She's making a weird animal noise and her face is tucked into her hands. She's crying.

"What's wrong?" I ask. We haven't been getting along lately, but seeing her this way hurts.

"Grant left."

"What?"

"He left. We had a huge fight and then he left. He's not coming back!" she wails.

I have a flashback of her being seven or eight and tucking her head into the couch. I used to tease her and call her an ostrich because every time she was upset about something, she would shove her head in-between the cushions and hide herself away. Back then, the sight of her headless body hanging off the couch could bring me to tears with laughter, but I can't find the joke here.

"Shhhhh . . ." I say, wanting to comfort and quiet her. I'd rather she not wake the entire house.

"Why did he leave?" I whisper, as I pat her head and smooth her tangled blonde hair.

"I'm pregnant."

Chapter 10

"What? How do you know? How did this happen?"

She stops crying long enough to crack a crooked smile. "Do I really need to explain to you how it happened?"

I blush. "You know what I mean."

"Aunt Flo hasn't visited for a couple of months. We weren't being careful. I was so stupid. How could I not know this would happen? It's like the thought never even entered my mind. And now he's gone!"

"What was the fight about? He didn't want the baby?" The room seems to be spinning. Why would I be so shocked about this? Maybe it's not shock. Maybe I'm hurt that this has been going on and we've never even talked about it. We talk about everything.

"No. He said he was fine about the baby, but I could tell something was wrong. Finally, I had enough of his silent treatment and we got into this huge argument and he told me he needed some time to think . . . That was two days ago."

"He'll be back, Kit. I'm sure of it. He loves you."

"I hope so," she says, and then she does it. She slinks down and puts her head between the cracks of the puffy brown cushions. It occurs to me that no matter how old we get, we're all still just children.

Kit has sworn me to secrecy. I don't think she wants my mom judging her. I can't help but think that Mom would tighten the reigns up on me if she found out about this, so

I'm more than happy to oblige and keep the secret locked tight. But I'm scared for her. What is she going to do when it's time to have the baby? If Jack were around, I wouldn't be so worried, but he's not. He's with the psychopath.

A few days have gone by and Kit has now started emerging from her room on a regular basis. Bentley has gone out a couple of times to try and track where Grant's trail might have led. Even Bentley's astonished at Grant's disappearance. I haven't told him why he's gone.

Kit seems antsy. It seems as though she wants to talk to me about something, but then just says, "never mind" and goes back up to her room. I finally decide to just corner her and figure out what's going on.

I find her lying on her bed, tears streaming off her face and into Grant's sweatshirt, her most prized possession. I take the sleeve and wipe her face dry.

"Kit . . . you can't stay in bed all day. It's probably not good for the baby to mope around all the time . . . stress and stuff."

"What would happen if I was too stressed?" she asks as she perks up.

"You could lose the baby, I suppose. It happens."

"Good." Her face is hard with bitterness.

"What?"

"I don't want it," she puffs out her lip in defiance.

"You don't mean that."

"Yes, I do," she persists. "Why would I want to raise a baby on my own? Why does he get to get out of it? Dani, you've got to help me."

"What can I do?"

"You've learned a lot from Jack. I can tell. You say medical things that I don't even understand. You could help me get rid of it."

"No!" Even the *thought* of getting rid of a baby has my heart racing.

"If you cared about me at all you would!" Her voice is reaching a high pitch and she is starting to get hysterical.

"You're not thinking straight. Just give it some time. If after a while you still don't want it . . . we can talk about it again." The idea of "doing" something about a baby makes me queasy, but she's so upset.

"Leave me alone." She hurls a glass jar at the wall and it shatters. She lies back down and turns her back to me. I leave stunned.

She's been in her room for three days. She won't get out except to go to the bathroom and I suspect she only does this when she thinks no one is around. I go in again, fully expecting her to yell at me to get out. She's sleeping, but I see a book open on the end table beside her bed.

It looks like she is reading about castor oil. Why? I haven't known Kit to ever read a book, not without being told to anyway. I scan the information quickly so I can figure it out before she wakes up, but when she starts to roll over I decide to slip out before she catches me.

I come downstairs to find Bentley fiddling with the TV again.

"More news?" I ask.

"Yeah, it's not easy to watch, but we should really be aware of what's going on."

He gets a station in, but all it's showing is some footage of a helicopter in flames. The volume isn't working, so it's hard to tell what the story is about. I sit down on the couch and start flipping through the pages of *The Hatchet*. I open to the part where the kid finds the dead pilot and throw the book back on the couch.

I look up to see Bentley frozen, watching the screen. His eyes frantically dart around at the bottom of the screen as he reads the captions. I sit down beside him in front of the TV and try to read the words that are scattered.

Fatal crash . . . General Burke . . . 3:03 a.m . . . updates to follow . . . fatal crash . . . General Burke . . . 3:03 a.m . . .

Then the screen pans to a shot from the compounds. Women and even some men are crumpled on the ground in pure devastation. I'm still not quite putting it together. I'm vaguely aware that my fingernails are digging into my thighs.

"He was trying to escape," Bentley says, more to himself.

"What's happening?" I ask Bentley.

"I'm not sure. Wish this stupid thing had volume." He goes to the back and removes the cover and starts messing with it again. While he is at the back of the set, I see another headline.

Second passenger in the helicopter believed to be the son of General Burke . . . Jack Burke . . . bodies being removed from the scene.

I get up and walk over to the kitchen and pour myself a glass of water. I glance over at Bentley who is struggling to get the cover back on the TV and then look back down to my leg. I've drawn blood. He's frantic now trying to get it to work. He has made a mess of the tin foil. He still doesn't know what I saw about Jack.

I sit down at the table. Numb. I know this isn't *really* happening. It's not possible. I outstretch my hands on the sturdy oak of the table. Even with the table's support, my hands are trembling. I really wish Bentley could get the TV to work.

"Stupid TV." He's so frustrated now that he has kicked over the TV set and it has landed with a dull thud. Really there should be more noise from it, as the glass cracks into an intricate spider web. He's so violent sometimes.

Bentley sits down beside me.

"This can't be real? Is it?" he asks. He puts his hands over mine to still them. "What will this mean?" He continues, "I mean I know I should be upset. But I'm not. I don't feel anything. Shouldn't I be upset?"

"Bentley," I say. He looks at me and I study him for just a second. Somewhere in me I'm pausing this second. The second before I change his world. I know what this feels like. I take a deep breath and touch his face one last time because after this, he will never be the same.

"Jack was in the helicopter."

Chapter 11

He stands up quickly, his sturdy wood chair scraping aggressively against the cabin floor.

"You're lying!" He looks at me one more time with confusion in his eyes and he's out the door in a flash.

I look around to see if anyone has noticed Bentley's blur of color as he sped out the door. He's getting careless with that. Does it even matter now?

I'm still not sure this is even real. It could be a trick. It has to be. How could someone so young be dead? But I know life doesn't follow those rules. There's an idea in the back of my mind taking root. When I think about it, it's more likely that he is dead.

Life was getting back to normal and I was even thinking about being happy again. Of course, he would be gone. I'm not allowed to live in a world where people I love get to stay alive. Love? I think I might have. I always knew I did though. I even know the moment I decided I loved him.

It was in the moment just outside the cave where Jessica had her baby. I had just witnessed the most amazing thing I had ever seen, watching the tiny baby enter the world and the boy who saved him. When Jack found me after the birth, he didn't say anything. We didn't have to. He just picked me up and spun me around. In that moment, as my head and soul swam with vertigo, I had decided that I loved him, even if I wasn't *in* love with him. I did love him. He was a beautiful person and I failed him. I didn't try to bring him home. And now he's gone.

I look back over to the TV, but in that condition, it can't possibly give me any more information. I find myself moving slowly from room to room looking for the radio. I have to find it to see if this is a big joke. It's still possible. I only saw a short blurb at the bottom of the screen. Who's to say that it wasn't a huge mistake? Maybe I'm dreaming.

I've located the radio and I'm so distraught over not finding the station, I don't notice that my family has rallied around me.

"What's wrong Dani?" Avery asks as she touches my cheek.

I've got the station, but I've decided not to listen. It's saying more of the stuff I don't want to hear. I get up quietly, in my own little world, and push through them all. Their faces are dripping with pity. Mom wants to follow me, but Dad stops her.

I collapse down on my bed. I breathe a sigh of relief when I glance over to Callie's empty bed. There's going to be something ugly that happens to me very soon. I wait for it.

Why isn't it happening? Why am I just sitting here? Where are the tears, sobs, and heaving for oxygen? I know how this works. When Drake died, I was a messy ball of tears every time I went looking for my dead brother in a game of hide and seek, only to remember he wasn't playing.

I'm only a little aware that I can't hear. I know I'm supposed to hear something because I feel the floor beneath me shaking. Then the door opens in a whoosh and a gust of air floats up my sheet.

“Dani.” My mother’s mouth pantomimes, but I hear nothing.

Callie comes in with a glass of water and Mom puts something into my mouth.

“Take this. We’ll figure a way through this,” she mouths, as she bares all her white teeth in a false, shaky smile, a move to comfort me, I’m sure.

But when she places the pill into my mouth, I'm barraged once again with memories of Jack. In this one tiny, white pill, she has reintroduced every memory of Jack that I have spent the last few weeks stuffing down. As the darkness seeps in like spilt black ink, I lean back down to my pillow. I let the darkness take me. It can gladly take me anywhere—anywhere, but here.

I wake with my face plastered to an old feather pillow with no case, little feather tips poking my cheek. I lift my head in a jerk, bottom lip sticking to a dried pool of drool.

I would never sleep on a pillow with no case. I’d rather sleep with nothing. It’s in this tiny little fact that I wake up realizing I’m not having another bad dream. Someone has been taking care of me. Not my mom. She knows my pillow case fetish. On cue, Kit pops her head in.

“Can I come in?” she asks, barely peeking around the door.

“Since when do you need to ask?” I croak out. It feels like I haven’t spoken in days.

“Can you hear me okay?” she asks, as she sits on the side of the bed.

“Yeah, why wouldn’t I?” I try to turn over, but every muscle in my body is sore.

"What's going on? Why does it feel like I've been hit by a truck?"

"You really don't remember?" she asks, as she surveys me. She lightly touches an angry, welty, bruise on the side of my leg, fully demonstrated in the slinky shorts I'm wearing.

"Did you dress me?"

"You don't like?" She winks.

"What happened?"

"Hmm . . . if you don't really remember. I wonder if it's some kind of amnesia . . ." She's lost in thought.

"Kit!"

"Oh, sorry. Well . . . after Jack," she stammers, "you must have gone into some kind of shock. You lost your hearing, blacked out, and sleepwalked, right out the door. That's how you got so many bruises. Your dad had to tackle you down last night just to get you stopped. Lucky he found you . . . I'm glad you're up now," she says, as she roams round the room, picking up loose items and putting them in their place. "Feel like a bath? Let me take care of you," she practically begs.

"How many days?" I ask.

"Huh?"

"How many days have I been out?"

"Only three."

"Three!" I stand to my feet much quicker than I should have. Immediately I'm swimming in dizziness. It feels as though invisible hands are pushing me back down to the bed as I try to catch my bearings.

"What's wrong with me?" I look at her confused.

"No one knows . . . Shock maybe? Are you feeling better now?" she asks, as my stomach growls loud enough for us both to hear.

"You need something to eat. I'll run you a bath and then I'll make you something."

"Fine."

I sit in the freezing water and as I slip down to immerse myself deeper, the grief fully sets in. Will I really never see Jack's gray eyes again? Never watch him skillfully examine someone in his quest for healing? I'll even miss the way he wipes his hands on his jeans when he's nervous. Images of him are playing out in my head like a movie and the last one I'm stuck on is him with a look of uncertainty right before he brushes the hair out of my eyes and behind my ears. He was taken from me. Another person Burke has stolen.

Kit slips in and she washes my hair as I sit shivering with my knees up and arms folded over. We don't talk. I don't even bother to close my eyes as she rinses the suds from my hair. I've decided to allow myself a little time to remember Jack for everything he was, and then for my own sake, I must find something else to do. Kit thinks I'm crazy when I tell her I want to go out for a run. Secretly, I'm wondering if I can find him in the forest.

"Why don't you do us all a favor and just stay put for a little bit? I've found some movies in the cellar."

"No TV."

"Huh?"

"Bentley smashed it, remember?" At least I'm sharp enough to remember that.

"Oh . . . he found another one. At Hannah's house. It's even better. It's a flat screen."

Bentley. How did I forget about him? Here I am wallowing in my own misery and I had completely forgotten Bentley lost his brother. His twin brother. How's he holding up? I knew Jack for only months but Bentley has years to grieve for.

I comply with Kit's orders and we walk down to Bentley's couch and find him sitting in his own world. He's flipping around a Rubik's cube he looks to have about solved. Kit busies herself in the kitchen, pretending not to be watching us.

As I sit down, he glances up. One more turn, puzzle complete. He tosses it to me.

"Cool," I say half-heartedly.

"I cheated a little. The algorithms were in the box . . . You okay?"

"You?" I ask, as he scoots a little closer.

"No," he says with no emotion, but with *so much* emotion.

I glance over at Kit who is eavesdropping with all her might. She almost drops her wooden spoon in her effort to lean.

"Want to get out of here?" I ask, trying to shake a case of cabin fever.

He perks up. "Where?"

"Anywhere," I say, and then in an attempt to encourage his flight with me, I tell him, "I want to try out my advancement."

"Really?" he asks, with eyebrows arched and his usual devastating smile, this time failing to make my heart skip.

I'm still faint with hunger when we leave the cabin and I notice a blanket of fresh snow as I step outside.

I start running before I even tell Bentley what I'm up to. Honestly, I don't know what I'm up to. I just want to run. And run and run. I feel like Jack's ghost is following me. It has taken root inside and I want to shake it out. It rots inside me like spoiled cabbage. I can outrun this.

Bentley keeps his pace with mine. I've only gotten three miles before I stop, defeated.

I sit down trying to compose myself. I hide myself inside my t-shirt and start sobbing. I'm so exposed. Bentley gently opens the neck of the t-shirt and peaks in on me cautiously.

"Don't look at me!" I shout at him.

"It's okay, Dani. We're going to be okay. He might not even be dead . . ." he shouts back, but then adds, "he doesn't feel dead," in only a whisper. He pins my arms down at my sides and almost crushes me as he pulls me in close. I bury my face into his neck and he loosens his grip.

"When is it ever going to be okay? When are people going to stop leaving? What's so great about living if all that ever happens is more people die? Why couldn't it have been me? He's so much better than me. He deserves to be here." I pull away, but he's not letting go.

I push some more and struggle to get away, but Bentley never lets go. Finally, I just crumple into his arms. With guilt, I feel myself realizing that I wish it were Jack holding me.

"You really loved him, didn't you?" he asks as he lifts my chin to look at him.

"I love you both," I say, before I turn around to go back, but he grabs my arm again.

"You love me too?" he asks, as he attempts an impish smile.

“Now’s not the time. How could you?” I’m so mad I take off without him, but not before screaming back at him, “Don’t follow me!”

I take a different route home because I was half serious when I said I wanted to work on my advancement, if I even have one. I’m not sure how this works though. Do I really just wish for something really hard? Can I get what I want?

I’ve picked out a spot by the stream and a chill rushes through me, sending goose bumps over every inch of my body.

Focus. If I want something, do I say it like a prayer? Do I ask Him? Is that how this works? I stay on my knees for what must be an hour because when I’m done asking, every exposed inch of me that was friends with the earth, is now angry and chastising. Red welts pulsate as I hobble back to the cabin. I know it is just a long shot, but I’m going to see if I really do have the power to change things.

I walk in and Kit gives me a dirty look. But she does bring me a plate of food and practically slams it on the coffee table in front of the TV.

I flip the TV on to find the coverage. I’m feeling the excitement build as I imagine the banners at the bottom: “News retraction . . . second body found not Jack Burke.”

I’m shoveling food in my mouth through all the capital propaganda. It’s some kind of weird meat with a red sauce that’s slimy and catches in my throat on the way down.

More commercials seeking the Golden Child. This is taking forever. Since when are there so many commercials?

Finally, it’s there. Only it’s not what I asked for. It’s funeral coverage. How can this be? I’ve asked to have him back. If I had a power, it had to work. I’ve never wanted anything so bad. I wanted this just as much as those other times. When I wanted Brody to heal, when I wanted Jessica to survive childbirth, I asked for it, prayed for it, received it. How can this be? How can Jack still be dead?

I can't help but start laughing. What a fool I was to think that I had a superpower! I've learned enough from Drake about superheroes to know there's no power for getting what you want. How could have I bought into all that crap?

I flip the TV off and wander up to Hannah's room. She's sleeping, but her color looks better. She has a few empty pill bottles strewn around about her. I clean them up and take out her old water bottles.

I get to the kitchen to find Mom cooking supper. She gives me a look of sympathy, but doesn't say anything.

"What was that medicine you gave me?" I ask, as I pour myself a glass of water, trying to forget that slimy red meat.

"Valium, to calm you down."

"That doesn't seem like your style. Where did you get it?"

"Hannah. And I don't see that I had much choice." She is dicing up some sort of game. Squirrel maybe? My stomach is churning in disgust. "You were out of control. Are you hung—"

As she is asking me if I want to eat, everything I just forced down has found its way back up. I'm close enough to her that it has splattered on her shoes.

"Oh, honey . . . Kit?" She calls from the kitchen. I head up the stairs, but not before I hear Kit retching in the background just as she enters the kitchen.

When I wake, I'm in bed again. This shadow of darkness even accompanies me in my sleep. It's so persistent that I don't even get a few seconds anymore to wonder if this is all real. I'm so antsy with unease that I feel like my skin is crawling. I go to Hannah's room.

Surprise. She's sleeping again. But this time, I'm actually glad for it. I glance around at her bottles on the floor, searching for words that start with V.

Got it. Valium. I remember a brief period where everything was kind of okay— almost happy—about ten minutes after Mom gave me one of these. I certainly didn't have this hollow feeling in the pit of my stomach. I sneak out of the room, guilt already setting in. I glance back at Hannah and shove the bottle deep into my pocket and walk in quick steps to my bedroom.

I search around, certain that there must be a security camera in here somewhere. Am I about to do this? One won't hurt. It's just an experiment. I want to see if it can make me feel better. I'm desperate to feel anything else but this, even nothing. Nothing is better than this. I slip one into my mouth and wait ten minutes. Nothing spectacular is happening, besides me feeling like a loser. I pop another one.

There it is. I know Jack's gone, but the sting of it is gone too. I consider just lying down and letting sleep take me, but I want to see what this feels like when I walk around. Can I run? Just imagining running feeling like this is giving me butterflies in my stomach.

But when I get outside, I lose all motivation to run. I put on my Walkman and an old pair of headphones and just begin to walk out into the trees. I know it's cold, but I can barely feel it. I've got some nice boots on and the fact that my feet are warm is enough to keep me happy. Yes, happy. I'm happy.

There are snowflakes floating down. I feel them disintegrate as they land on my hot skin. Bentley doesn't think I notice him watching me, following me, but I do. And I don't mind. The music in my ears has created my own personal world and I'm dizzy with the joy of it. Even he can't take it from me. Billy Idol is shouting at me and all I can do is smile. I might not have chosen this, but it was either Idol or Roxette. Two tapes are all I have left. I can't even believe it still works. Antiques that function, who knew?

After about an hour of wandering around, he stops me.

"Want to turn around? It's getting pretty cold out here and you're hardly wearing anything . . ." he stammers as he pushes the headphones off, knocking them to the ground.

"I love you Bentley," I say with a tipsy smile.

"What's wrong with you? What's going on?" he asks. I can almost see him wondering if I've lost my mind.

"No, not like that! Remember Bentley? Just like you said. I can love you, even if I'm not *in love* with you right?" I'm shouting and it feels obnoxious, but it also feels wonderful.

"That's enough horsing around. We need to get back. Everyone's worried about you." He's keeping his voice even and I can tell it's taking a lot for him to cool his temper. I giggle at the thought of it.

"You're so irritating!" he shouts back, face as red as a beet.

"Is that why they call it beet red?" I wonder aloud as I giggle again. He slings me over his shoulder and nausea creeps its way from my stomach to my throat, settling in my head.

We get back to find our rather large family all staring at us as we enter the cabin. Dad gives me a disapproving look and Kit is scratching nervously at her neck.

I don't really care what they think of me. I go to my room and pass out.

Days, maybe weeks—it feels like weeks—go by like this. I spend most of my time alone. I even ignore Hannah, which I do actually feel guilty about. I can't seem to shake the funk I'm in now that I know Jack's gone.

It's just another ordinary day and I slip two more pills into my mouth and stare out the window. Huge snowflakes are landing on my window and it occurs to me that I should be outside helping Brody build a snowman. I lay back down.

Jack is talking to me. I know it sounds crazy, but when I'm sleeping, he comes to visit me. Logically, I know that he's in my dreams because I think about him so much, but it feels like something more. These dreams aren't of things we've done in the past. He's in my present. We are doing things that haven't happened yet. His hair has grown long and now touches his shoulders, making the similarities between him and Bentley striking. But as sweet as the dreams are, they always end the same. I'm reaching out for him and I've almost got his hand when he bursts into flames.

I wake up in a start, sitting up and out of breath, sweat plastering my hair to my neck. Just as I'm about to reach for my almost empty pill bottle, Bentley opens my door.

"Don't you knock?" I say with a scowl on my face as I slip the bottle under my pillow.

"Do you know what day it is?" He smiles.

"Oh, I don't know, Tuesday? Does it even matter what day it is?" I ask, voice heavy with sarcasm.

"It's your birthday, Dani."

"So?"

"So, we've got something special planned for you. Why don't you come on down? We're all waiting for you. Well, Kit's in her room, but the rest of us are."

"Grant's still not back?"

"I'm not sure he's coming back."

"Why would he do that? It doesn't seem like him."

"Enough about Grant. This is about you," he persists.

I puff out my lip and shake my head. "I'm not going anywhere."

"I thought you might say that," he says, "and I'm glad. This is more fun anyway."

Before I can stop him, he slings me over his shoulder and is bounding down the stairs. It takes only three seconds to reach the bottom.

"Someone feed her," he shouts. "She can't weight much more than 100 pounds."

He means it as a joke, but I see a look of worry cross my mother's face.

"Happy 18th birthday, sweetheart," my dad says, as he walks over to me and squishes a wet kiss on my cheek.

"Gross, Dad," I scowl at him.

"I love you too, peanut," he replies with a wink.

The birthday dinner goes by in a bit of a blur. I eat, because truthfully, I'm awful hungry. I even polish off two pieces of cake, sans frosting. Mom apologizes profusely for not having it. She says they didn't have the supplies to make the sweet topper.

"What's wrong with Kit?" I ask, as I'm rubbing my belly. It's so full, it actually feels like it's protruding.

"She's sick," Brody says, as he hovers by Mom, asking, well begging, for another piece of cake.

"What's wrong with her?" I ask Mom.

"I'm not sure," she answers. "She won't let anyone in there. She says she doesn't want to get anyone else sick. She hasn't taken any food for two days."

I leave without any further explanation. She's probably doing this on purpose. Her defiance at Grant leaving her alone. Once when we were young, she was grounded for a week and she tried to boycott the punishment by not eating. She lasted 12 hours before she was raiding the fridge.

I don't even knock. She has the door barricaded, so it takes some time to get it open, but finally I do and she has her back to me, folded up on the bed in the fetal position. Fetal. My heart skips.

I take a seat on the bed and try to stir her.

"Kit, it's me. Wake up . . . Are you okay?"

She's silent, but I can tell she is awake. Her breathing has sped up and I can feel her heartbeat at her shoulder where my hand rests. Then she lets out a stifled sob. It's only now that I see a half empty bottle of castor oil on the nightstand, sitting next to an empty, oily, glass mason jar.

"You didn't!" I say with a shrill in my voice. How could she?

My mind is racing at what she has done. She's tried to get rid of the baby. And I didn't stop her. What has she done? But then the anger switches to worry like the click of a lock. I'm not even sure what it does to you when you consume castor oil, but it can't be good.

"Kit, look at me. What have you done?"

She doesn't answer me, but she turns around and I see someone else.

It's not Kit. Kit is beautiful, spirited and full of life. This girl is a shell of a person. It's hard to even see Kit in this girl beside me.

"Don't look at me!" she sobs.

"I don't understand. What is this?" I ask as my hand reaches up to her angry skin, but she shrinks away.

I take in fully what she now looks like and I'm not even sure my mind can process it. Her skin is covered in hot, red boils. As painful as they must be, I know what's bothering Kit more.

"You were right," she says in between sobs. "I never should have done it. Now look what's happened to me. That book said it would take care of it," she says in disgust, as she picks up the book and slams it into the wall.

"Are you in pain?"

"What do you think?" she growls, while lightly patting her cheek where the reddest boil resides. Heat radiates from it. "Don't look at me."

I leave to go to Hannah's and pick out a pain killer. She asks me what's wrong, but I only answer with asking her to meet me downstairs. I hope she doesn't notice when I swipe another bottle of Valium.

I give Kit the medicine and pray she finds sleep and relief soon. I'm bothered that the boils are either going to kill her or leave her scarred for life. She'd probably prefer the former.

I've called a meeting in the living room and everyone but Callie is there. She's been disappearing more and more and no one can seem to ever locate her.

I fight the urge to protect Kit and not tell anyone about what she's done, but I'm scared. This seems too big for me. I need help. I need to know if there is a way to reverse this. I'm wishing for Jack now more than ever.

Everyone listens as I tell them about Kit and as I finish, I plead for a cure.

Jonah speaks first. "The castor oil is not what did it."

"What do you mean?" I ask.

"Castor oil doesn't do that. If she really drank it, it would only cost her a few trips to the bathroom . . . if you know what I mean. The boils are from God."

"What? That's crazy," I say back. Even though everyone else is in the large living room of the cabin, this is a conversation for only me and Jonah.

"How else could you explain it?" he asks.

"Are boils in the plagues?" Even as I'm asking, I'm feeling foolish for not learning all of the plagues. "Can you tell me about them?"

Mom goes to tell Avery and Brody to play in the other room when Jonah stops her.

"Today's world no longer allows for ignorance. Let them stay," he says to Mom.

I look at Jonah as if I'm seeing him for the first time. He is calculating and slow in his speech, commanding our attention.

"As we all know, the plagues are not following the order of the original plagues in the Bible. These are different times. The first plague is of blood. We've already seen that in the river. The second is frogs," he says as he paces the room.

"We're going to have frogs?" Brody asks, and I find myself a little in love with his innocence. I can imagine the idea of thousands of frogs is fascinating to him, but it sends a shiver down my spine. Brody seems to realize that this is story time and quiets down, satisfied without an answer for now.

"The third would be plague of lice or gnats. All the dust throughout the land would become lice. This could be translated as lice, gnats, or fleas. Fourth would be plague of flies or wild animals. We've seen that back at Tent City with the rabies infestation. Fifth would be plague of pestilence. This is a pretty bad one. It would present as an epidemic disease wiping out all livestock. If you think you were hungry before . . ."

I'm sitting on the oversized brown couch numb. I hear what he's saying, but when he explains it, I feel like I'm still dreaming. How could this be? If God were so unhappy with us, why doesn't he just kill us all now?

"Sixth," Jonah continues, "plague of boils."

As soon as he says it, I know it's true. The condition of Kit's skin is so surreal that there could be no other explanation for it.

"Seventh, plague of hail. This one doesn't sound so bad, but it could be devastating. Number eight is locusts. We've seen this come as the first plague. Number nine, plague of darkness. God will turn off the sun and we will be forced to live in complete darkness. This would have more consequences than we could ever comprehend."

The room is heavy with the silence of each member of my family contemplating what this means for them. Jonah seems weighed down with the burden of it all when I ask him one final question.

"I thought there were ten plagues."

"Maybe we could save that one for another time," Jonah finally relents after a painful silence.

"You said today's world no longer allows for ignorance," I challenge.

He looks at Avery with fear in his eyes and then back to me. "Death of firstborn."

Chapter 12

Everyone seems to be shook up about all of the new revelations, except for maybe Jessica. She has been in high spirits ever since Hannah healed her baby. When I asked her about how she could be taking this all so lightly, she responds, "It's God's will."

"Why does only Kit have the boils? What about the rest of us?"

"That does seem unusual. Maybe it's some kind of lesson," she says. I catch myself before I roll my eyes.

"Is there anything we can do about it?" I ask back.

"Well, I have a theory," she says.

"This, I've got to hear."

I take her out to the porch, even though it's freezing and we take our spots on the rocking chairs. I run back in to get a couple of blankets and some tea and when I come back she's shivering in her chair. A cold breeze shoots up the back of my shirt and I throw on a parka and give the big blanket to Jess.

She settles in as she takes her first couple of sips with only a slight tremble of a shiver as her drink vibrates in her hand.

"So?"

"Hmmmm . . ." she says, as she looks out into the trees. I take a peek at what she is looking at and I see Waite scatter through the pines. The only difference from his normal cryptic appearances is that Duke seems to be following him. Weird.

"He's still here?" she asks.

"He never left," I reply. "So what's this theory of yours?"

"Are you sure you're up for this? It's going to sound bizarre."

"Can't be any crazier than what I just heard in there," I say, motioning to the cabin door.

"Well, all right. You asked for it," she says, as she takes another sip and burns her tongue. She spends a few moments cursing herself for drinking too soon before she says, "I think the plagues are happening because the world has gone to shit."

"Jessica!"

"What? There really is no other way to put it. If you go back to the beginning times, God made people in reflection of himself. He set out the rules, and all us humans seem to do is muck it up."

"Hasn't it always been that way? You know, the human sinning thing."

"Yeah, but it's gotten worse. All God wants us to do is be kind to one another, love Him, and follow His rules. But us humans? We think we are bigger than Him. We don't want a baby? We have a solution for that, a legal one even. And then with all the school shootings that used to happen. And all the bombings at the sporting events, and that's just in America. You might be too young to remember, but there used to be professional sports games. People used to pay big money to watch. He wouldn't admit it, but Jonah misses that. Basketball was his favorite."

"I remember. My dad was a fan of Michael Jackson."

"You mean Michael Jordon I think," she says with a smile. "Anyway, people were afraid to go to any kind of sporting event for fear of another bombing, so they shut that down too. It started at the Boston Marathon . . . It's too bad. I could have seen you doing one of those. You can practically do a marathon in your sleep," she says.

"Not anymore," I say with sadness. "I've lost my touch."

"Probably because of all that poison you're putting into your body."

"I don't know what you are talking about." She has startled me. I wasn't expecting this. I thought it was my secret. I get up and walk back into the house before she can say anymore. Looks like I need to be more careful.

I go inside hoping to find Bentley. I don't really want to talk to him. I just want to be around him. He's comforting.

I find him and Hannah on the brown couch with some papers spread out in front of them. He is writing frantically and she seems to be in awe of him. They barely notice as I take my seat beside Hannah.

I surprise him and he almost covers up what he is writing.

"Whatcha guys up to?" I ask.

"Bentley's taking inventories of advancements," she says with a smile.

"You look great Hannah. Are you feeling better?" I ask. And she really does. All the color has come back to her cheeks and she even seems to be putting some meat on her bones.

"Yes, much."

"So?" I ask, as I lean over to look at Bentley's list. I see a list of all the people he thinks to have advancements, but don't see my name.

"Have you changed your mind about me?" I ask with a smirk.

He returns the smile. "Maybe."

"What are you going to do with all that?" I ask. Hannah has lost some interest in the conversation and nestles herself into the couch, absently watching the movie that's on the TV screen. It looks like Mighty Ducks.

He looks around before saying, "I'm going to try and fix this, Dani. I'll find a way."

"Battle with God? That's not a mismatch or anything," I say back, as the words David and Goliath float through my head.

"That probably wouldn't be wise, but I have to do something." He's got worry creased deep into his face.

"I wouldn't worry about it too much," I say. "Doesn't it seem like whatever is going to happen, is going to happen? It would be nice to know what to expect though. Too bad the Big Guy wasn't doing them in order," I joke. It's hard for me to take this seriously, even after witnessing the full effects on Kit. I think it's easier to laugh it off. Well, maybe not easier, but I'm giving it a good try.

"How can you take this so lightly? Didn't you hear Jonah? We don't know which one is coming next. What if it's . . . never mind."

"What?" I ask as I glance over at Hannah who is now sleeping. She must have good dreams because there is a faint smile on her lips. Lucky girl.

"Don't worry about it," he says as he gathers up his papers, and stalks off to the other room.

His mood swings don't even bother me anymore. I find myself excited to be alone again. I go up to my room and dress for a walk out into the woods again. Maybe even run if I feel up to it.

I pack my bag and my precious pills and head out for a day to myself. Mom has even stopped asking me where I'm going. I know I'm not far from Tent City, but it will still take me most of the morning to get there.

It's tougher than I thought to get through the areas I want to. I find myself wishing I had some kind of snow shoe with me, as my foot sinks all the way through the deep snow. Waite is trailing along beside me in the trees, gracefully trotting, making me look even clumsier.

He has grown even bigger with a winter coat. His yellow eyes never leave me. He's not even shy anymore about making himself known. As far as I know, he will only get close to Avery, Brody, and me. I still don't know why he's around. As comforting as he is, his presence still bothers me. I know that this big pile of fur is around for a reason. The reason is usually danger. I try to shoo him off and shout at him to look after Brody. He stops for just a second, but continues on with me.

I've decided to run and I'm still at least a couple of hours out from Tent City. I don't know why I want to go back. Maybe I'm hoping to find peace in losing Jack. It's probably even halfway dangerous. The last I knew, the camp was overrun by The Council in search for the missing children.

I'm foggy and exhausted from running and probably the Valium I can't seem to get enough of. I set my pack down by a huge downed pine tree and rummage around for something to eat. I find some dried jerky and swallow it down with some fluffy snow.

After another grueling two hours, I find Tent City. It's so strange to see it with all this snow. It looks sad and abandoned. I walk carefully into camp, noticing Waite is no longer with me.

All of the tents are caved in with piles of slushy snow. The limitless piles of wood are now covered and unseen, only tiny, white mountains covering what they used to be. I want to walk in further, but I can see from footprints that someone has been here . . . recently. The hairs on my arms stand up despite being covered by layers of clothing. I want to scan around quickly, but find ease in only slowly turning my head. Maybe if I move slowly, whoever is here won't spot me. I'm cursing myself for not wearing the white camouflage. Instead I'm wearing a bright orange ski jacket that makes me stick out like a target.

I'm itching to get into one of the cabins. I want to find Jack's medical books to find a cure for Kit, but the danger is high. I know it. Whoever is here is watching me. I don't know why I know this, but I do. If I had Waite with me, I might just go for it. But I don't. So I do the last thing I want to and turn around and run as fast as I can back home. Is it Wes? Is it other Tent City campers? Might even be Rigby, or The Council. I need to get back there, but now's not the time.

When I come back, I find the house in pure chaos and I can't believe what I'm seeing. It takes me too many seconds to register who's here. He's a huge man with blonde hair, slight gray streaks at his temples. He's mid laugh and it's in the laugh, that I realize who it can't be.

It's my uncle Randy. It's been years since I've seen him and he still looks as good as he always has, maybe even better. My dad claims he has always been a ladies' man and it's easy to see why. He glances my way and his crystal clear blue eyes light up.

He doesn't even give me a minute to register all of this before he comes up to me and engulfs me in a huge bear hug.

"Dani? This can't be you! I can't believe how you've grown." He laughs, huge grin spread across his face.

I take a step back to look at him. If it wasn't for his voice, I wouldn't be convinced it was him either. He looks the same, but different too. His skin is tanned and even for as old as he is, he's still got muscles popping through his t-shirt. He is a massive, towering man, but somehow not intimidating, just friendly.

"What are you doing here?" I ask in astonishment. "How did you find us?"

For a moment, I'm afraid that if he has come here, The Council now knows where we are. But then I remember, it's Randy, and how he's better at surviving than anyone. He wouldn't bring danger here.

"We have time for that later," Mom calls from the kitchen. "For now, let's eat!"

The day out has made me ravenous and now that Randy is here I feel like I can breathe a sigh of relief. He'll have a plan for us. Maybe now that Burke is gone, The Council is gone too.

“Where have you come from?” I ask, as I pass Randy the instant potatoes.

“The capital, of course,” he responds. Mom hands him the pitcher of water, but he declines. “Got my own.”

“What?” Dad kids. “Our water not good enough for you?”

“Nah, it’s just fine. I’ve just been on a vitamin water kick. Found a whole stash of it in a warehouse. Been stuck on it ever since. It made some rapper rich and famous. It’s got to be good for me,” he says, as he chuckles and unscrews the lid to his bottle. It does look refreshing. It’s got a picture of a waterfall on the side. Is that what keeps him looking so good?

“What will happen now? Now that Burke is gone?” I ask almost shyly, as I glance over at Bentley.

Randy looks pained when he decides how to answer me. “I’m afraid not much will change, sweetheart. Burke was only one man and The Council still stands as it is. But I can tell you this, I think things are getting better.”

“How can you say that?” Bentley now asks, distrust in his eyes.

“What do you mean, son?” he answers back.

Bentley bristles at the word son, but then says, “what about the plagues? There are still more to come. That seems to be the bigger threat right now, don’t you think?”

“Shoot. You gotta die of something, right?” Randy laughs and it feels oddly inappropriate, but then stops to say, “I did want to thank you for letting me know where my family is. It really means a lot to me.”

“You told him?” I ask Bentley. I don’t know why this shocks me so much. They did have a relationship while we lived in Tent City. Bentley claims that his ties to Randy were the reason we did as well as we did. Randy would tell him good raid spots, and Bentley could come in quietly and come out safely because of Randy's Intel.

"How?" I ask, as I impulsively kick Bentley under the table. Why is he always keeping secrets from me?

"Propane store had a phone, remember?" he responds. But actually . . . I don't care. I'm just so happy Randy has found us and maybe he can find a way out of this mess. I want to ask him about Jack so badly, but I can't bring myself to do it.

"I'm going up to my room," Hannah says, after barely touching her food. A flash of worry creeps across my mind. I'll check on her later.

Okay, it's now or never. "How do you know?" I ask Randy, as I watch him swallow his last bite.

"Know what sweetheart?" He winks with a smile.

"How do you know Burke is really gone?"

"Saw the bodies myself. No need to worry," he says as he grabs for my shoulder. "All your worries are gone."

***

It's late at night and I'm restless again. It feels like there are coils of energy bound deep within the fibers of my leg muscles. I stretch them, do leg squats, and kicks before I go to leave my room out of frustration. I'm just about to leave my room when I hear voices in the hallway.

"Shhhh . . . you'll wake the house," Randy says.

"Can you prove it?" my dad asks.

"Yes. I don't have it with me now, but it's true."

The sounds become muffled as they lower their voices more. I can tell they are right outside my door. I place my ear to the door.

"How come we didn't know about this before?" Dad asks. "How do you know it's you?" I can almost picture him shaking his head in disbelief.

"I know. I need you to have a little faith in me, brother. It's me. I just know . . . I know what you're thinking . . . this isn't an ego thing. We are direct descendants. We've found the book of Judah. There is to be a new King. Do you think I want this responsibility? It's a lot to take on."

Dad seems to be thinking about this. "Can you prove it? Does this have anything to do with the Davidic Descendants? You know that's all crazy. Do you have actual proof?" Dad asks, as his voice starts to rise.

"Why do you need proof? Isn't it enough that I'm telling you?"

"If that's true, why is . . . why was Burke looking for the Golden Child?"

"The Golden Child isn't really golden at all," he says back.

"What do you mean? What about The Council? They've had bulletins running for days. They're convinced there's a Golden Child," Dad asks.

"Well . . . even if there is," Randy stammers, "we are the descendants. I have a job to do. I can feel it . . . Some child isn't going to be able to run the country. Jeeze, can you even imagine?"

"What makes you—" Dad starts to reply, but I lose my footing a little and the door gives just a bit, but it's enough to quiet them. Damn, why didn't I stay still just a little longer? What are they talking about?

I open the door to find them looking at me, heat coloring their cheeks.

"Hey," I say quietly.

"What are you doing up? It's late," my dad scolds.

"Couldn't sleep. What are you doing up?"

"Just catching up with your dad here," Randy says, as he grabs my dad by the back of the neck, a friendly gesture. "He tells me you've become quite the runner. You'll have to show me what you can do later. Maybe tomorrow?" he asks as he stifles a yawn. "I'm bushed. See you in the morning kiddo," he says as he lightly punches me in the arm.

I wait until I know Randy is gone before I ask, "Dad . . . what are the Davidic Descendants?" Even the sound of it makes me think of cartoons or maybe vampires. I'm so confused.

"You don't need to worry about that," he says, as he puts his thumb to my cheek, something he hasn't done since I was small.

"Dad," I persist. I'm not leaving without an answer.

"Just a crazy group who thinks they are King David's descendants," his voice low.

"What's so crazy about that?"

"I suppose it's not really crazy. They just think they're better than everyone else, that they have rights over others: the right to lead, right to power. Your uncle used to be a part of it. I thought he quit, but maybe he hasn't," he answers, but then looks at me as if maybe he has said too much.

He takes me off guard by squeezing my forearm and leaning to whisper in my ear, "Don't ever tell him." He leaves without another word to join my mother in their bedroom. A shiver that moves like electricity shimmies up my spine.

What does he mean, "Don't tell him"? Don't tell him what? That I know? Dad seems to be afraid of Randy now. It's a very bizarre feeling. Randy is my dad's older brother and as far as I know, Randy has always taken care of my dad. Their parents died when they were younger and Dad claims that without Randy, he never would have survived. Why is Dad acting so weird all of a sudden? And how could Randy think he's to be the next King? Has he gone crazy?

The next morning I find Bentley on the porch cleaning a pistol.

"Hey," I start.

"Hey. I'm glad you're up. I was just coming to look for you . . . It's time we trained you with one of these. I was an idiot not to do it before . . . you know, when Tent City was attacked. Sorry about that," he says, as he clicks the safety back on the gun and places it on the railing with a steady hand.

"No. Don't be. And don't bother. I'm not training with one of those."

"Why?"

"I'm just not."

"Come on. Be serious. Things are getting bad again. I want you prepared."

"Why? You'll just come save the day anyway," I say, voice dripping with sarcasm.

"Dani, please."

"No." I leave without another word.

Jessica's words about all the school shootings and mass bombings are still haunting me. It's probably dumb not to train with a weapon, but the idea of the gun leaves a bad taste in my mouth, almost like gun powder. I've done all right before, I'll get by.

The only reason I may have wanted a gun before is to finish off Burke. But now that he's gone, it seems pointless.

I'm surprised Randy hasn't planned to stay long. He says that he has to get on the road after lunch. Of course he will stay for lunch. I've never seen anyone resist Mom's cooking.

"Hey, big guy," he says to Brody, as he carefully wipes his mouth on his napkin, "looks like you need a haircut. Can you even see?" he chuckles. "Cost of a haircut too steep around here, John?"

"He likes it long!" I practically shout.

"Can I be excused?" Brody asks Mom.

"Of course, honey. Don't go far. There's a storm coming in."

He and Avery are out the door before she's even done yelling instructions and I breathe a sigh of relief. Is this what Dad was talking about when he said, "Don't tell him?" Does Dad know about Brody too?

I want to continue to look at Randy as a hero. I've thought of him this way for so long. When I found out it was him that helped out Bentley and Jack while we lived in Tent City, I almost burst with pride that it was my uncle that helped us survive. But why is he acting so weird now?

After Randy leaves, Bentley and I get ready to go over to Hannah's to get supplies before the incoming storm hits. I can't believe how much has been stocked up in Hannah's old house. They even have an old root cellar that has enough canned vegetables and government packaged food to last all winter. We avoid the packaged food and bring all the cans back.

I ask Bentley to take one more trip back with me to get Hannah more of her medicines. He's happy to, probably happy to have something to do. He spends most of the second trip showing off running up to the top of the hill and back so many times, I am dizzy just watching.

"Show off," I say.

"Wouldn't you?" He laughs. He's not even out of breath.

"Yeah," I admit with a smile.

We spend most of the afternoon in the basement of the house. We have gotten caught up in looking at all the photo albums. I see an album with medical certificates and it looks like the woman who lived here was a pharmacist. So that's where all the medicine comes from. She must have been hoarding it after the locusts.

I see a lot of photos of Hannah's old boyfriend. It's easy to see why she fell in love. He was quite handsome. I even see a picture of Hannah. It's hard to tell that it's even her because she looks so different now. In the picture, she is the epitome of health. Her cheeks glow and she has a wide grin that spreads across her whole face. The boyfriend has his arm around her and all seems right in her world—a happily ever after, if only for a moment.

"Well, you ready to go?" Bentley asks me after what must be hours. He checks his watch. "Wow, it's late. Do you want to bring any of that for Hannah?"

"Um, no. Probably just bring back bad memories."

We get up the stairs and it's dark out. Panic pinches at me when I realize there is no reason it should be dark out. The words of Jonah talking about the plague of darkness are lingering at the back of my mind, slowly shoving to the front.

"It can't be," I say.

"What's going on here?" Bentley asks, as he puts down his box of canned vegetables and runs over to the window.

"It's snow."

"What?"

"Snow. How is that possible? How long were we down there? Could've only been a couple hours. What?" he asks as he skims his fingertips across the glass of the window.

Snow is blocking out all the outside light and appears to have swallowed the house. Bentley rushes to the open the door, only to find us trapped.

"No way." He is frantically working out how this happened, and I stare in awe at the big mound of snow blocking the door. The lights flicker. The word igloo floats inside my head.

"We're stuck," he says, as he sits down on the edge of the end table where a lamp sits. The lights flicker again before going out.

"Solar start box must be damaged. Looks like we are not going to have any light," he says. I hear him get up and start rummaging around.

What a peculiar feeling. There is not an ounce of light in this old, creaky house. My hand instinctively goes out to reach for Bentley. The house moans in disapproval.

A loud crack booms at the ceiling and I let out a shriek. "What was that?"

"I don't know. A tree maybe landed on the roof. We need light."

He takes my hand and leads me to the kitchen. We're stumbling and tumbling over each other, but finally we find the drawers that hold the flashlights. He's clicking them on and off and they are not responding. I open one to check for batteries. In the dark, I examine them by touch. If I had to guess, they are corroded and worthless.

I stumble my way around Bentley and go to the refrigerator. I remember seeing candles on the top. I feel around until my fingers land on the glass bowls filled with wax. One comes crashing down as I clumsily try to catch it. I'm careful with the next one.

I've found three candles, but no matches. We spend the next ten minutes searching for matches, but come up empty.

"The stove," I say, as I reach my way over there.

I turn the gas knob. It clicks a few times before it ignites and gives us just the smallest bit of light. I roll up a paper I found on the counter and light the end in the open flame on the stove and then light the candle.

"Smart thinking," Bentley says, and I see a faint smile in the little bit of light we have.

We spend the next few hours lighting every available candle, but it's still not much against creepy darkness. The house has grown cold in the little bit of time we lost lights and heat. I'm not sure what we are going to do, but I'm wishing desperately we hadn't made the second trip back. Now we're trapped here, and everyone else is trapped there. How did so much snow come down so fast?

Bentley has barricaded the kitchen off so we can keep the little heat we have in the one room. We spend so much time in survival mode, we don't even eat supper and I fall asleep shivering in his arms on the kitchen floor.

I wake to find him trying to dig through the barricade at the front door. His hands look raw and bloody from his frantic scraping.

"I'm so sorry, Dani. It won't budge. Can you look around and try to find a shovel?"

"Basement?"

"Yeah, take a candle and see if you can find one. Hurry back."

I take my time down the creaky stairs. There's only one shovel, but it's better than nothing. I scan around and see a pile of books a little further in. I scoop up a few and bring those and the shovel back. Might need something to do if we're going to be here a while.

Bentley and I take turns shoveling ourselves out of the snow wall. We take what we've scooped out and store it in the corner of the house. We're at least eight feet beyond the door with no end in sight.

"How about we take a break?" I ask him, as he is more like just banging the shovel around than really pulling out any new snow. He seems reluctant to quit, but does after I remove the shovel gently from his hands.

We barricade ourselves back in the kitchen and he looks through the books as I cook us a lunch of green beans and an old can of pork and beans. The expiration on it was five years ago, but I think it will be fine. I can feel him watching me. A shiver creeps down my spine, but I'm not sure if it's from the cold.

"You're so beautiful," he says quietly.

I pretend not to hear him. "Anything good there?"

"Bible?" he asks, and I almost choke on my green beans.

"Can you look up anything on kings?" We have every candle burning in the kitchen and the lighting is mysterious, ominous, romantic. Why am I feeling so pathetic?

"What do you want to know?" he asks, as he leans in toward the limited light and leafs through the paper thin pages. Of course they would be paper thin; they're paper.

"I don't know, anything."

He tells me about all of the kings, but I feel a special pull towards King David, even if it's in a creepy way. The mood has lightened despite our circumstances. I watch Bentley intently as he tells me the story of David and Goliath. He reads quietly to himself for a few minutes.

"Now what are you reading?"

"A story about King Solomon."

"Care to share?" I ask with a little giggle. I'm a little dizzy with the drugs I have taken or lack of oxygen, either one is fine with me.

"Okay . . . so King Solomon was a very wise king. One day, two women came to him and staked their claim on the same baby after one of the women had smothered her own child in its sleep,"

"That's awful," I interrupt.

"There's more," he continues, as he holds one finger up as if to silence me. "This same woman who killed her own baby has taken the child of another woman that she shares a home with. When she wakes up, the mother of the living child finds she's holding the dead baby, who she knows is not hers," he says.

I'm lost in thought. I am just noticing the smooth rhythm of his voice and what a good story-teller he is. I get lost in the way his mouth is moving with each syllable and he notices. My chest becomes heavy with guilt.

"You listening?"

"Um, yes, sorry, go on." Heat flushes my cheeks. What am I thinking?

"Well, since the woman cannot convince the mother of the dead child to give her back her child, they go to King Solomon for a decision. The king hears both sides, which are identical, and decides that the best course is to cut the baby in half so both mothers will have a share," he says and I gasp.

He continues, "To do this, however, means to kill the child. The mother who has already lost a child is happy with the solution, but the real mother cries out and begs Solomon to let the other woman have her baby."

"Then what?" I ask.

"King Solomon sees that the woman who was willing to give up her baby in order to save it is the true mother."

"Solomon was a pretty smart guy huh?" I say, as I give him the last of the green beans.

"I guess so. But he's not the true hero of the story. It's the mother. I suppose if you love something enough, you have to let it go."

"In her case anyway."

"Should we start digging again?" he asks, as he shoves the green beans to the side.

"You get started and I'll clean up."

We spend the rest of the afternoon, at least what I think is afternoon, digging out of the glacier we found ourselves in and collapse back into the kitchen seeking warmth for the night. We've got a pretty good tunnel, but it seems never ending.

This time Bentley makes supper as I sprawl out on the kitchen floor with my eyes closed taking in all of the sounds. I open my eyes when I no longer hear the clattering of dishes to find Bentley hovering above me.

"I'm sorry, Dani, but I have to do this."

He leans down to kiss me and I startle myself by kissing him back. For a minute, I forget I'm trapped inside an old house, probably never to emerge. I forget that the world is coming to an end. I forget that my family is trapped in another house and I forget that I'm not even sure if they're alive. And Jack. I've forgotten about Jack.

All I can think about in this moment is Bentley's lips touching mine. Why do I always shy away from this? It's wonderful. It leaves me feeling scared and safe at the same time. My heart has lodged itself in my throat and my stomach is all twisted up. It feels like I'm on a Ferris wheel. He makes a small groaning noise and it shakes me back to reality. I push him away.

"We can't do this," I say, out of breath.

"Why?" Even in the dim light, I can see hurt on his face.

"We just can't." I bite my lip to keep back the tears.

He sighs. "Is this because of Jack?"

My tears are brimmed up into my eyes, heavy, and I realize I don't have an answer for him. I find myself thinking about how easy it would be to just give myself to Bentley. But I can't. I don't know why. It hurts just thinking about it. The tears are slipping out now and he has my chin in his hand.

"I can wait for you. Take all the time you want." He gently kisses my forehead and then bunches up our sweatshirts for pillows. Despite the guilt and Jack's face in the back of my mind, I scoot toward Bentley and tell myself it's only for warmth.

We wake in the morning to scratching sounds. Something is in the tunnel! I'm still in Bentley's arms and we are tangled up. We bang heads in our rush to see what's coming.

We run out to see a hole of light peeking through the top of the tunnel. We hear scratching and chunks of snow are starting to cave in when I see a paw poke through.

"Waite!" I shout. "He's here, Bentley! I knew he would come," I shout, never feeling so relieved.

"Who's here?" Bentley asks me with confusion in his face. He has picked up the shovel and stands in a defensive position.

"No, don't. It's fine. It's the wolf. He's come to get us out. Put that down," I say and he sheepishly drops the shovel.

Bentley runs down to the basement and comes up with some tennis rackets.

"What's that for?" I ask, as I work on the small hole Waite has dug for us.

"Snow shoes," he says with a grin.

He gets to work on those and adds straps to fasten to our shoes. When we emerge from the tunnel, the sun is blinding. I shield my eyes, but everything is already black and splotchy.

"Wait here," Bentley says, as he crawls back inside. He comes back with two hideous pairs of sunglasses.

"This house has everything," he says and then laughs.

He pauses just before we reach the exit, "I kind of wish we had more time. I feel like I sorta wasted it."

I look at him and hesitate, before I say, "Let's go, everyone must be worried."

The homemade snow shoes actually work really well. It's strange walking 20 feet higher in the world and at a height above the houses. It looks like Waite has scattered after breaking us free. I'm eager to get back to the cabin and see if my family is still trapped.

As we clear the area of Hannah's old house the snow starts to fade. By the time we get back to our cabin, we notice that they didn't get nearly the snow we did. How is that possible? It's only a couple miles from here. It's as if an entire snow cloud hovered above Hannah's house, trapping only us. Why?

We stumble into the house, laughing and Bentley catches me in his arms as the shoes catch on the front rug.

"Where have you been?" Mom shouts from the kitchen.

"They were at my house," Hannah answers with a grin.

"Yeah, how did you know?" I ask her.

"I've seen what's there," she says.

Then I notice it. Hannah is pale and worn down again. She sits herself down quietly on the couch.

"What happened?" I ask her, as I feel her forehead. She is on fire and I have my answer.

"How could you? You know what it does to you. Who was it?" I'm burning with anger.

"I didn't have a choice," Hannah answers back.

"There's always a choice. Who was it!"

"Me," Dad says, as he comes in with his entire right arm bandaged up and in a sling.

"What happened?" My face must be ugly with accusation.

"Chainsaw. I'm really sorry, honey. I tried to stop her."

"Chainsaw?" I ask. "You're saying a chainsaw attacked you?"

"It got away from me. A tree came down on the house in the ice storm and I was clearing it away when the blade caught on a knot and swung back on me."

"You don't need to be mad at him. It was my choice. And I would do it again. I saved his life," Hannah says with pride.

"Yes, you did," Mom says, as she comes and puts a hand on Hannah's shoulder, "and I will be thankful for the rest of my life."

Hannah smiles shyly and I help her to her room. I know I should be grateful that she saved my dad, but for some reason, I'm not. I'm tired of people using her. She looks completely exhausted.

"I'm curious." I start. "I thought it was just for sickness. You can do that with injury too?"

"Yeah, I wasn't sure it would work . . . and it definitely feels different."

"How?"

"Well," she says, as she adjusts the blankets twisted up at her feet, "with sickness, I just feel yucky and gross . . . but with your dad, it was more like pain."

"You know, you can stop doing that. We still love you, with or without your powers," I say to her, as I tuck the blanket over her shoulder and under her chin. She's shivering despite the multiple layers I pile on top.

"I know. That's what makes it so easy. I would give it all up for each and every one of you," she says sleepily, as her eyes flutter shut.

The snowshoes have given me an idea. I'm going to use them to get back to Tent City. This will make the going much faster. I almost ask Bentley to go with me, but I like these little trips by myself. I get time to think . . . alone. I'm confused at what happened in the old house. It needs some sorting.

I've doubled up on the Valium today and the snow is exhilarating. I'm still wearing the ugly sunglasses and I sneak up on the outskirts of Tent City. I see more fresh tracks inside the perimeter. How can I sneak around without being seen? I did wear the white camouflage today, so I choose to watch from the outside.

There is a fire that looks like it has recently been put out as the last of the smoke wafts into the air. Mom and Dad don't keep track of me anymore, so I decide to camp out for the night and see if I can see more tomorrow.

I've built a snow fort far away from Tent City that protects me from the wind and snuggle in for the night. When I wake, I make my way back to Tent City.

I crouch down to get a better look at who is in Tent City. I see a guy tending to the fire, but it is too far away to see who it is. There only looks to be one. I wonder if it's Wes who has made his way back. I've decided that if it is, I'll tell him he needs to come back with me. It would be good for Bentley to have him around. I don't even care anymore if he's a peeping Tom.

I'm packing up my stuff to make my way closer when someone grabs me from behind. I yelp in fear. The stranger covers my mouth and I yank free to see who's got me.

"Jack?"

Chapter 13

"Are you alone?" he asks, but it doesn't even look like him. He's got a full-grown beard and his eyes are hard with distrust. But, oh God, it *is* him.

"What is happening? Am I dreaming?" I smack him as hard as I can in the shoulder with an open hand and it makes a loud thud.

"Are you alone?" he whispers this time.

I feel lightheaded and dizzy. I drop to my knees and try to steady my breathing. He drops to his knees to match me.

"I knew you'd come," he says softly.

"What are you talking about? How is this possible? The helicopter? The crash. I don't understand. Jack, what's going on?" I reach for my pocket and pull out the pill bottle. I put two in my mouth, eager for the effects.

"What's this?" he asks as he takes the bottle from my hand. "What are you doing?"

"What's it to you!" I yell, surprised that my first emotion is anger. "You left! You left me to sit around and think you were dead! How could you?" I snatch back the bottle and put it in my pocket.

I sit quietly for a full minute. What's this new feeling? Giddy? It worked? It really worked? I got him back? I've got to be dreaming. In the past few weeks, I've made deals with God and deals with the devil. Who took me up on my offer? There were times I promised if I could just have him back, I would give up everything. I even had this crazy idea that if he came back, I could put the Bentley/Jack dilemma to rest. I would choose Jack. I wouldn't even care about who was right for me. I would take it as a sign that I belonged with him. And he's here.

Jack is talking to me, but I can't even put any of his words together. I'm distracted by movement behind him. The man tending the fire comes jogging up and I'm on my feet before he can reach us.

"You!" I scream at him. I hadn't anticipated this. How could I?

I look back at Jack and burn with betrayal. I'm on fire with rage. Before I know what I'm doing, I'm racing towards Burke and I have leveled him to the ground with a leg sweep Grant taught me. I'm on top of him now and smashing punches into his face. Blood is spurting now either from his lip or his nose, but he's not fighting back.

"Monster!" I scream at Burke as Jack pulls me off.

"Dani, you have to give me some time. I can explain everything. Please, just give me some time," Jack says.

The two pills I just took are taking effect and my vision is speckled. Black spots are dancing around like butterflies.

Burke seems wary of me now, always keeping a few feet away from me. He has shoved a dirty handkerchief up his nose to stop the bleeding. I look around and see in the days I have been gone Jack and the monster have cleaned up camp, but I still can't get used to seeing it with snow. I ache for how it was in the summer, when the stars were flirty and winked all night, and even the brown, dirt-covered trails felt warm. I take a deep breath in and notice the pine smell that I came to know as home is gone.

Jack tells me to sit. He and Burke find chairs beside the crackling fire, but I'm standing with my arms crossed. I'm debating taking off, but the Valium has made me slow and it would take Jack only seconds to catch me. I'm aching for Bentley. As much as he has lied to me, he would never do . . . this.

"Listen," Burke starts, "I know this must be difficult for you, but if you could just let us expla—"

"I don't owe you anything." I'm practically snarling.

"No. You don't." He stands now. "But maybe you owe Jack. My son here has done everything he can for you."

"I never asked for that," I spit back.

"Is she always like this?" he asks Jack. "I'm sorry, but I don't see the appeal." Burke shrugs.

"I've had enough of this. I'm leaving." I spin around, more difficult because all my senses are slowed, but I'm determined to leave. Burke stays back at camp, but Jack follows me as I march off, trudging through the snow. I'm thinking about a way I can kill Burke before Jack can stop me.

"Hey, can you just wait," Jack finally says when we are far enough away from Burke that I can no longer see him. "I've been waiting what feels like *years* to see you."

I stop. "Jack, I don't understand what's going on." I reach for my pocket when he stops me.

"What is all this?" he asks. "Who gave this to you?"

"That's not really any of your business," I say in defiance, but I do put the bottle back. I can get to it later.

"Okay. How about an easier one. Is Bentley with you?" he asks as he glances back towards camp.

"Why are you with him?" I ask back. "How could you? What happened with the helicopter?"

"See? That's why you should stick around. We've got lots to talk about."

"I can't."

"Why?"

"I think you know why."

"Is that the only reason you won't stay?" he asks, as he glances back again.

"Isn't that reason enough?" I fire back. I still can't believe Jack is here in Tent City with that evil madman, even if Burke is his dad.

"Do me a favor. Stay here. I'll be right back."

I tell him I will, but as soon as he's out of sight, I contemplate bolting. I feel the urge to get back to Bentley and tell him his brother is actually alive. But I've missed Jack and I really would like to know what's going on. In the end, curiosity wins and I stay put.

Jack jogs back and the memory of all of his kindness comes flooding back. Of course, if I were to see Jack again, it would be in Tent City.

"He's gone," Jack shouts, "Come on."

"Gone? What do you mean?"

"I told the old man to scram," he jokes, and since I'm eager to see camp and everything I've left behind, I follow him. I still can't believe Jack's alive.

We sit around the fire and it brings in a comforting warmth. I spend the first five minutes back in Tent City just looking around in wonder at my old home—and sneaking peaks at Jack. I'm still not sure this is real. The cabins seem to be intact. The storm must not have hit here. Even the swing Bentley built for me is still here, swaying in the breeze.

I settle in as Jack stokes the fire. I'm watching him in disbelief. I'm waiting for him to reach out for me and burst into flames. The only thing that even half way convinces me that he's real is the beard. He's never had one in my dreams.

The medicine is working overtime. It has now provided a lullaby of music in my mind as I watch Jack skillfully work over the fire. He arranges the wet logs single file by the fire, encouraging them to dry up. My eyelids are becoming heavy with the sensation of peace that can only come from being able to stop grieving for the boy with gray eyes.

When I wake, I'm convinced I'm still dreaming because I'm handcuffed to the bedpost of my old cabin. I scan the empty cabin frantically.

"Jack!" I call, but he doesn't answer.

Panic and fear are pulsating through me. I'm having trouble catching my breath, despite being stuck to a bed. Has Burke taken over and done something to Jack? Or worse, could Jack be in on this? What's going on? I can't even fathom a single reason I should be hooked to a bed.

Just then the door crashes open. It's Jack.

"What's going on?" I ask, as I hop to the side of the bed and the handcuff pinches at my wrist. I'm his prisoner. Why?

"Sit. I will explain everything," he says. He seems to be gauging my reaction, unsure, but yet so confident. How does he do both at the same time?

I sit and he digs into his pocket. He's got my pill bottle.

"We're going to do something about this," he says, as he shakes the bottle in front of my face. Is he taunting me?

"You can't do this!"

"See, that's where you're wrong. I can and I'm going to." He seems almost angry.

He stands and starts pacing. "You know, I never figured you for the type. What's going on with you?" he says, as he looks at me with what kind of looks like disgust.

I bow my head and start to weep. He's right. It's been my dirty little secret. But I'm not sure that I would have done it differently. When I first found the magic in those, I could forget about Jack. Forget about the crash. Forget about Drake.

He leans down by where I'm sitting on the bed and brushes the hair out of my eyes. I jerk away.

"I'm going to take care of you. This will be over soon. Can you tell me how much of this stuff you were taking?" he asks.

"Enough."

"Can you be more specific?"

"Barely enough."

"Funny," he says, but I won't give him anything. He's watching me in this vulnerable state and as I'm crashing with every emotion, he is cool.

"Okay. Here, take this," he says as he hands me not two pills, not even one, but one that he has cut in half. "This is 5 mg, which would be enough for most people. We are going to get you off this stuff. It's not going to be fun, but I'll get you through it."

I take the meager portion and lay my head back down on the pillow and look up at my handcuff. The skin around it is raw and red and I look back at Jack with a silent plea to take it off.

"Okay. When I'm with you, it can be off, but when I'm not, it's gotta stay," he says, as he removes the cuff and my wrist sighs in relief.

I'm fighting tears of frustration. How did I get to this place? I know Jack is disgusted with me, but it's nothing compared to how I actually feel about myself. It makes me even sicker to know that if I could take more pills, I would.

"My skin is crawling," I finally say.

"Come," he says as he stands. "I have an idea."

I see that he's going to lead me outside and I follow him. I'm wondering if I will have a chance to bolt. I'm shaky, but I also feel like the energy and angst bound up in my legs will probably make me faster. I could be back to our cabin in no time. If I'm as fast as I once was, there's no way he could catch me.

He takes me by the hand and I change my mind. I'm trying to remember the deals I've made. I've gotten what I've asked for. He's back. Now it's my turn. I can do this. My hands are shaking. He squeezes to steady them.

"We have to take the quad. It's way too far to walk."

"Okay."

Where is he taking me? I trust him, so I just wrap my arms around him and close my eyes. I'm embarrassed to admit I find myself thinking of my pills more than him. What have I done to myself?

I open my eyes as I feel he is starting to slow down and it looks like he has brought me to some sort of pond or small lake. It's freezing out, so I'm surprised it's not frozen. He sees my confusion.

"It's a hot spring . . . Shoot, I should have asked. You didn't have a suit with you? Back at the cabin?" he asks.

"What are we doing, Jack?"

"I think this could be good for you. It's just a theory I have. Like water therapy. I suppose it depends on if you like water or not. Water brings us back to our most infantile state. Think of this as a safe womb." He smiles, and I can't help but laugh.

"You said your skin was crawling," he says almost shyly.

"I think it's brilliant," I say with a shaky voice. I know he's trying to help me. Why do I always fight him about everything? I can give this a try. Anything's worth a shot. I feel like I'm at war with myself. If I'm lucky, I'll drown.

I realize I'm in jeans and a long sleeve shirt. Drowning seems like a good possibility.

"Turn around," I say.

"Of course," he says, and it's like he can't turn around fast enough.

I get down to my bra and underwear and prepare myself for the assault of cold water. Only it's not cold. If I didn't know better, it would feel as if I was in a heated pool. This is amazing. I never even knew such a thing existed. Why don't we have camp set up here?

Despite the warm temperature, my skin almost seems to sizzle as I make my way to the deep end. Every inch of crawling, sweaty skin is being replaced by something that's not mine. I don't feel like me. I can't resist and I let the water fully cover my head and I start to sink to the bottom my arms up, invisible, free. It feels like I was on fire and now I'm drifting in rain clouds, wet, cool, nourishing. When I'm down pretty far, I feel weightless. My hair feels magical, floating around me. It's as if I'm a mermaid and I could stay down here forever. My lungs start to burn and I'm finally reminded that I need air. I breach the top and I'm surprised to find Jack gone.

"Jack?"

His head bobs up beside me and he looks furious. "What are you doing?"

"What do you mean?" I ask, breathless and choking. I'm not sure if it's from the panic of Jack being gone or the mouthful of water I took in.

"Are you trying to kill yourself?" He's struggling in the water and I wonder how well he can swim.

"I'm fine," I laugh. "You were right. This water is like magic. Can you even swim?" I ask as he continues to struggle. "Go back."

"I can swim. It's just that I have all my clothes on. It's harder."

"Take them off."

"What?"

"You have boxers?"

"Of course," he says, choking on his own mouthful of water.

"Take your other clothes off before you drown. I won't look, I promise."

His face reddens, but he makes his way back to the shore. I do take a quick peek before he catches me and I turn around. There is a weird feeling I'm having. It feels sort of like power. Usually, whenever I'm around Jack, I feel weak, incapable. He's the smart one. The good one. The one who always knows what's right and what's best. I feel small around him, but seeing him shy and awkward about swimming with a girl in her underwear has given me an idea. Maybe I can even the playing field.

It takes him a while to get comfortable, but once he does, we actually start to have fun.

"So where have you been?" I ask, as I splash him. He ducks and gives me a flirty smile. Jack is different when he's having fun. He should try it more often.

"Making my way back to you," he says with more confidence.

"So, am I your prisoner now?" I back away so I can see his face when he answers, but all he does is go under. I search for him, sure he will come up soon, but he's nowhere to be found. I wait patiently because I'm sure he's repaying me for scaring him.

I let out a shriek as I feel hands around my ankle and I barely have time to close my mouth before I'm pulled under. He's getting braver.

He comes up and I decide it's time for payback. I swim over to him before he has a chance to get away and I dunk him, shoving him down by his shoulders. He comes up quickly, as I realize he has moved us to an area where his feet can touch the ground. He lifts me up, but doesn't let go. He's got his arms wrapped around me and the shock of his hot skin against mine sends an unexplainable feeling through my entire body. I start to shake.

"Are you okay?" he asks, his voice shaking too.

"Are you?" I ask, as I touch my hand to his face in my urge to touch his beard. It strikes me odd that I could be in such close proximity to a man with a beard. "What's up with the beard anyway?" I joke, trying to break the tension, even though neither one of us seems willing to let the other go.

He doesn't answer. It's like he's somewhere else. He brings me in closer. His hand cradles the back of my neck and he looks down. Before he can look back up, I press in and let the water lift me to where I need to be, letting every inch of my body cover him, including my lips. He almost crumples when our lips meet, but then he changes. His hurt seems to change to want. He brings me in even tighter, so that there's not even water between us. My skin gets even warmer.

He backs up to the sandy beach and we fall to the ground. He is feverish, yet respectful when we get to the sand. His hands have not started wandering yet and I'm strangely grateful and disappointed at the same time. He kisses me softly again, as if he's afraid he will break me. He seems to be taking in every second and slowly starts to work down my neck and to my collarbone. I finally realize I'm only in my bra and underwear and that he only has boxers on. I know I'm in a place where everything could change for me . . . forever. I'm not sure I want it to change yet. And then I do the worst thing I could possibly do to ruin the moment. I think of Bentley. A flash of him watching from the tree line sends a tidal wave of guilt through me. I scan around, but see nothing.

"I'm sorry, Dani," Jack says, as he brings me back to attention. "Was that too much?"

"No, don't say that. I wanted it too." I get up and I almost tell him to turn around so I can get dressed, but it seems like if I do that I will make this more awkward than it is so I try to act like it's no big deal and I slide my shirt over my head. The jeans were a little tougher and I sort of laugh to myself as I realize how unattractive I must be now hopping around trying to get a pair of pants on.

"What are you laughing at?" He smiles as he seems to just glide into his jeans.

"Thanks for bringing me here. I think it helped," I say, as we start to walk back to the four-wheeler. I can already feel the itch in my need for more medicine and I find myself wondering if it's time for my meager dosage of Valium, but I'm too embarrassed to ask.

***

"Now what?" I ask, as I hop off the four-wheeler and make my way back to the campfire ring.

"So you don't like the beard huh?" he asks, distracted as he looks into a handheld mirror and rubs at his beard.

"Well, it is different. I kinda miss your face."

"Well, then I guess it's time to shave." He smiles.

"You don't have to do that for me," I say, kicking my feet around the ground, finding it hard to look him in the eye.

I don't know why, but this feels awkward. Is it because he has seen me in my underwear? I only had power for a couple of minutes and I've already lost it. I need it back.

I watch him cut down the bulk of his beard with scissors and then get out a pan of water and heat it up. He is already starting to look more like Jack. I need to be brave. This is part of growing up right?

"Here, let me help," I say, as I take the blade from his hand.

He doesn't deny me. He just looks at me with a healthy dose of caution.

"I'm not going to hurt you." I smile, the beginnings of my confidence coming back. I place the bowl and the shaving brush on the tree stump and instruct Jack to sit on one of the lounge chairs. I stand behind him, like a real barber would do and lather his face up.

"It's time someone took care of you," I say, as I finish up the lather. Now he resembles Santa Claus. Just missing the belly.

I start with smooth strokes and the blade is surprisingly sharp. I steady my hand and hope that he doesn't notice it trembling. I'm feeling sort of ill, but I want to finish the job. I feel the need to sit down. I'm lightheaded, but I don't want to admit that I'm weak again. I don't want him to have to save me. The angles are getting harder and I accidentally nick his jawbone.

"Sorry."

"It's fine. I trust you."

I walk over to the front of him and surprise the both of us by sitting in his lap, straddling him. I feel a slight blush creep up my neck. "Easier," I say when I see him looking at me with a smirky grin. Sitting has already taken away some of the nausea. I bow my head down to take a deep breath when Jack sits up straighter and removes the blade.

"I think you've had enough for one day. You need some rest. You've already done wonderfully. I am really impress—"

I put my finger to his lips to quiet him and then bring his face to me. I press my lips to his and my skin heats up again. I'm not sure what I'm doing. I've never been this forward before. I can smell shaving cream and it's smearing all over my face, but I don't care. I press in further. I can't believe I have Jack back. I would do anything for this. Why does it feel so good and so bad at the same time? He doesn't give me time to wonder for long.

He stands up, still carrying me and he makes his way to the cabin. My heartbeat picks up and I just realize what I've done. I can't deny him now. I'm the one who came on to him. What kind of hypocrite or tease would that make me? He opens the door so quickly I don't have time to figure out what to do. He's making his way towards the bed, kissing me and holding me so tight, I think he will never let me go. So he surprises me when he lays me down on the bed, alone.

"You're burning up," he says, as he walks back over to the bed and sits down beside me. He reaches into my bottle and gives me my half a pill and some other white pills.

"What are those?"

"Tylenol."

I start to cry.

"Are you in pain?" he asks.

"What did I do?"

"Oh . . ." he says, as he pats my leg. I couldn't possibly feel more pathetic. "Listen," he begins again after he clears his throat. "Today is going to go down in history as one of the best days of my life . . . really, but this can't happen now. You're vulnerable. I don't think I would like myself if you and I did this, and it wasn't something you really wanted. Dani, if it's right between us, it will happen. It can't happen until I know you're really mine. I can tell when you're thinking about him."

Oh, my God, I feel like a predator. I hadn't even considered he wouldn't want me. I lean over and let out a groan. This was all wrong. How did Jack do that to me again? Make me feel small. I feel crazy when I'm around him. I don't know if that's a good thing and it's just chemistry, but it's enough to always have me on edge. How foolish to think that I could actually be the one in control for once. The medicine kicks in and I'm relieved that only a half a pill can lull me into sleep. I don't think I can be around Jack right now . . . at least not conscious. Maybe when I wake up, this will all have been a dream and I didn't just humiliate myself.

I wake startled and drenched in sweat. Jack is over in the corner of the cabin reading a book. When he sees me, he puts the book down and walks slowly over to me.

"How are you feeling?" he asks, as he pulls his stethoscope out of his bag.

"Like shit." My heart is beating wildly and every inch of my clothing is sticking to my body. A look of worry flashes across his face. He reaches into his bag and gives me the other half of the pill and some water.

"Drink the whole thing," he says, as he hands me the cup.

"Jack, I'm scared," I say, and I am. My eyes must be bulging out of my face because what I feel is real, raw fear. I know it's irrational and that nothing is actually happening to me, but my hands are trembling and I feel nauseated.

"I'm going to be sick." I try to sit up straighter and before I even get up all the way vomit has bubbled out of me with enough force to splash everywhere I wish it wouldn't. For only being in my throat a second, it has set my esophagus on fire. I'm annoyed as I see the half pill has been ejected out of my body.

"Damn," he says, as it only makes it partially into the empty bucket and more onto his clean flannel and jeans.

"I wish you didn't have to see me like this."

"It's fine. I want to take care of you. Just let me do this."

"How long is it going to be like this?" I practically wail, as I try to steady the room from spinning.

"Not long," he says, as he starts to clean up. "This is the worst part."

I moan and lean back over so he can't see me. I vaguely realize that there are pieces of vomit left in my mouth, but I'm too weak to care. I'm shivering and tremors seize my body. I know I have no control over this. It's hours of tremors, and what feels like the shakes. I keep my back to him because I must look disgusting. He never leaves. I can feel him hovering. Finally, when my whole being including my consciousness can't fight anymore, I find sleep. I can't really keep track, but I feel like this goes on for days.

Chapter 14

"Good morning, Dani."

I open my eyes and my heart beats in a slow, terrified thud because that's not Jack's voice. I don't know who it is, but he's staring at me with compassion.

"Let's take this off," he says, as he unlocks the handcuff that has chafed my skin raw.

"Who are you?" I ask.

"I think you know," he says with a smile.

He looks to be just a couple years younger than me, but somehow so much wiser than I could ever be.

"I don't, honestly I don't. Should I be afraid of you?"

"Hardly," he laughs.

"Where's Jack?"

"You've grown into such a stunning woman, if that's not too weird for me to say," he says, as he ignores my question.

I blush and look to the ground. When I look up again and look deep into his eyes, my entire body explodes into goose bumps. This isn't possible. It's him, but he's grown. How is this possible?

"Drake?"

"I was wondering how long it would take you to figure it out. How's Mom and Dad?" he asks, looking more like the little boy I know.

And I'm not even able to answer his question. I burst into uncontrollable sobs and there isn't one ounce of me that's embarrassed. Because there's nothing I could possibly do about it. How is he here? How is this happening? I'm sure it's him, and he's beautiful.

"Are you real?" I ask.

"Am I?" he asks back.

"Am I dead?" I look down at myself, half expecting to find some kind of ghost-like appearance, but it's me, covered in sweat and goose bumps, growing more aggressive with each second. And then I can't help myself.

I shoot out of bed and run to him so fast that I've knocked us both over and we are both laughing wildly.

"I can't believe it's really you! How is this happening?" I say, feeling lighter than I have in years. Maybe I really am dead.

I close my eyes to steady myself and when I open them again, he's gone. I run out the front door to see where he's gone only to find Jack chopping wood.

"Where did he go?" I shout at Jack.

He stops chopping and comes back to the cabin.

"Who? My dad? I told you he won't come back while you are here. It's safe. Go back to bed."

"No," I slump down feeling defeated. How could he be gone? He was so real. "Drake. It was Drake. He was here. I know he was."

"I'm so sorry, Dani," Jack says, as he rests his axe against the wood stump. "He's not here. He never was. You're having a hallucination. Let's go inside so I can check you over." He looks at me with pity.

"No! I swear he was here. He's the one who uncuffed me. How can you explain that? Did I just magically unlock the handcuffs?"

"Dani,"

"Explain that!"

"You were never cuffed. I took them off days ago, remember?"

I'm losing my mind. I can almost believe it was a hallucination if I saw Drake when he was young, but he was grown. He looked sixteen. I don't know how much more of this I can take.

I collapse back into bed and find sleep, but not before praying for no dreams. The next time I wake, I find Jack beside me.

"I think it's over," he says.

"What?"

"Withdrawal. All your vitals are stable and you haven't had any medicine for two days."

"Two days? How long have I been here?"

"Seven."

"Seven? My parents must be worried sick." I go to stand up, but I feel dizzy.

"Easy," Jack says. "You must be starving. Let me make you something to eat and you can be on your way."

We sit around the campfire and I eat enough for three people. My belly is full and I feel half way normal, but I can't shake the vision of Drake. I haven't gotten any of my questions answered about the helicopter crash or why he's still with Burke, but I've promised to come back after checking in. He has made me promise not to tell anyone about his return. Not even Bentley. What will I say when I see Bentley? Will I tell him the truth? I should be glad to get it over with and move on, but I feel sort of a sense of loss.

"I don't know if I can keep it from Bentley," I tell Jack.

"You have to. Just for now," he replies.

"I don't think you understand how unfair that is," I say, as I am strapping on my snow shoes.

"This will all work itself out, I promise," he says, as he kisses me on the forehead and shoos me off. It was a cool sort of friendship kiss. Did I imagine the other stuff too?

"What about Kit?"

"Just do what I told you."

As I walk home, I'm kind of kicking myself. Why didn't I just stay and find out what the story is. From what I can guess, either Jack staged the helicopter death or got lucky. What I can't seem to figure out though is why he's still hanging around Burke. Is it just because that's his dad? Or is there more to it?

Mostly, I'm just grateful to be free. Because that's what I am. I've caught myself reaching for my pocket out of habit, but I actually find relief when I find it's empty. Jack has told me I need to be careful. I believe him. I even daydream about restarting my training. I miss being strong.

Chapter 15

As I get closer to the cabin, I see Brody out swinging from a tree. I almost can't believe what I'm seeing. He's jumping from branch to branch.

"Brody!" I run to him and stand below him, ready to catch him if the branch snaps. "Come down from there. What are you doing?"

He hops down in a big mound of snow, barely leaving an imprint.

"Hey, where have you been? I haven't seen you since last year." He giggles.

"Huh?"

"You missed the new year. Where were you? Mom's mad."

"Just had stuff to do. Where's Bentley?"

"He's with Grant."

"Grant's back?" I had almost forgotten about him.

Most everyone is gone including Mom and Dad. I go to Kit's room to check in with her and as many times I see the new Kit, I will never get used to it. She has her hair hanging wildly, and she looks crazed. I get out some warm packs that only need to be massaged to activate the heat.

"Here, put this on the worst ones," I tell her.

"Where did you get these?" she asks, as she places it on a particularly bad boil on her cheek.

"Oww." She winces and I hand her some pills.

"Take these," I say. Jack has given me some pain pills with hesitation, but did so because he says Kit must be in agony.

"I heard Grant was back. Want me to help you get cleaned up?" I ask.

"What difference would it make? I'm ugly now. He won't ever love me again."

"Who says you even want him?" I ask. "He left you, remember? I wouldn't expect you to just take him back."

"I would, if I didn't look like this."

"Have you seen him?" I ask, as I look her over without being too obvious. The boils still look bulgy and hot, and seem to have a life of their own. I try to take notice if they are firm or soft and filled with pus. They still seem firm, but I can see the beginnings of a white center.

I know I'm not supposed to tell anyone Jack is back, but I feel compelled to tell Kit. I wait for now. I want to find Bentley and Grant. I tell Kit I'll be back and she barely seems to notice. She just lies back down and stares at the ceiling, but at least she is complying with the heat packs.

I don't find anyone but Hannah downstairs. She is sitting on the couch, watching a fuzzy screen.

"Hey you," I say as I sit close to her. She looks worse than when I left. "Are you okay?"

"I've been better," she says.

"Is it harder to heal wounds than sickness?" She looks weak and fragile.

She surprises me when she starts to weep.

"I've only got one left."

"One what?" I ask, as I feebly pet her leg.

"One more time. I can feel it. I only have one more."

"One more healing?" I ask frantic. "How do you know?"

"I don't know. I can just tell. I don't think I ever fully heal from them. I don't know why it took me so long to realize that I don't really recover. I can just do it so many times . . . You know, in a way, it makes it easier. I hated what happened to me with the cancer and I hated Jimmy so much for what he did to me. It's better this way. I did save his mom. I didn't waste it on something else. She would have died."

I'm stunned. If Hannah has only one more heal in her, she won't live long. I know her. She will save the next person who needs it.

"Hannah, you have to promise me something."

"I can't promise that," she says.

"How do you even know what I was going to say?"

"I know. Can you help me to my room? I'm so tired."

I get Hannah to bed and when I'm faced with all the pill bottles on the floor, I spend just a second scanning them to find the ones labeled Valium, but the memories of how sick I was lead me out the door empty-handed.

When I come back downstairs, I find Grant and Bentley home.

"Where are my parents?" I ask Bentley. Seeing him for the first time in days brings on a fresh coat of guilt.

"Nice to see you too. Where have you been?" He pauses to look me in the eyes, almost studying me. "Good to have you back." I feel more than one meaning there. Did he know? He picks me up and spins me into a hug. Grant's watching, so I squirm out of his arms.

"More like where have you been?" I glare at Grant.

"Long story," he says.

"I've got time," I reply.

I learn that my parents are gone scoping out another cabin. It seems the search for another cabin is easier than the search for propane, so we'll be moving. I'm lost in thought and not paying much attention to Grant and Bentley, but something Grant says perks up my attention.

"You have to help me get it out," he tells Bentley.

"How do you expect me to do that? I think you might just need to move on. You're putting everyone in danger."

"I know. That's why you need to get it out. I can't leave her again," Grant says.

"What are you guys talking about?" I ask, after it's clear I'm not going to figure it out.

"Kit didn't tell you?" Grant says, as he glances up towards her room.

"Obviously. What is it?" I'm annoyed with him and making no attempts to hide it.

"I know what you think. I never left her. I was captured. And now they've put this device in me under my skin and I've got to get it out."

"Where is it? What kind of device? A tracking device?"

So Grant tells me his story and I find myself no longer angry with him. Instead I feel sorry for him. It's true, he did leave after the big fight. But he says he went to town to get baby supplies. When he was in town, he was captured and he's been living on a compound for the past month.

"I'd rather die than go back," he continues. "It's nothing but a cult. All they do is sit around and worship nothing all day. If I ever have to hear another word about being saved again, I'll punch myself in the face!" He's waving his hands in the air and his face is red with anger.

"And the device?" I ask again.

"They are putting it in everyone. Even the common citizens not breaking any laws. The Council says it's for safety. There were some other non-crazies at the compound too. They called it The Mark of the Beast. I don't really know what that means exactly, but it's not good. Eventually, they will use it as a way to trade goods. Like credits that read out from your arm. The whole thing is creep—" He stops midsentence. "How is she? She won't let me see her."

"Not good." I say.

"The baby?" he asks, his eyes moist with tears I know he won't let go. I shake my head.

He puts his head in his hands and silently trembles. It makes me uncomfortable so I get up and start rummaging around for something sharp. It's hard for me to see Grant like this. To me, he has always been rock solid. He never flinches, never wavers. His training is what led me to be as strong as I was. It looks like Kit is his Achilles heel.

I can't find anything remotely close to appropriate for slicing human skin.

"Bentley, I need your knife." I know he keeps it razor sharp.

He hands it to me without asking. We are out of rubbing alcohol so I spend a few minutes sterilizing it in boiling water. I clean the fishhook needle. No telling how deep I'm going to have to go. Grant knows what's coming and he doesn't seem to be nervous.

"Lie down," I say, as I wipe the last of the steam from the glistening knife.

"Here?" he asks, as he is standing by the long oak dining table.

"You got a better idea?" I ask.

He does as I ask. He takes off his shirt and I'm not prepared for what I see. He's covered in scars. I know what he's supposed to look like. I've seen him enough without his shirt to know these scars don't belong here. New scars.

I can't help but bring my hand over my mouth.

"Sorry. I should have warned you." Grant chuckles.

"I don't find this funny. What happened?" I ask. Bentley is watching and I see rage building in him. I understand.

"I told you. I got caught. They wanted information. But don't worry, they didn't get anything from me," he says with confidence and I believe him. "Too bad too. I had just found this baby store that had everything we could ever need. Sweet little crib, bottles, everything . . . Suppose it doesn't matter now. Can we get this over with?"

I scan the area he told me they implanted the tracking device. The puncture wound is so tiny, I'm not sure it's even there.

"Are you ready?" I ask, before I make the cut.

"As I'll ever be."

I cut into the first layer of skin at his forearm and immediately it starts to bleed. It doesn't seem to be on the surface, so I go a little deeper. I see him wince and ask him if he wants pain medicine. He doesn't. "Just get it over with," he says again.

I go in about a quarter inch and have to pierce through muscle when I find it. I place my fingers on it and wiggle it back and forth until it pops free. I place it on the table and close him up.

We all stare at it. It looks like a tiny light bulb.

"It's got a number on it," Bentley says.

I crack the delicate glass and the mechanism on the inside has a long serial number on it with a latching system. I pull it apart and nothing happens. I click it back together, fighting the urge to do it over and over again. It's so tiny.

"What do we do with it?" Grant asks.

"Smash it," Bentley says, as he picks it up and rolls it through his fingers.

"Maybe we could find a better use for it," I say. But Bentley's impulses are quick and he crushes it before I can stop him.

"Hey." I poke him in the ribs.

"Safer," he says with confidence.

"We have to do something about this," I say as I look up. They are both grinning at me in agreement.

"I half thought with Tom gone, things would get better," Bentley says, "but it's like it got worse." It always throws me for a loop when he calls Burke, Tom. I wonder how many years he's done that.

"What can we do?" Grant asks, as he places his shirt back on and begins buttoning from the bottom up.

I clean up the pieces to the device and try not to think about just how bad things have gotten. Just as I'm finishing up, my parents walk in. Mom doesn't even seem that surprised to see me.

"Hey kiddo, we've missed you. Glad you're home," Dad says, as he gives me a peck on the cheek.

He looks like my dad, but I'm sad to realize that the vision I had of Drake was probably just me imagining he would look like Dad, as I see the resemblance more than ever. When I think back to the Drake I saw in the cabin days ago, it's easy to imagine him being Dad at that age.

***

A month has gone by since I've been to Tent City. We've moved from our cabin into a new one just outside of Deadwood. Dad tells Brody about a man named Wild Bill, as we make our way to the new cabin. It's almost the exact same setup, so it doesn't even really feel like we've moved. It's like the citizens of the Black Hills had a building plan for all the cabins and built them the same.

At first, it was almost impossible not to tell Bentley about Jack, but we are just so busy with moving, it almost seems harder to tell him. I fear the consequences of not telling Bentley will be a divide between the two of us, as he will see it as me being more loyal to Jack. Not that it will even matter in the long run.

Kit is now ready for me to cut into her boils. Jack told me I had to wait until they were full of pus and ready to "lance" as he put it. If I'm honest, doing this is harder than any of the small surgeries I have performed.

For one, she's in excruciating pain. No amount of pain medicine is helping her. Her screams shake the cabin walls, at least that's what it feels like. I sneak quick glances at the door and wait for Grant to rush through the door and force me to stop. I can feel him pacing outside the door.

There are actually only five really bad ones, the saddest being the little volcano on her cheek. I start there. Kit grasps her sheet as I cut into the first one and squeeze it until all of the white, mushy substance is pushed out. I am certain I will never eat mashed potatoes again. I feel confident that the scarring will be minimal as the skin I broke into was thin and almost seemed to peel off as I removed the infection.

The bright spot in the boil procedure is that as soon the tiny mountain is deflated, she lets out a sigh of relief. It gives me the courage to continue with the other four.

When I am done, she almost looks worse than when I started, but I can tell she's no longer in debilitating pain. She lets me wrap her back up so that only her eyes are showing and only then does she allow Grant back in the room.

Kit's depressed because she thinks she has lost part of herself: her beautiful part. But it doesn't seem to push Grant away. If anything, he seems more dedicated to her than ever. I think he's even forgiven her for getting rid of the baby.

It's February now and we're in the really cold part of winter. We spend most of our days just hanging out in the cabin. I'm going stir crazy. Grant and Bentley are in town getting supplies. Bentley is excited about this trip as they are going to check out some of the casinos. Grant seems hesitant; I imagine he's remembering the time he had been caught. I will use the opportunity to go back to Tent City. I take a snowmobile since it's now too far to walk.

When I pull up and see Jack exiting the cabin, it's like no time has slipped by at all. I jump off the sled and take a look around. I'm waiting for the awkward part where I have to tell him I want Burke to leave.

"He's not here," he says with a smile. "Let me take a look at you."

"I'm clean, I promise," I say with a shy smile.

"That's not what I meant. I knew you would be. But it took you long enough to get back to me. Where you been?" he asks, as he scratches at his face.

"Why do you have to be a secret? Why can't you come back with me?"

"Here, come on in. It's freezing out here. I've built an indoor stove in your old cabin. Come check it out."

I walk into the cabin and not much has changed. I'm surprised to see that most of my old stuff is still here. The only difference really is the wood stove he has built with a chimney leading outside.

I sit down after stripping off my snow suit. I peek through the hair hanging in my face to see him watching me.

"Sorry," he says when I catch him, "I just can't get used to seeing you . . . in the flesh."

"It's weird being back here," I say. "I don't really remember much of last time." I sort of blush then when I realize that there are memories from last time that I'll never forget.

I scoot closer to the wood stove and hold out my hands, hoping to steal some of its warmth. Jack is busy opening up cans of soup and placing them near the flame.

"How's Kit?" he asks.

"Better . . . So where is he?" I let my mind wander to the knife I have in my back pocket that burns against my skin every time I think about Burke.

"Not here. Isn't that enough?"

"No. I can remember a time when you promised me no secrets."

"He's not who you think he is."

"Is he the man responsible for Drake's death?" There I've said it. I don't even like saying Drake's name out loud. I feel even the memory of Drake is too good for this place now that Burke has tainted it with his presence. A part of me feels as though I have betrayed Drake by allowing Burke to slip away and live.

"I'm still sorting all that out. I've been here in Tent City by myself for a while now. Lots of time to think. I will say this . . . there's more to the story. My dad isn't who you think he is. He's been through a lot too."

"Ha! How can you say that? He's taken everything from me. Maybe it was a bad idea that I came." I get up to put my suit back on.

"Wait, I have something to tell you."

"What?" I'm annoyed and not looking at him. I would like to just get dressed and go, but he's persisting.

"I'm getting this place ready for you," he says softly. "This is all for you. I've put up stoves in the other cabins too. You can bring your whole family here. I've just got one cabin left, but they could come now."

"What makes you think I'd want that?" I scowl.

"He's not coming back if that's what you're thinking."

"Why all the secrecy? Why couldn't I tell Bentley you were alive? Did you even stop to think about how much this was hurting him?"

Jack starts laughing and I find myself losing my temper because I'm actually contemplating smacking him in the face. The idea is getting more and more appealing the more I think about it.

"Bentley doesn't think I'm dead," he says after a bit.

"How do you know that? Have you seen him?" How could Bentley not tell me? I realize how self-righteous that sounds even in my head. After all, I've been keeping the secret from him for a month.

"Did you ever hear those stories about the twins who feel each other's pain?" he asks.

"That's not real."

"Not for all of them, but we've always been that way. He'd know if I was gone. He broke his leg when we were seven and I was so convinced that I had broken mine too that Mom casted us both," he says with a smile as he remembers the story.

I let it all sink in. Is that why Bentley didn't seem upset after that first day? I remember thinking it was weird that I was the only one grieving. Why didn't he tell me? Couldn't he see how much pain I was in?

"Speaking of your mother, I thought you said your dad was responsible for her death. How can you forgive him?"

Jack sits down in the chair and lets out a huge sigh. I sit down beside him as I crawl out of the pants of the snow suit. I want to stick around for this.

"Are you sure you're up for this?"

I settle in with my soup, but almost drop it when I hear noises just outside the cabin. I stand up so quickly to look out the window that the scalding chicken noodle soup spills on me and for a second I'm only worried about getting it off. Jack doesn't seem too alarmed. He just goes to the window and pushes the curtain to the side and I see his body go rigid, every muscle tense.

"Bentley's here."

Jack exits the cabin and I quickly change into different clothes I had left behind. I had forgotten about this sweatshirt. How could I have left it behind? It was my favorite. The only pants I can find are a pair of jeans that are now too big, but I pull them on anyway and head out the door.

"What are you doing here?" I ask Bentley.

"Maybe I should ask you that? Why does it feel like you're cheating on me?" He winks, and before I can stop him, he leans in for a quick peck on the cheek.

"How did you find me?" I feel like I've just been caught.

"Tracks." He smiles as he points to the trail that leads right up to the cabin. He then turns his attention to Jack.

"You been here the whole time?" he asks, and surprises me by walking over to Jack and shaking his hand.

"No. Here and there, but I've been fixing up the place. It's nearly ready to go."

"Go?" Bentley asks, as he shakes snow from his shaggy blonde hair.

"Yeah. Come check it out," he says, as he and Bentley start walking around camp.

I sit down on the swing and try to figure out what just happened. I watch them walk from cabin to cabin and find myself in awe of them. They're quite the pair.

I can't help but feel jealous. I remember my beautiful brother too and I wish he was here. Even though my hallucination of him was drug induced, or rather lack of drug induced, I can't shake the memory and I'm not sure I want to. It had been so many years since I last saw him that I had almost forgotten what he looked like. Now I have a new memory.

I take some time to go back inside and straighten up my old cabin. Most of the stuff in there is mine anyway.

I'm putting clothes into neat piles and making the bed when I stumble across Jack's journal. It takes everything I've got not to open it. And then I cave. I open it to a random page and then I see my name and my face heats up. I slam it shut.

It's kind of weird that Jack lives here among my things, and now he has a journal where he's been writing about me?

Chapter 16

The next few days go by in a blur, even though I could tell you it's been three days and twelve hours since Bentley showed up at Tent City. We spend it moving everyone back to Tent City. I'm still not sure it's a good idea. The memories of the day Rigby attacked our camp are still fresh in my mind and I can't help but think it's only a matter of time before he returns. Brody seems to think it's a good idea and for now that's good enough for me. I asked him why, and the only thing he said was, "it's where we belong."

Burke has not returned. I haven't seen him since that first day when I leveled him. I haven't been able to get Jack alone to ask him about the crash and what is going on. He and Bentley spend almost every waking minute together. I won't admit it, but I don't like it.

Kit is healing. She will probably always have some little scars, but at least she no longer has the boils. She usually has her face covered with a scarf and Grant tries to convince her to take it off. Their wounds are slowly healing.

I still itch for the medicine sometimes, but I've decided it's time to get back to running. That's the blessing Jack has given me. The medicine stole every ambition I ever had and my body has gone soft.

I bundle up and head for the trails that have been worn by Jack and Bentley's trips to the streams and find myself running at a good clip. Maybe I'm not in as bad as shape as I thought. I would love to get out to the waterfall to see how it looks in this crystallized beauty, but that may require a snowmobile. For now, I'm happy just to try and get a couple of miles in.

After only about two miles at a nine minute pace, I slow down. I'm exhausted, and I'm depressed. The time I took off to wallow in my misery has taken its toll. I am weak. All those months of training have been wasted on what?

I slow down to a brisk walk and take a look around. Something seems off. Everything is still and quiet in the snow-covered forest. Even the enormous pines are precariously quiet. Usually there are noises of squirrels scattering or animals burrowing or at least something. I feel like I'm in a snow globe and I've been deprived of sound.

I'm trying to be quiet so I can hear the trees speak, as they do right before they release their limbs. When the snow and ice settle on the old, rickety trees, sometimes it's too heavy for the branches to hold out and they crash to the ground. Learning to listen to the sounds is paramount for not getting crushed by a heavy branch. I'm straining harder to hear, waiting for the cracks and crackles that will announce the fall when I see a blur pass through a belt of trees. I steady my breathing. It's probably only Waite.

I continue to walk, still not shaking off the feeling of something watching me. I start my trot again, eager to clear the area where I feel too exposed and that's when it happens.

It happens so quickly, I'm not even sure it has. Everything is silent except for the sound of my body collapsing to the ground. Something is grasping and clawing at my back. I'm aware that the back of my neck is exposed as I feel a breeze rush in, followed by the hot breath of whatever has me pinned. I quickly cover the back of my neck just as it bites down slicing through the top of my glove and puncturing the top of my hand with a fat fang.

I struggle to turn over, hoping to flip it off me when I see it. It's a mountain lion. My heart is ready to explode out of my chest and I'm weighing my options. I briefly consider playing dead, but decide not to since it would probably just start eating me. I scan around frantically searching for a weapon. I'm hysterical with silent screams. I manage to get it off me and I reach to the back of my pants to find the knife I don't leave home without, only to find it missing.

The cougar doesn't waste any time and lunges for me again. It has pushed me to the ground again and knocked the breath right out of me. I'm flailing around trying to protect my face and neck. One bite to my jugular and I'm finished. All I can think about is how much I've been through only to be killed by a mountain lion. I'm so stupid. Why didn't I see it coming? I close my eyes and wait for the inevitable when I hear a deafening snarling sound.

I open my eyes again as I stumble to my feet to see Waite charging on the mountain lion. The lion no longer has its appetite focused on me. The big cat is hissing violent meows at the wolf while swatting at him with enormous paws. I don't know why the sound it makes is so startling. It mostly just sounds like an overgrown housecat. Waite doesn't waste any time and lunges at the cat, just barely missing its thick neck. The lion takes off and Waite is close behind. No amount of old reruns of Animal Planet could have prepared me for watching this play out within ten feet of me.

My emotions change from fear to excitement, although my heart pounds just the same. I find myself thinking *attaboy, Waite, get em*' and I even chuckle at the thought of it. I think the fear of it has made me insane.

Instead of backing away to seek safety of camp, I am running after Waite. He has treed the cat and it is hissing and meowing at Waite. My wolf looks crazy with thirst to get at the cat and for the first time, I feel fear towards Waite. With all of his teeth bared and snarling, it's not a pretty picture. I am not seeing him as the gentle creature that quietly watches. He is a fierce monster with huge scary teeth and guttural growls. It reminds me that he is a wild animal, not my pet dog.

This time, I do take the opportunity to run. I run away from the scene, checking back every couple of seconds to see what's happening. The cat seems almost irritated that I'm getting away. It makes a jump far out of the tree and past Waite, bounding towards me. It didn't stand a chance.

I stop as if watching a horrific accident. I can't seem to stop watching. Waite has clamped onto the back of the mountain lion's leg and it hisses and swats at the angry wolf. Waite takes less than a second to move up and chomp down on its neck and the lion goes still. It's over. Waite looks up at me and regards me before dragging it away.

I crash to my knees and wonder if what I've just seen is real. My heart is still thudding in my throat and I realize why Waite has been around. Is this what he was meant to save me from? Was it me he was to save and not Brody? Does this mean Waite will leave now or is there more to come?

The cat's behavior seemed strange to me too. I used to be a big fan of Animal Planet and I would have guessed the cat would have stayed in the tree all day. It must have been pretty hungry to take a chance on me with Waite in the way. The animals are acting weird.

I decide not to tell anyone about my animal encounter. It might just make Mom squeamish and overprotective. I do give Brody and Avery a quiet lecture of my own, but they brush it off and run off to play.

Everyone but Bentley seems to be off doing their own thing at different places in the snow-dusted forest. I take a seat beside him and the dancing fire.

"Whatcha working on?" I ask, as I see he has some rope that moves quickly through his fingers.

"Knots," he says, without even looking up. He grunts a little in dissatisfaction as he tries to get a loop that is sticking.

"You really are a Boy Scout aren't you?" I ask, only half-interested. I still can't get the picture of the snarling wolf out of my mind.

"Wanna learn?" he asks, as he looks up and shoves the rope my way.

"Why would I ever need to learn how to tie a knot? On second thought, I suppose if your dad ever makes it back here, we may need to tie him up."

"Hmmmpph," he scoffs at my lame joke. "I don't disagree there, but here, watch."

He shows me all the knots including a bowline, double fisherman's knot, square knot and even one called a monkey's fist. I take special interest in this one, if only for its name. He then hands me an extra rope and when I don't take it, he shoves it in my bag that's by my feet.

"Never know." He smiles.

"So, I can never seem to get Jack alone," I start, but feel embarrassed by my choice of words and he looks about as embarrassed as me. "I mean, what happened? Did he tell you?"

"What do you mean?"

"Helicopter." Even saying it brings a shock of grief, which is ridiculous because if he's no longer dead, why do I still feel a sense of loss?

"Faked, obviously."

"How did they do that?" I'm wishing I had the rope back in my hand, if only for something to keep my hands busy and break our eye contact.

"Hired a guy I guess. When you have the means, it's not so hard to fake your own death."

"What about the bodies they buried? Who were they?"

"I didn't ask," he replies, as he contemplates this. He must not have wondered. Why does he trust Jack so completely?

"Won't The Council figure it out? I mean, Burke's pretty high profile, someone is bound to see him."

"Jack says he's hiding out in Williston."

"Coward."

"Hey, you're preaching to the band."

"Choir."

"Whatever. For now, I'm just happy he's gone. We can get to him when the time comes. Enough about that, I want to show you something," he says as his face lights up in excitement. I get a vision of what he must have looked like when opening Christmas presents.

He takes me down to the wide stream we use for fresh water. He leads me over the deeper part, lies down on the bank and submerges his arm deep into the chilly water. He is on the very edge of the bank teetering on the boulders and it's making me nervous how deep he's slipping into the rapids.

"What are you doing?" I cross my arms in irritation and wait for him to finish his game. Why does he always have to draw everything out?

Five minutes have gone by and I see his body is starting to convulse in shivers. He's determined though and has shown no signs of giving up whatever it is he's doing.

I'm being so stubborn about our outing and lost in my own world, I don't even have time to react when a fish comes flopping my way and smacks me in the face. It's cold and a bit slimy. Bentley bursts out laughing in a deep roar. I let out a small shriek and hold my hands out, fearing he's about to toss another one my way. He's laughing so hard, tears are coming out of his eyes and I can't help myself, I start laughing too.

Finally, after I have caught my breath I ask, "What was that for?"

"I'm teaching you how to fish."

"That's not fishing. I believe fishing requires a pole."

"Well, I think I've dispelled that theory," he says, as he glances at the fish losing its fight in this world. It gives a few last efforts of a wiggle before it goes still, eyes still bulging. For the first time in my life, I wish fish had eyelids.

"All right then, what's the secret?" I ask. It was pretty impressive.

For the rest of the afternoon, we pull in fish after fish. I guess the trick is to use your finger as the bait, a concept I could not bring myself to do until after his third fish, and I wanted in on some of the action. Bentley tells me to hide my arm in the water and wiggle my finger tips. The first time I feel the nibble, I jump like a spawning salmon, but by the second one, I decide that it isn't a man eater and allow the nibbling. When you feel the first nibble you allow just a split second before it decides you're not food. Then you grab as quickly as you can and fling it out before it escapes in its slime. There's even an art to how you fling it. By the time I get to my fifth fish, I'm certain I am the better fish flinger.

"My arm's frozen. I think I'm done," I say, as I stand and count the fish.

"Want me to warm it up? You can stick it in my shirt. I promise I can take it," he says with a smirk.

"I'm good."

"I'm not trying to put the moves on you. It's survival 101. Share body heat." He is still smirking.

"Fine. But let's put a bet on it. I'll stick my hand in your shirt and if you flinch, you carry all the fish back."

"I would anyway." He laughs and so do I.

"Okay then, no need for the bet."

"Hey, I didn't say that. Go ahead. Do your worst." He lifts his t-shirt and I contemplate which part of the skin would be the most sensitive.

I try to find the area that has the least amount of fat, but there's just not much fat anywhere. I avoid the six-pack, as I feel that the muscle keeps him warm and walk behind him. I can feel his anticipation. I aim my forearm near his side and place the coldest part of my hand into his armpit. He lets out a small grunt and backs up just the slightest bit.

"Hey, that's not fair. I wasn't expecting that."

"You lose."

"I wouldn't have won that one either way. It's the only ticklish spot I have."

"Good to know," I say, and it is.

We walk back to camp with fourteen fish, and as soon as we arrive, we see Jack. He notices we are together, but doesn't give us his usual death glare. He even seems happy at the haul.

Callie's finally back. I'm not sure where she went, but as soon as we walk up she takes the fish and gets to work on cleaning them. She says she has a recipe for trout that's "to die for." As she takes them from me, I notice she gives Bentley a sad smile. They must not have mended their fences yet.

Jack avoids us for the rest of the day and I can't bring myself to mind. I do miss him, but it's like it used to be when Jack and Bentley were both around. One on one, they're amazing. Put the three of us together, it's just awkward and weird. Knowing Jack's alive is enough for me.

I've considered telling them I'm not choosing either one of them, despite the nagging feeling I get about going back on a deal. There's two parts to this. The first part is the logical part that knows "my deal" with God or the devil, whoever it was that took me up on it, was not real at all, and the only reason Jack is alive is because he was never dead at all. Even when I convince myself of that, a little part of me is still bothered by the coincidence. The other part, sometimes the more persistent part, tells me that there was a deal made and if broken, there will be consequences. I think fear runs that part.

Not choosing either one of them seems like the only way I can keep them both, if only in friendship. I just don't see any other way around it. If I choose one of them, the other will leave and it's not an option I want. I can't picture life without either one of them.

Kit's actually the one who makes the decision for me. Well, not directly. I saw how stupid she got over Grant and decided that I wanted nothing to do with it. She used to be free and uninhibited. Now, she's practically a housewife. If falling in love makes you act like a crazy fool, then I want nothing to do with it.

I haven't seen Waite since the incident with the mountain lion. I have already given myself to the fact that he was my guardian. I wonder if now that he has fulfilled his job, he'll disappear.

Hannah seems to be getting better. She has a cabin to herself and she rests in bed most of the time. Jack and Bentley have gone on a mission that they won't tell me about, so I decide to spend the day with her.

She's sitting up in bed by the time I get there and looks excited for some time outside.

"Want me to brush your hair?" I ask, as I notice it's been a while and it's plastered to her face.

"Sure."

I try to ignore the fact that big clumps of hair are coming out and quietly toss them to the side before she can see. She looks back to me to see why I've stopped and an idea comes to me.

"Are you sure there's really only one time left?" She knows what I am talking about. It's all she ever thinks about, I'm sure. I know I would.

"Yes. And I want you to know that it's oka—"

"No, it's not okay and you know it, but if you won't stop, I want something from you."

"Yeah?"

"Two things, actually."

"Okay," she says, as she focuses her eyes on me, sparkly and curious. She turns around and takes the brush from me and continues the job herself. "Well?" she asks. She looks so thin it makes my stomach ache.

"Well, first, you hafta promise that you won't do it for me." The idea of her using her last heal on me actually has me feeling nauseated.

"I can't promise that."

"Why! That's not fair. It's not like I'm asking you not to do it . . . because I know you will. It just can't be me . . . okay?" There are tears in my eyes because I know she doesn't have much time left.

"I can't promise you because then I would be breaking a promise to someone else."

"What?"

"I already promised Bentley I'd save it for you," she says quietly.

"You know that doesn't count, right?" I say to her.

"What do you mean?"

"That's disgusting. He can't make you promise that. It's not his right. When I find him—"

"Dani, I want to," she says, as she touches my arm. Then another thought comes to me. If she saves it for me and nothing happens to me, she won't use it on someone else.

"Why would he do that?" I say more to myself.

"He's afraid."

"Afraid of what?"

"The plagues of course."

"We all are. That doesn't give him the right to—"

"Just listen. He made me swear I wouldn't tell you, but he thinks the plague of the firstborn is next. He's afraid you'll die."

The weight of it all hits me at the same time. Why do I keep discounting these plagues? Of course, it's only a matter of time before the next one.

"He's the firstborn too," I say, as I recall Bentley taunting Jack about being the older twin in their fraternal bond, if only by a few minutes.

"You're thinking about Jack now, aren't you?" she asks, and I blush.

"How do you know that?" My head is cocked in curiosity and I study her face.

"Wild guess." She smiles. "Get this," she says, as her grin spreads even wider, "Jessica has a theory about your little love triangle."

"Puh-lee—" I try to interrupt, but she returns the favor.

"Shut up, you gotta hear this." Still grinning, she continues, "Jess thinks that you were meant to be with Tom and Emma Burke's first child, but that since they are twins, the lines are crossed somehow."

"What? She's so weird. Sometimes, I feel like just returning her to the compound."

"She does have some pretty strange ideas. She says that God has a hand in three things: births, deaths, and who we end up with. Hence, the crazy love triangle."

I'm silent while I consider this. Just when I think I might have something to learn from Jess and Jonah, something else comes up that is too strange to even process. Why can't things just be black and white? Why?

"You said two things," she says, interrupting the flurry of thoughts in my brain.

"Huh?" I'm so confused. My head is spinning at it all.

"You said you wanted two things from me. And don't worry about the first one. Nothing is going to happen to you. I can feel it." She smiles and squeezes my hand.

Her smile brightens my mood a little and brings me back to the second thing.

"Well, as disturbing as this sounds, if you don't have a lot of time left, I want you to do everything you always wanted. Tell me, Hannah, what is it you've always wanted to do?"

"Oh, you mean a Kick the Bucket list?" she asks. I smile remembering the term people used to use when their whole lives were ahead of them and they didn't need to worry about survival, just their next vacation.

"Yes. Make a list. We'll do all of them."

She's quiet for a long time before she says, "I'd like to fall in love again."

"Oh, Hannah."

"I know, I know, but you said wish for whatever I want." She lies back down and looks completely drained. If only talking does this to her, will she even have anything left to save anyone else? “I’ll think of something . . . if it will make you happy,” she says as she drifts off to sleep.

I leave her to rest and dream of her list. I consider that maybe I don’t know what I have gotten myself into. I was hoping she was thinking more along the lines of “write a book” or “visit Mount Rushmore.” I can definitely handle Mount Rushmore.

Chapter 17

Days go by and there is still no sign of Jack or Bentley. I can tell Grant is pissed that Kit asked him to stay. He's trying to be domesticated with her, but I know Grant well enough to know that he's better suited for being in on the action.

With Jack and Bentley, there used to be a time when I would just sit and worry, but I've come to find that worrying doesn't do any good. I know it sounds morbid, but I'm trying to figure out a way to live without the people I love, as sort of a preparation. I've created a scenario where I can half way accept the loss of the people I love . . . all except Brody. I don't even go there.

Hannah was ecstatic about my idea of Mount Rushmore. She couldn't believe how long she had been in South Dakota and had never gone to see it. After raiding the gift shop (never know when you might need a satchel full of pretty rocks) we sit down in the tourist area that allows optimal viewing of Mount Rushmore. We sit in silence on the frosty benches for a while. The mountain that contains the heads of four dead presidents seems so out of place now. I know it's a part of history, but it's hard to picture a time when there was nothing better to do than to sit around and stare at something that has absolutely nothing to do with surviving to the next day.

Mom, Dad, Avery and Brody are with us. Dad teaches Brody about the four presidents featured, but Brody is more interested in the guy who carved them, a guy named Borglum.

"So he never got to see it finished?" Brody asks.

"No, sadly, he died before it was complete."

Brody looks upset by this before Dad adds, "It's okay Bro, his son saw it completed and do you know what his name was?" Dad asks with an impish grin.

Brody looks up at him with innocent eyes before Dad answers, "Lincoln."

Brody considers this and I find myself wondering when Dad became the history buff. But more than anything, I'm happy to have completed this task on Hannah's list. If I can't get her to change her mind, we're at least going to give her a good life now. After all, none of us really know how much time we have.

I had hoped to use this time to ask Brody some questions. I want to know what he thinks about the plagues and if we will see them all, but he's having such a good time, I leave it alone for now.

Hannah's requests for her bucket list were odd, but everyone obliged. Callie is even performing a Native American sweat lodge ceremony for Hannah. It is just the two of them and they are set to stay in the makeshift tee-pee for hours.

Callie sends me for a list of supplies. The firewood and red willow were easy to find. It took quite a bit more time to find sage, and sweet grass. I never did find bitterroot. She makes do.

Steam and strange smells, as well as Callie's murmuring escape the tent as I watch from the outside. I had hoped Hannah would invite me in, but this is something for just her and Callie. When they finally exit the tent, Hannah looks even weaker, but a strange content smile is spread across her face.

"Are you okay?" I ask as I help her out. The cool breeze seems to shock her system as her breath catches and she makes a squealing sound. She doesn't answer me, only looks to Callie.

"I can never repay you for that," Hannah says to Callie.

"No problem," Callie fumbles out. She looks like she has been crying. Finally, Hannah looks to me.

"You can take me to my room now," she says as she takes her first step, but then stumbles to the ground.

"Dad!" I shout toward the cabin and he comes running out. "I need your help. Can you carry her?" He comes and scoops her up and I catch a glimpse of her back through her flimsy ceremony dress. It feels like I've been slapped in the face. I knew she was thin, but after seeing what I see, I'm not even sure how she's still alive. It looks like she just walked out of a concentration camp.

I can see every rib from the back and her skin is so thin I can see the veins, pulsating and shiny from the exertion of the sweat lodge. She catches me looking at her and I look away, but she knows I've seen. She folds her head into the crook of my dad's neck and allows him to carry her inside.

I sit on her bed and watch her sleep, at least I thought she was sleeping when she says, "It's okay, Dani.

"What's okay?"

"I can go now."

"No!"

"I've had a good life. I'm happy. I've seen the dead presidents. You don't have to worry about the bucket list anymore. In fact, please don't. Just let me enjoy the time I have left." She's so weak that it appears to take the last of her energy just to speak.

I leave before she can see the tears slipping off my face. Life is so unfair. Why do guys like Burke get to walk around free as a bird when a girl like Hannah lies on her deathbed?

I come back outside after I tuck Hannah in to find Callie sitting by the fire. It crackles and smolders, leaving a trail of smoky hunger reaching for the sky.

"Will that help her?" I say with a touch of anger in my voice. "Looks like it took more out of her than was it worth."

"What do you mean?" she asks, as she clears some of the ash residue from her arms.

"Will it heal her? Isn't that the point of those rituals?"

"She wasn't looking for healing," she says. I want more information, but she's not giving it up.

"What's your deal anyway? You hardly talk to anyone, you disappear for days and all you ever do when you're here is sulk around camp. If you hate it here, why are you even here?" I feel childish, but I can't shake the anger I feel about Hannah.

"I think you know why." She's not on the defensive even though I've gotten into her face. She actually just looks tired. "You won't have to deal with me too much longer."

"What do you mean?" I ask.

"You know, you can get off your high horse. You're not the only one who cares for Hannah. She asked for the ceremony. Do you know how bad I wanted it to work? It's funny," she says with her face all pinched up, "I find myself hating and liking you at the same time. You've taken everything from me, but somehow it seems okay too. Maybe he was never mine in the first place."

"Bentley?" So, I guess we are going to do this now. Might as well get it over with.

"What else?" she scowls.

"I don't mean to pry or anything, but if . . . if what you had before is gone, why stick around? What's so great about him that you can't forget?" Is Callie one of those desperate girls or is he leading her on?

She's quiet in thought for a while before she answers me. "You know, I keep asking myself that same thing. This is going to sound lame, but he's my Chief."

"What?" The confusion contorting my features must have my face in a map of wrinkles.

"Well, that's what I can't get over about him. He's like my chief. The most important part of my world. The chief would be like your center, what you look to, who's strong and in charge. Basically, like the boss of all things," she finishes and I almost choke on my own tongue.

"You can't be serious? Are you?"

Her face heats up under her mahogany skin. "You wouldn't understand," she says in a voice so soft it's almost impossible to hear. "All these people are here for you . . . in some way or another, but he's all I have . . . or at least all I had. He saved me when I was nothing." A tear slips out from her eye and she wipes it away. I've always imagined her as so strong, but to hear her talk of Bentley as being her chief is almost laughable and it would be, if there wasn't so much pain in her face. Chief? Center? One in charge? Seriously?

I almost wish she hadn't said anything. No, not almost. I was hoping that she'd gotten over him, but maybe she's truly in love with him. And by stringing him along, I'm actually stringing her along too. It occurs to me that if I tell Bentley that I choose Jack, Bentley would be free to move on. And I know Bentley loves Callie too, maybe not the way he thinks he loves me, but I don't doubt that if I had never come along, they would probably be together. I can't believe I didn't realize that by telling the both of them that I choose no one, it's possible they could still both wait for me. I shake my head in disgust just thinking about it. I try to knock myself down a peg, but deep down I know it's true.

"What do you want me to do?" I ask.

"Can you let him go?" she says as another tear slips out and drops off her chin.

"I have. I told him I don't see him that way."

"Do you?"

"Do I what?" I'm playing dumb because I'm not sure how I feel. I have to admit that seeing Callie so hurt does make me feel bad, but imagining them together doesn't make me feel much better.

"It doesn't really matter. I'm not sure if I want him if he's going to be pining away for you. That's why I've got to get out of here . . . I'm leaving."

"What? Where you going?"

"I've been checking places out. I actually ran across another place kind of like this. Not sure what it's all about, but maybe they need a cook," she says with a weak smile.

"So what's the deal with you two anyway? What happened?" I'm not sure why I'm asking. I don't even think

I want to know, but it's sort of eating at me. "Were you in love?"

She puts her face in her hands and lets out a frustrated sigh. She looks small and I see her as a child, maybe sitting in her mom's lap after she's scraped her knee.

"I was . . . you know I can't even believe I'm talking about this with you of all people . . . I don't even know what happened. One day, he just said he wanted to be friends. He said I wasn't 'the one'. I don't think there's anything else he could've ever said that would hurt more. I mean, how does he even know?" She finally gets up to pour water over the fire and I am reminded again of her beauty. Her dark hair falls into her face as she struggles to empty the boiling pot.

"Can you do something for me?" I ask, as I get up and help her heft the big pot, spilling its contents. She looks at me with skepticism. "Can you just stick around for a little longer? Things might change," I say as the water hisses in the fire.

She looks hopeful for a second. Maybe she's wondering if I will release him from whatever hold she thinks I have on him and in that instant I decide that I will.

"You'll let him go?" she asks with a small, hopeful smile.

"Yeah," I say, but I'm not sure what I've done. Have I sealed the deal? By promising to someone else, is there no going back? It has to be what is best for everyone . . . I can't stand this anymore.

"Promise?"

"Promise," I say, but it makes me sick even thinking about it.

What have I done? What will Bentley say? Will he be relieved? The happiness in her face helps a little, but now it's just a matter of getting it done. I'm just not sure how to do it or how he'll take it. She goes in and I think about it for so long that I'm astonished when the solution becomes so clear it practically smacks me in the face.

Chapter 18

Even though I have my plan, I can't execute it because Bentley and Jack are still gone. It's been two weeks now and signs of spring are everywhere. Birds have started to chirp again, even if it's in just nervous twitters. Patches of green grass sprout out of spotty ice patches. I haven't seen Waite since the incident with the mountain lion. I guess he's gone. Dad's so excited by the new change in weather, he's decided to take Brody and me fishing.

"Ice fishing?" I ask, with my eyebrows raised. I think I would rather show him the way I fish.

"Yeah," he replies. "I've wanted to teach Brody and you might as well come with." He smiles.

Brody is more than excited. Avery stays at home, which is surprising since she and Brody are inseparable. It reminds me of an old country song Dad used to listen to called "Don't Take the Girl." We go to a lake called Deerfield Lake since Dad says its higher elevation keeps the water frozen longer.

We drive the snowmobiles to get to an area where the ice is still rock solid. Even though the trees are sweating ice from their branches, the lake is still firm and dad gets to work on the holes. Brody loses interest after the second hole and I find myself alone with Dad. The sun glares at me off the lake and I'm wishing for my sunglasses.

"So, how you holding up?" he asks, as he drops a line in. I see him scan for Brody and then satisfied, looks back to me.

"What do you mean?" I am almost smiling. Strange question.

"With all this," he says, motioning to the land around him. Something seems off. I feel danger despite the mask of an innocent spring day.

"Fine. Why wouldn't I be?" My skin is starting to itch. I feel a father/daughter talk coming. I'm not in the mood.

"Oh, I don't know. I guess I still can't get over it. You're not the same girl you were ten months ago."

I don't say anything. I check his line to distract myself.

"Don't get me wrong . . . it's not a bad thing. I'm just sorry that you had to go through it by yourself."

"It's fine, Dad. Really. Can we talk about something else?" The itchy skin has turned to prickly sweats despite the breeze rolling through.

Just then he darts to his feet and shouts, "Brody, back off that ice! It's too shallow!"

He's running towards him when I yell, "Dad! Don't go any closer! It won't hold you!" I can see the terror in his face and it's provoking mine. I vaguely notice the tremors in my hands.

I can fully see now what has Dad so alarmed. The ice we are fishing on is sturdy, even in color, blue and steely. The ice Brody is teetering on is near the edge of the lake, and is slushy and gray. There are cracks and crevices dangerously teasing near his boots. Brody looks up confused. I see what has brought him there. He's chasing a frog. When I look closer to the edge, there are hundreds of them, just below the surface.

Before I can stop him, Dad has foolishly run towards Brody. It's like he has lost all good sense. He's only gotten about half the distance to him when I hear it. First, it's a whisper; it's the tiniest sound of crackle. Then it explodes into a thunder of shattering ice and he breaks through ice and the water swallows him whole.

"Dad!" I look over to Brody and he's scampering up to the bank. He's safe, but he looks stunned. I see him drop the frog and look to me to do something.

"Stay back Brody!"

I have a million thoughts in my head. I know I don't have long. My heartbeat is thrashing so violently that I can hear it in my ears. I can't catch my breath and I'm not even in the water yet. The tremble that was in my hands has taken over my arms and my whole body is shaking uncontrollably. This is my dad and I'm about to lose him. It's seconds, seconds I have, I repeat in my head. He'll drown, or die from hypothermia.

I see his head pop up and he's gasping for air. How can I do this? I can't run out there. We'll both die. But I have to try. It registers in my head that this is going to end very badly. Worst case scenario? Brody watches us both die. Specks of green float across my vision as I see hundreds of frogs being released from the ravaged ice, broken free in my dad's desperation. This can't be happening. He goes under again and my panic has become debilitating. I scan around and search for something to throw to him. I growl to myself. Why are we not at Sylvan Lake? I know they have flotation devices in safety glass. I could have broken through by now and gotten something to save him with.

And then it hits me. The rope. I frantically search around for the rope in my bag, and in the background I can hear my dad has come up again, gasping for air. I can hear Brody shouting at me, but I'm too disoriented to decipher any of it.

There it is. I've found it. Seeing it has brought me one second of peace. I just need a few more to remember the knot. What was it again? Something about a monkey. I'm picturing Bentley's smiling face, teasing me, encouraging me to try again. "Get it right." He pushed until I did. I've gained enough composure to figure out a plan. I know I only have a few more seconds. I run about 10 feet away and pick up a stone the size of my hand. This has to work.

I place the cool rock in my palm. In my mind, I won't have enough time to do this. Every time I practiced it took me at least five minutes to get it right. I only have one shot at this. If the stone is not secure on the inside, it will flail out and detach from the ropes. I give the rock a squeeze and start with my first three thin strings and wrap them around the stone. I know I am cutting corners because I should build my knot first and then place the stone inside after it's firm and secure, but there's no time for that. I wrap in triple. And then I do it again, weaving it in and out, hoping I've done it right. I can almost feel Bentley whispering, telling me which way it goes. I finally finish and take a look at my crude work. I can already picture the stone staying put in the rope where it is should be and then in a cruel sense of luck, dislodging from the rope and slipping out at the last second. Even worse, the stone could come loose and actually hit my dad.

But I don't have time to worry any more. I take a deep breath and close my eyes. I do allow one second for a quick prayer, begging is more like it. I even have time to think for a second how pathetic I am for only doing this when I'm in trouble.

When I open my eyes I see my dad has surfaced again. He looks desperate with terror and I stifle a sob that is heavy in my throat. This has to work.

I work my way up to him as far as I can go without getting too close. I close my fingers around the monkey's fist and give it a squeeze. And then I go for it. I'm careful as I twirl it, trying to keep the stone within. I finally give it a forceful toss and it lands just inches from his fingers that are clawing at the edges of the ice.

He goes under again. This wasn't part of the plan. I got him the rope. Now he just needs to grab it. What do I do now? Do I go in? I can't just stand here. I have to go in.

I'm taking steps even closer and I hear cracking beneath my own feet when his head pops up again and he strikes his arm out in front of him, and misses. For a split second I see a look on my dad's face that is unacceptable. Acceptance. Is he giving up?

I look up at Brody to see him frozen in fear. I look back to my dad to see his fingers finally clasp the monkey's fist. Yes! He has it! He pulls the rope toward him and clamps down on it hard. I scurry over to the deeper part of the ice and start bearing down. I'm pulling and pulling in the biggest game of tug-of-war of my life. My hands are on fire, but I'm gaining on him. He is gasping, but he's actually emerging from the water. I slide the rope over to the bank where Brody is and together we pull Dad the rest of the way in. Tears cloud my vision as I see Brody pulling with all his might.

I pull Dad to the bank and he's crushing frogs underneath him and they are leaving a sludge in their wake. I get flint from my bag and search for kindling. Damn, everything is wet. My hands are raw and I'm bawling out of frustration of not getting a fire lit. If I don't, he'll die. The rest of his skin is starting to match the blue of his lips. I only have a few minutes left.

Brody runs back carrying some sticks and cattails. I hadn't even noticed he left. I release the white cotton fluff from the brown, velvety covering and almost instantly the fire is lit. Dad is seizing up on the bank, but within seconds after using the cattail kindling, I get the fire going and it's becoming healthy, hungry. I tell Brody to go get more and the fire continues to eat.

I strip Dad of all his clothes. I can't even remember the last time I saw him naked, but there's no time for embarrassment now. His lips are still blue and I take my dry shirt off and lay it over him. I take my pants off too and try to put them on his legs, but they are so small, they catch at his knees. I'm shivering in my bra and underwear, but after about 20 minutes, his convulsions have slowed down and his shivering even seems to match mine. Brody and I massage heat into his exposed skin. When I see he's going to make it, I let out a sigh of relief and actually laugh at the situation.

"Here," he says, as he kicks at the pants and they stick to his ankles. Now Brody's laughing.

Finally, he notices. "Frogs," he says, as he looks around at the hundreds of frogs released from the ice.

I'm not even sure how this is possible. Were they hibernating underneath the ice, waiting to be released by the stupidity of some fishermen? I'm trying to think of it as a natural phenomenon, but I know the truth. It's another plague. It seems like a rather harmless one, especially as Brody now delights in trying to catch them along the bank. I can't see how this could possibly be a bad thing, except that it's another warning and if I admit it, another step closer to the plague I *am* afraid of: Death of firstborn. The plagues are coming quicker now. As harmless as the frogs are, they are a sign of things to come.

This plague of the firstborn bothers me for obvious reasons, but the biggest is that I don't think there's anything to fight against. When I allow myself to wonder about what it will be like, it seems like maybe the firstborns just don't wake up. How are we to even know when our last day is? Do we just go to bed for the night and never wake up?

We get our stuff together and Dad actually seems to be okay. He lets Brody capture some of the frogs to bring back to Tent City. He loads him onto the snowmobile and then turns and looks at me.

"Thanks," he says, as he looks down, embarrassed. I've never seen him this way before. He's the most confident man I know, annoyingly so, well maybe besides Bentley.

"It's okay Dad, it was just an accident."

"Yeah," he stammers, "but I'm supposed to be the one taking care of you." He looks to the side with his face full of anguish. A tear actually drops from his eye. I've never seen that before either, not even when Drake died. "You can't know how proud I am of you."

Before I can stop it, a shudder of a sob has escaped from my chest. I don't know why I'm crying. I should be ecstatic from the way this turned out. Joyful, full of happiness. Dad takes me in his arms and he lets me cry. He keeps murmuring over and over, "I'm sorry."

As he holds me, I'm aware of something happening. I'm letting go of something. Ever since he sent me off, I've been angry with him, and Mom too. I couldn't believe they could just send the two of us off to fend for ourselves. If I'm really honest with myself, I resented that they couldn't find another plan, one that didn't involve shipping us off. And then all the lies he told me about Drake. I don't think I'm letting go of that. I'm not even sure I can. I would if I could, but it's a deep wound that will stay with me forever. If I could take a pill to remove it, I would. But it has taken root in me, much like Hannah's cancer. It's when I think about this, I release him and pretend like I'm in a hurry to get home.

"Mom must be wondering where we are," I say, as I brush the hair out of my eyes. It's now wet with salty tears, a combination of us both I suppose, but I want to compose myself before we get back. The puffiness in my face will reveal my weakness again.

Chapter 19

We pull into Tent City on the snowmobiles and as we dismount Dad and I make eye contact in our pact not to tell Mom about what happened. I think he dislikes her tears as much as I do. Jack and Bentley are back and scurrying around the tents.

I help Brody off the snowmobile and whisper into his ear, "Was that a plague?" I look around nervously, hopeful no one's listening. He only nods.

"Why? What's it for?" I've probably opened up a conversation too big for us now, but I can't help but ask.

"It's a sign," he says, and looks to me to ask more questions, but I just tousle his hair and tell him I will see him later.

"There you are!" Bentley says. "Where have you been?" He seems nervous and scattered. Jack looks calm and is already helping Brody unload his haul of frogs.

"What's going on?" I ask, as I watch him pace around and I unload my stuff to dry it off. He notices the monkey's fist and smiles despite his obvious unease.

"You know that camp Callie found?"

"You know about that? I thought you guys weren't speaking?"

"That's not really the point . . . Anyway, it's not just any camp. It's Rigby's camp," he says as he grabs my shoulder.

"Are we leaving?" The idea of it exhausts me. We've been moving around so much lately that even the thought of it makes me weary and then I'm disgusted because I realize I'm only thinking of myself.

"Hannah's too weak to move," I say.

"I know. We're not leaving. We're getting ready."

"Ready for what?"

"Anything," he says.

I go in to check on Hannah, but before I'm at the door I ask, "Where's Callie?"

"They've got her."

Everything's so chaotic around here, it's hard to find a second to think. Hannah is bedridden and Jack fears moving her will kill her. She tries to convince us to leave without her.

The guys are making a plan to go and get Callie back. I don't know why she didn't know it was Rigby's camp when she went there in the first place. Maybe he wasn't there when she visited, but it was still dumb to go there, not knowing who they were.

Grant finally seems to be himself again. He is trying to act like he's worried, but I can tell he's not. He's putting on a good show, but it's clear he's having a good time by the good-natured shoving he does with Bentley every time he walks past him.

They're so busy making their plans that they don't even see her walk up. Her beautiful features are broken and swollen, yet she still manages a smile.

Bentley rushes up to her and I see the rage cooking inside. "What have they done? I'll kill em'," he says as he rushes over to her, and I'm overcome by two feelings, jealousy being the one I'm ashamed of. I'm sickened to know that even relief at her escaping doesn't even compete with it.

"What happened?" he asks her.

"I got away, that's what." She smirks. "Good thing too. What were you guys planning?"

"Did they follow you?" Grant asks.

"I don't think so," she says, but she doesn't sound certain.

"Jack?" Bentley asks.

"I got it," he says, and he takes her into the old medical cabin. She walks with a limp, but for the most part she seems okay. I kind of smile thinking of what she must have done to whoever captured her. They obviously didn't know Callie well enough to know she'd give em' hell.

"What are you going to do?" I ask Bentley.

"Nothing. Yet. We have to get the area secured." He leaves me and meets in his cabin with my dad, Grant, and Jonah. He comes out only minutes later. They must just be reaffirming a plan that has already been made.

"So we are just going to sit around in defense?" I ask.

"For now," he says.

"When are we going to start doing something about this? Fight back." I sigh as the exhaustion sets in. I'm so sick of not doing anything.

"Soon," he says, as he runs his thumb down the side of my cheek, but then leaves in his busy hustle of things.

I stay with Hannah in her cabin. I'm overcome with grief that she may not get better. I didn't know her long, but I'm not ready to let her go. Dusk is setting in and I take my place outside by the fire. It's only Jack and Bentley up and I consider going back inside. Bentley even looks slightly irritated when I sit down.

"Am I interrupting?"

"Don't be ridiculous. Sit down," Bentley says.

I ignore his curtness. "So what's going on? What's going to happen?"

Silence.

"Why aren't you guys speaking?" I say, looking back and forth at the two of them. They look like naughty schoolchildren caught in the act.

"He's here," Jack says.

"Who? You can't be serious! He can't be here. Where is he?"

I look up to see Burke unloading his bags from his snowmobile. What could he possibly be doing here, especially now with my parents at Tent City? How could they think this is okay? That's fine. I'm not going to find out. It's time.

I walk calmly so they don't stop me. I scan around, watching for any other obstacles that could get in my way. I don't see any. I'm quietly thankful my parents and Brody aren't here to see this.

I've taken four large strides his way before I remove my knife from my back pocket and I'm gaining speed. Burke doesn't seem alarmed yet. That buys me at least a few more seconds. I don't wait any longer and I pick up more speed. I'm almost on him when I'm grabbed from behind.

"I told you she was going to do that!" Bentley says to Jack. "Do you even know her at all?"

He has cranked on my arm pretty hard and I turn around and glare at him, tempted to spit in his face, although I've never done that to anyone in my life. I've always found that repulsive, but it seems fitting now. How can Bentley be holding me back? He wants this as bad as I do.

"No, Dani, not like this," he says. "You won't like it."

"Like hell I won't, let me go," I scream. Bentley removes the knife from my hand and says to Jack, "You're going to have to do something about this."

"I know."

Chapter 20

So the big plan is to keep Burke locked in a cage, although I'm not sure it's for him as much as me. He sits handcuffed to the bed in one of the cabins, much like I was not too long ago. The absurdity of it makes my stomach churn.

My dad comes to find me after everyone else has gone to bed. I suspect that he has been given baby-sitting duty for tonight. He finds me seething on the front porch of my cabin. I'm unable to sleep knowing Burke is alive just a couple of cabins away.

"This is pretty tough stuff, huh kiddo?" he asks finally after we sit in silence for a while.

"How can you stand it?" My fingers are curled around the edge of the decking and my knuckles are white from the strain of it.

"I don't like it either, Dani, but you can't kill him."

"Why not? He killed Drake and got away with it."

"Is that who you are now? Are you a killer?"

"I've killed people," I say, as I look down. I haven't told him about the raid with Rigby and the lives I took. He doesn't ask and I'm grateful. He sighs and looks to the ground.

"So how should we do it then?"

"Huh?"

"Well, are we going to come up with a plan at least?"

"We?"

"What, you mean you get to have all the fun? That doesn't seem fair. Come on, let's really figure this thing out. It'll be fun."

"That's not funny, Dad."

"You're right. This is serious. If this is something you have to do, you better think about it long and hard. And while you're at it, think about the fact that everyone's got a story. You know what I can't put my finger on?"

"What?"

"Why hasn't Jack or Bentley done it first?"

"Maybe they can't. I couldn't do it to you . . . no matter what you did."

"Well, why don't you think about that first, and what it might mean if you were the one who did it. Good-night kiddo. Just remember this," he says, as he pauses, searching for the right words. "It'll change you." He gives my shoulder a gentle squeeze and walks to the cabin he shares with Mom.

Crap. He's got me there. How would Jack and Bentley feel if I was the one to pull the trigger? Seems like Bentley would accept it, but Jack? I'm not so sure. But it doesn't change anything. I know I should head to bed, but I can't get myself to. I head over to the cabin Burke's in. I'm surprised to find him alone.

I step inside and the shock of seeing Bentley's face in his almost has me dropping the knife.

"I've been expecting you," he says, with no fear in his eyes.

"Where's your guard," I ask.

"Jack? I've sent him away. I think we both know you won't do it," he says, as I'm wondering if he's mocking me or challenging me.

I sit down. I've got time to figure this out. He hasn't yelled or screamed for anyone yet. I'm surprised that I haven't just jumped on him and finished the job. The sick part I think is that I'm sort of enjoying dragging it out. Why shouldn't he have to suffer first?

"I've got questions."

"Shoot."

"I wish."

"Ask."

"Did you kill my brother?" There, I've said it. I'm surprised at my lack of emotion. My breathing is steady and my voice is monotone.

He's silent, seeming to search for the words. I'm annoyed at his lack of enthusiasm for our conversation, but then he lowers his head in . . . what is that? Shame? I have to give him a little credit . . . he's an amazing actor.

"Not directly."

"How then?"

"What difference does it make? What's done is done, and I can't change it."

"Did you poison the food?"

"No," he says, as he looks me in the eyes. Okay, now he's starting to irritate me.

"Then what was it! Why can't you just say it? What game are you playing?"

"It's not a game, Danielle."

“Don’t call me that,” I say, as I get up to leave. If he’s not going to give me answers and I can’t kill him now, there’s no sense in staying.

I reach the door when he says, “Wait.” It’s not so much what he says, but the way his voice sounds. Just as I see Bentley in his face, I can hear Jack in his voice. This is really messing with my mind. I stop with my hand lingering on the cool doorknob.

“Please sit,” he says, as he adjusts himself on the bed, clearly uncomfortable as the handcuffs pinch at his wrist. I smile at the small justice of it.

“I lost someone too,” he begins, “someone very important to me, someone who meant more than life itself. Cliché’, I know, but it’s the truth. She was the most beautiful girl I had ever seen. And smart too, that girl. You know, I can’t even believe she took a chance on me. I was just a poor boy trying to make it as a minister. She could’ve had anyone, but . . .” I don’t like the way his story is making me feel. I zone him out for a minute as I start to see him as a human. This scares me.

“Wait, if this is going to be a while, why don’t we take those off?” I say. I take the key from the table across the room and walk over to him and slowly unlatch the cuffs, releasing my tie to cold-blooded murder. If he attacks me, isn’t it self-defense?

“Go on,” I encourage, as I take the knife out from my back pocket and take my seat across from him. I’m not afraid of him. I’m actually hoping he makes a move.

“As I was saying,” he says, as he rubs his wrists and extends his feet across the bed. Is he comfortable with me? Why does he seem so relaxed?

"As you can guess, it was my wife, Jack and Bentley's mother. She died when they were 11. They changed that day. Sometimes I think that was almost worse than her death."

"How did she die?" I want to see if he will admit it. That he has killed her too.

Instead of answering me, he lowers his head again and stifles a sob. It's strange to see him in this condition. Every time I have ever seen him, whether it's on TV, or back home in the sheriff's office, he has commanded the room. I can't help but think it's a ploy. I'm not buying it.

"Save it. What happened?"

He composes himself. He looks up at me and shakes his head and almost smirks, "She would have loved you. You know, I didn't see why Jack was so . . ." he says, twirling his finger in the air and rolling his eyes as if to say coo-coo, "but I do now. You're a lot like her."

"You don't know me." I'm glaring at him, but losing all fight in me to kill him. But now that I've uncuffed him, it seems awkward to lock him back up and walk away.

"I can see this is hard for you. Why don't you just let me tell my story and you can decide for yourself. Let go a little. I can tell you've already decided not to kill me."

I look at him with confusion and he motions to my hands. I hadn't even realized I had put the knife down.

"If I could go back and do it all over, I would. I got mixed up with The Council and by the time I figured out what they'd done, it was too late. I'd already lost her. I lost them too really . . . the boys. They couldn't forgive me. By then, The Council had me by the balls." He looks up for a reaction. I give him nothing.

He continues, "Threatened to expose me, have me thrown in jail. I was a coward. I didn't stop it."

"That seems pretty hard to believe. I don't even know anyone else on The Council. You were the 'General' after all. You really gonna say that it was everyone else and you were an innocent bystander?"

"Hell, no. I didn't say that," he says to me, looking almost angry. "I just said I didn't know the extents they were going to and by the time I did . . . it was too late. I lost my Emma."

"Jack said she was digging around where she wasn't supposed to. Is that how it happened?"

"Yeah, there's a lot more to it actually. That son-of-a-bitch killed her when she wouldn't back down. Only I didn't know it, until recently. I thought she died just like everyone else. I'll kill him if I get the chance."

"Who?"

"We'll get to that. Anyway, I don't know if Jack told you, but his ma, she's real smart, doctor and everything. She used to work for the United Nations. She was an ambassador. Well, she was looking in on some of the illnesses, and cause of the locusts. The Council advised her to stop poking around. She figured out what caused all the deaths and when he confronted her, she wouldn't let it go. I think he had her killed." He clears his throat and looks around, as if he is searching for something. He glances at the knife.

"Sure, it looked like an accident, but it's just all too convenient. I should've gotten her out when I could've," he says, as he pounds his fist into the side of the bed.

"You said he? Is it someone on The Council?"

"Yeah, you could say that."

"Enough of the mystery. Who did it?"

"You sure you wanna know?"

"I'm asking aren't I?" The hairs on my arm stand up and I almost know what he's going to say.

"I believe you guys call him, Uncle Randy."

"Randy? I thought you said it was The Council?"

"Danielle, he *is* The Council."

How is this possible? Randy has done nothing but say terrible things about The Council. He's the one who kept us safe from them. This can't be right. It must be a trick. How could I possibly have been buying anything he said? Burke must have everyone under his spell, including Jack.

My head is spinning at the ridiculousness of it and before I know it, I've retrieved my knife and placed it at his throat, knocking him hard against the back of the bed. I don't even remember taking the steps to get to him.

"You're lying!"

He is rigid, eyes wide. I can't tell if he is planning on a counter attack, but when he tries to speak it comes out garbled because I'm cutting off his airway. I let up a little.

"I'm not. How do you think he got away with all he did? Do you think it's easy to make fake death certificates? How do you think he got all that info to Bentley?"

"Is he planning on killing the Golden Child?" It's slipped out before I can even think of the consequences. By me asking, he's going to figure out I've got something invested in the Golden Child and he would be right to assume it's Brody. I'm such an idiot. I'm seriously considering just slicing his throat now, but I don't get the chance.

I turn around when I see the door open and flushed with guilt, I drop the knife.

It's Jack and he scans me and the knife that has just hit the floor. He looks . . . almost disappointed.

"It's Hannah. She's asking for you."

I lean down and swipe the blade off the floor and run out the door.

"Is she okay?" I ask breathless. Here I was about to take someone's life and she's hanging onto her own.

"She's fine," Jack says, as he keeps his pace with mine. We get to the door of her cabin and he tries to follow me in, but I stop him. He seems to understand and leaves me be.

"Where were you?" she asks.

"Nowhere. Are you okay? You look better. Can I get you anything?"

"Sit down," she says, as she sits up all the way and pats the bed.

"You don't want to do what you were gonna to do."

"How do you know what I was gonna do?"

"Does it matter? Can you trust me on this one? It's something you can't take back. It won't make the pain go away."

"It might."

"It won't. You need to let it go."

"Why? He admitted it was his fault. He needs to pay."

"I'm not asking you to let it go for his sake."

"What? Mine?"

I laugh. She must be crazy if she thinks it won't make me feel better. I could tell her all the ways it would make me feel better. "He's going to try and convince everyone that Randy is The Council."

"He could be."

"What? He's gotten to you too? When did you talk to him? How could you possibly know?"

She doesn't even answer me. I don't really need an answer. For now, I'm so exhausted with all of it, all I want to do is crawl into bed and forget the world for a while. I drag myself over to the other bed and even though my mind and body ache for sleep, all I can think about are all the times Randy pulled in special favors for us. How could he act like our friend after what he's done?

The story has carried through camp by morning. My mom has shut down and buried herself away in her cabin. My dad seems to be in shock, but he's not denying it.

At least they're still keeping Burke locked up. I'm not sure how I would feel passing by him at camp or sitting by him at lunch. Can you even imagine. "Hey, Burke, pass the salt." The idea pisses me off so much I try to forget he even exists.

The guys are getting the camp locked down. Bentley has passed out all the guns he's salvaged. It's not much, but it's better than nothing. They've taken down all the extra tents and either burned or buried them. They have barricaded the windows. I'm not sure why. If The Council or Rigby come in, it wouldn't take much to tear it down. I've decided to call a meeting. The time for secrets is over.

Everyone is seated around the campfire and I'm finding it difficult to breathe or even swallow. Am I about ready to do this? I've felt for so long that keeping Brody's secret is what has kept him alive. If it gets out that he is the Golden Child, will he now be hunted? Even if it's not just The Council hunting him, are there others out there who don't want him around? I'm thinking about all the stories of the presidents who have been assassinated. It seems like it was the ones who had some sort of controversy about them. If Lincoln was shot because he wanted to end slavery, what will the people think of the boy who's supposed to change the world?

Everyone is seated and looking at me expectantly. For a second, I change my mind. That little voice in my head says no.

"What's the big announcement?" Bentley finally asks.

"I don't know if I can do it," I say honestly. I look over at Hannah and she is nodding in encouragement. Seeing her out in the fresh air brings me some confidence.

"Go on, honey, just tell us," Dad says.

So I do. All the members of my family and my Tent City family watch me and listen carefully as I tell them about how I discovered Brody's marking the last time we left Tent City. I tell them about how he got sick, but he wasn't really sick, just his transformation. I tell them about Waite. I even tell them about how Brody seems to know things already. Wise beyond his years, I tell them. Brody gives me a little smile.

"It's him . . . Brody is the Golden Child," I say again. I look around at them and not one of them is saying anything. They all just stare at me like I'm crazy. Maybe this was a bad idea. I had never even considered that they might not believe me.

Then they all start laughing. Every one of them.

"What are you all laughing at?" I'm so confused, but as their laughter carries on, I find myself getting mad. Why aren't they saying anything? This is serious. Brody being the Golden Child changes everything . . . for all of us.

Finally my dad speaks up, "Oh, honey, sorry . . . it's just that . . . we already know."

"What?" How is this possible? I've kept the secret locked tight. Hannah?

I look over to Hannah. She has betrayed me. She promised not to tell anyone. How could she after we promised all of our secrets to each other.

"Don't look at her," Dad says. "You can't really believe we wouldn't know, would you? We're not that blind. Hang around Brody long enough . . . and you can *feel* it." He's still laughing as he scoops Brody up and places him in his lap. I can't find it in myself to even find it a little funny.

"Why didn't you say anything?" The idea that I could have unburdened myself months ago is devastating.

"Thought you didn't want to talk about it," he says, "you don't like to talk about the advancements either . . . and I have to tell you, I've been dying to ask you about it. We're just trying to respect your wishes."

Jonah nods, and he and Jess move on, as well as everyone else, but Dad and Bentley.

"You knew too?" I poke Bentley in the shoulder. He just smiles. "Why didn't you tell me?"

"No offense, but you're kind of a hothead. Every time you are upset about something, you just run off. I've kind of learned it's better not to piss you off."

"I'm the hothead?" I feel the heat flushing my neck already and I want to remind him that he's the one who shattered the TV, but even in my defense, I realize he's right. Instead I cross my arms and look away. Stubborn, childish gesture.

"Now that we're all out in the open, can we talk about the advancements?" Bentley asks.

Dad walks away, but not before saying, "We'll talk later."

"What's there to talk about?" I say, but I'm not really listening. My mind is still reeling that everyone here has known about Brody this whole time. Why wouldn't Hannah tell me?

"Well, for starters, I figured out what yours is," Bentley says. I don't bother telling him that whatever I had before is gone. I could feel a sense of something before, but now it's gone.

"You're the reason we're all here," he says confidently and I find myself blushing, even though I don't believe him.

"What do you mean?"

"Think about it," he says, as he takes a seat close to me and grabs the tail of my shirt. This is somehow even more comforting than if he had taken my hand. He's got me without invading my space. How does he know just what to do?

"We're all here because of you in some way. You found Hannah. You brought Brody and Kit here. Jonah and his family—you were responsible for saving their baby, and now they are a part of your forever family. And Jack. Don't worry about him," he says with a wink. "I can't help but think something big is going to happen and I think your advancement is getting everyone here. You're really important, you know."

"Why do you think we all need to be here?" I've always seen Bentley as a reliable source, but now I'm having my doubts.

"I don't know. You know, I haven't even really figured out if it's Tent City we're supposed to be in, or if we're all just supposed to be together."

"Are you supposed to be here?" I ask, as I am thinking about all the things he's been teaching me. How could I have been so stupid? He's getting me ready for when he dies.

"What do you mean?" He has let go of my shirt and now slouches back into his chair.

"Oh, I don't know. Why the sudden interest in teaching me everything? The fishing, the knots, the guns? I know what you're thinking."

He stands up now and lets out an exasperated sigh.

"What are you planning? Some kind of suicide mission?" I persist with a condescending smile.

I stop smiling when I see the glisten in his eyes, and then I say, "I'm sorry, I didn't mean to . . . I know this place makes you crazy sometimes . . . You don't have to stay for me."

His face changes. Now, he's smiling.

"You think I could leave you . . . willingly?"

Embarrassment catches in my throat. "I mean, you don't have to stay, I'm not forcing you."

Now he's laughing. "For such a smart girl . . . Dani, I'm not *leaving* you."

"Oh." He's right. I am kind of acting like a moron. Why does it feel like I'm always one step behind when it comes to him? "Bentley, you don't *really* think?"

"Have to prepare for everything," he says.

And now I pull on his shirt to bring him closer to me. "If it really is the firstborn, you don't have to prepare me for anything. We'll both go. In a way, wouldn't it be easier? Neither one of us would have to know about the other. Bonnie and Clyde, going down in flames." I'm being playful with him now, but he's not taking the bait.

"No, don't ever say that! I've got it figured out." He forcefully backs away releasing my hand from him.

Hannah . . . of course. Now I'm not so playful, as I remember what he made her promise.

"You know," I say, as I move closer. He is inches away from me. "You had no right!"

Instead of meeting my anger, all he says is, "I know" and walks away.

Chapter 21

"Are you serious?" I am replaying it in my head again to figure out if what she has just told me is true, but after seeing Hannah, the proof's in the pudding, or the milk at least.

"Don't look at me like that." Hannah laughs as she finishes the rest of the cupful of Jessica's breast milk.

"How does Jack know that will even work?"

Just then Jack walks in with another cup. It looks watery and weird, and certainly not sanitary.

"What is this going to do?" I ask him.

He seems slightly uncomfortable as he hands the cup over to Hannah, his fingers barely touching the plastic rim. Hannah doesn't seem nearly as offended as she should. Essentially, she is drinking human milk that came from . . . well, you know. The word cannibal floats in my mind, but that's not what this is, babies drink it all the time. But Hannah's not a baby and Jessica is not her mother.

"It's called the HAMLET method and I don't see we have much choice. We've scanned Hannah's old house and it looks like the old bat used up all the cancer meds. It's the only idea I could come up with."

"Old bat huh? You told him the story too?" I don't know why I feel offended by it. I guess I just thought Hannah kept all her secrets for me.

"Well, it was pretty cruel. The nerve of that woman," he says as he wipes his hands on his jeans.

"So how does it work then?" I ask, because at this point, I'm just generally curious.

His face lights up now as he starts his medical speak. I get him to speak regular English and he tells me that it's some sort of antibody in human milk that fights cancer cells. Hannah finishes her milk and I walk outside with him.

"Will it work?" I ask.

"Truth?"

"Of course," I say as I fold my arms over my chest. I'm a little annoyed that he has her drinking Jessica's milk if it doesn't even give her half a chance.

"It could," he says with a child-like smile. "Back before the locusts, they were making huge strides with it. It's funny you know, they used to use a lot of chemotherapy and radiation, when the answer was in the human body."

"But, she's so sick. Is it too late?"

"No. I don't want you to ever say that around her. Half of this is going to be how hard she fights. I can tell she thinks an awful lot of you . . . so do me a favor, don't say anything to her unless it's positive."

"Breast milk?"

"Hey, like I said, it's the best we got."

"Okay. Hey, just one more thing," I say as I'm trying to suppress the smirk, but finding it impossible.

"Yeah?"

"How do you get it out?" And even though I was trying to be totally serious, we both start laughing and Jack doesn't seem like Dr. Jack. He is back to being the 18-year-old kid he should have been before all this plague stuff.

"We went and got a pump from that baby store Grant was at. Got lucky too. Battery powered."

I'm so caught up in just enjoying Jack that I don't notice Bentley watching us from across camp. When I make eye contact with him, my heart jumps and I blush in shame. I'm not sure why. I'm not tied to either one of them, but it probably has to do with the look on his face. He looks hurt. He has more than given me his blessing to give me time to choose, but I can see from the look in his eyes that I've hurt him. I can't even really blame him. Callie can bring those feelings out in me too. What am I going to do about this?

***

Everyone seems to get into a routine of things. Spring has brought a new energy to camp. Cabin fever has finally broken and people walk around with a new purpose, despite us all wondering about the next plague.

Jessica spends her time between nursing DJ *and* nursing Hannah, if you want to really get down to it. Jack spends most of his time tending to Hannah as well. If I'm brave enough to admit it, I think she might even be getting better. I don't want to put too much hope there because deep down, I'm afraid one more heal will kill her and knowing her, she'll do it.

Bentley, Dad, Jonah, Callie, and Grant spend most of their time getting camp ready. Kit's even helping out. She said she's tired of feeling like a victim. They think an attack is coming. If they are so sure about it, I don't know why we don't just pack up and leave. Hannah seems well enough to move and I'd like to get both Hannah and Brody out of here. The idea of Brody being around if an attack comes brings me back to memories of the last time camp was attacked. By some stroke of luck, we came out of it okay, but I haven't seen Waite in weeks and not having him around makes me uncomfortable. Strange, since it used to be the other way around.

Everyone ignores Burke locked away in the cabin. I think by pretending he's not here, my parents can put away thoughts of Drake and the fact that his killer lives here at camp.

I should say everyone, but me. When I find everyone else is busy, I sneak back in to see if he can provoke me today. The sight of him doesn't help. He sits with his back against the wall and his arm hanging from an uncomfortable cuff. Even from here, I can see the wrist is fat and swollen.

"Jack okay with this?" I ask as I turn my wrist in the air indicating the cuffs.

"No, not really. He wants me to take it off, but I know it will make everyone uneasy."

"Save it. Why did you come back? I thought you took off to Williston. Isn't that where your wife was from? They didn't want you either huh?"

"More or less."

"Why come back?"

"They're all I have left," he says as he drops his head. He's really keeping the act up. What is he hoping? That I will feel sorry for him and let him go?

I sit down in my usual chair and notice with some disgust the pot he must be using to piss in and choke back a dry heave when I actually picture what else must go in there.

"So . . . I have some more questions," I start. He doesn't respond, just shoots a glare my way.

"Feel like talking?" I ask. More silence. Fine, play that way. I get up and head out to the door. It worked before, so I'm hoping it does again.

"Wait," he says. He's so predictable. Being in here alone all the time must be getting to him if he's willing to talk to me. We have an obvious dislike for each other.

"What have I got to lose?" he finally says.

"That's better. I want to know about the missing book of Judah."

"Wondering when you would get around to that," he says with his first smile since I've entered.

"Is it real?" I've got my knife out and I'm flipping it around. I've gotten quite good at maneuvering it around and right now I find it more entertaining than him.

"I think so, but I haven't seen it. It's also called the Missing Book of Kings," he says as he raises his eyebrows and motions to his empty water cup on the floor.

"You don't think I'm going to wait on you, do you?"

"Throat's kind of dry. Hard to talk . . . you know." He's got a full blown smile now. Is he messing with me? I'm torn between stalking out of the cabin and getting him some water. If I don't get him the water, I won't have my answers and he knows it.

I'm practically growling at him when I hand him the water. I do it so forcefully, some of it splashes on him and I see irritation float across his face. I sit back down, only slightly satisfied.

"Anyway," he begins, "this missing book, if it's real, would reveal who the next king was going to be. Haven't had kings for a long time, but then again, haven't had the plagues for quite some time either. Word has it, the new king is the descendant of King David, God's favorite King."

David. Wasn't that the one Bentley and I were reading about in the snowstorm . . . and also the one Dad talked about with the Davidic Descendants? I seriously feel like this belongs in a comic book.

"You must know a lot about this . . . why the plagues?"

"You want my honest opinion?"

"No. I want you to lie to me so I can sit around and try to figure out the truth from the lies," I say with so much sarcasm, I'm almost embarrassed.

"Okay," he chuckles, "I think He's wiping the earth. You know, like Noah's Ark?"

"Come again?"

"You know, sinning gone rampant, God wipes the earth, starts all over, two of every kind? Never heard of it?"

"Sorry, must have missed that one."

"Makes sense to me. We've gone and screwed everything up. God set up the commandments and humans don't really feel like following the rules." He's starting to sound a lot like Jessica and Jonah. Maybe it was part of the religious doctrine handed out at the compounds.

"So what's the point of even trying anymore, if he's just going to kill us all anyway?" I can't believe I'm even buying into what he is saying.

"You of all people should know." I'm starting to feel like Burke is toying with me. I look up and he is looking at me with curiosity.

"Your brother. That's the point," he finally says when I don't answer. Goosebumps the size of bowling balls flash across every inch of my body.

I leave and go sit on the front of the porch. He calls out for me to stay, but I'm spooked. I'm going to have to kill him soon. I'm losing some of the drive to do it, but I know it needs to be done. He's trying to come off as smooth and maybe even remorseful, but I can tell he's hiding something. I feel like he's trying to win us all over so he can be released. For all I know, he's the one who was sent to kill Brody.

The next morning, I wake in sweats, dreaming of Randy. I hate that Burke's in camp, but realistically, he's the only one who can give me answers and I want them before I kill him. I head back over there even though the sun is barely rising. Maybe he's an early riser.

When I get closer, I hear a ruckus in his cabin. Is he trying to escape? I hear some shouting and it sounds like someone has been slammed against the door. I try to shove it open, but it won't budge. Finally, it comes crashing open and I look to the bed. He's still there and he's still cuffed? What is going on here?

I look over to find Bentley and Jack wrestling on the floor and before I can stop them, Bentley has smashed his fist into Jack's eye. I wince, as if I had been hit.

"What are you doing?" I rush over to pull him off Jack, but it's like he's possessed. He keeps swinging. He jerks me off, as if I'm a ragdoll.

"Uncuff me! I can help," Burke yells. I'm torn. Is this part of his plan? What should I do?

I look back to Jack and Bentley and they're both bloody and raw, filled with rage. I've never seen Jack like this before, but I have seen Bentley. And that's why I do it.

As soon as I uncuff Burke, he is on top of Bentley and removes him with ease. "Bentley, that's enough!" Burke commands.

I think Bentley is so surprised by it, he stills. He looks up at me and then looks down, breathing hard, and almost appears embarrassed.

"Asshole," Bentley says as he storms past me.

Jack is feeling his face, obviously dazed by what just happened. They must be fighting about what to do with Burke. Jack probably feels that he is being mistreated and Bentley probably feels the punishment isn't enough.

"Jack," I start, but he barely looks at me and he leaves the cabin.

"You gonna make this hard on me?" I ask as I pick up the cuffs and twirl them around.

"Nope," he says as he sits back down on the bed. He's giving me the opposite hand to cuff to the bed. It will make it awkward for him to sit, but give him reprieve for the other that is still red and swollen.

"You proud of yourself? Look at what you've done to them? Just when they were starting to get along," I say as I latch the cuffs, tighter than I should.

"You think that was about me?" He laughs.

"What else?"

"Sweetheart, they weren't fighting over *me*."

Chapter 22

I need some time to think. I don't even dare look around for Bentley or Jack. I don't want to see either one of them. The biggest thing I can't seem to figure out is why I let them be an idea that gets stuck in my head. Given the current condition of the world, why don't I spend my time sitting around thinking about plagues, the fact that my brother is supposed to be the new king, or that there might be an attack coming, maybe even a plan to fix this. Leave it to me to act like some stupid girl and worry about guys. Maybe Kit and I aren't that different after all. But I know the truth of it. They're my friends, and I don't want to lose either one of them.

It's almost dark, but I've got to get out of here. Maybe I'll take a snowmobile and head into Deadwood. That's the last place they would expect me to go and I don't want anyone to follow me or bug me about leaving. The idea is getting more appealing as I realize I could find more baby supplies for DJ. Maybe a teddy bear. He doesn't have one yet.

I leave mostly because I want to stop thinking about Burke. He's getting into my head and I'm losing my resolve to kill him. The funny part is that deep down I know he's faking it. Sure, maybe he feels torn up about losing his wife, but he doesn't seem to really care that he was part of killing off half the population of the United States. Over 150 million were lost the year Drake died. How did they do it? How is it possible no one found out?

It doesn't take long to get into Deadwood. If I'm honest, I've spent most of the time thinking about the things I'm running away from. I'm starting to wonder if there is something wrong with my brain. I take the sled down Main Street, hoping to find a baby store, but right away I'm drawn to an old saloon. It says Saloon Number 10 on the door, but that's not what has my attention. There's music coming from inside and if I was more familiar with parties, I would call this a party.

I park the sled in the back because it must have something to do with The Council. No one else would dare be so loud. I take a peek inside the window, careful not to be seen. I'm taken aback by what I see. I scan from face to face. Why are they all kids? A flashback of Tent City comes into my mind of when I first walked into camp. The same feeling of being astonished by a lack of adults is back. How could they be doing this? Aren't they afraid of getting caught?

I walk inside now. It feels like I'm being drawn in. Here I am thinking about that Pied Piper again. I can't control myself. It's the music. It's pulling me in. I've never experienced anything like this before. I touch every item lightly with my fingertips as I make my way slowly through the back, absorbing every sensation. It smells like beer and smoke, but it's not unpleasant. I study everything. Dusty chairs, old lottery machines, stacked crates, old pictures of old outlaws. Stale sawdust covers the floor.

The only music I've ever been exposed to comes from an old headset and it sounds NOTHING like this. My whole body is vibrating with the sound. I can feel it start at the wood floor, flow into my boots, and travel out my fingertips.

Before I know it, I've lost all fear and all sense of control and I'm in the middle of a huge pile of kids just dancing. This is dancing? Everyone's moving and elbows and knees are crashing into me with synchronized motion. We all jump together to the beat. This feels almost identical to Valium. Have I taken something without realizing it? The guy on the stage is belting out lyrics and I'm as lost in them as I am in the rhythm.

I stay for hours. I would've stayed longer, but kids are starting to scatter and I don't want to be the last one. I don't speak to anyone. I feel a hollow sadness knowing it's over. I take one last look before I duck out the back door and I make eye contact with the boy who was singing. He smiles and nods and I slip away.

I'm soaked with a combination of what feels like hundreds of other kids sweat as I mount my sled. It's sending a breezy chill up my shirt and I start shivering uncontrollably. My hair whips back and I accelerate the snowmobile. I'm alive again.

I sneak back into the cabin I've been sharing with Hannah and breathe a sigh of relief because she's still asleep. Why don't I want to talk about this with anyone? Not even her. If I told anyone about it, it would be Hannah, but I feel like I would be flashing something in her face that she can never have. Even if she were with me, she could have never done what I've just done.

I go back for the next two nights. It scares me to know that I wouldn't care if the world did end tomorrow.

Somehow I've pushed the anger to the side. When I'm here, I forget to hate. I've started to talk to a few kids who I see on a regular basis, but I'm not eager to share anything about my life or where I live. I think they feel this way too. But actually, I don't think anyone comes here to talk. As soon as I walk in the door, I lose myself in the middle of the dance floor. I let the crowd swallow me up and for a few hours, I pretend I'm not me.

I'm sneaking out the back door again on my third night, when I'm startled by the singer.

"Hey you," he says as he stands in front of the doorway, blocking my way.

"Um, hey?" I try to push my way past him, but he doesn't budge.

"You ever gonna stick around for the after party?" he asks. I've looked at him a couple of times before as he belts out song after song, but never for this long and never this close. It just occurred to me that I never really thought he was a real person.

"I gotta go." There's a split second when he smiles that I feel alarmed, but there are other kids here and I don't think he really means any harm. But I don't know these other kids. For the first time, I'm feeling foolish about being here.

"I've seen you here for the last couple of nights. It looks like you have a pretty good time. What's your name?"

He's looking at me waiting for an answer. I don't know what to tell him. I take just a second to study him. I think I'm trying to figure out if he's good or bad. He's not really what would be the standard good looking, but there is something about him. I think he gets extra points for his voice that absolutely commands the room when he's onstage.

"Tilly."

"Tilly? Now, don't be silly. You're lying," he says with almost a laugh.

"How would you know?" I say with a scowl. My heart is thumping and I'm regretting lying.

"Your mouth twitched," he says as he studies me.

"Dani," I say, embarrassed, but when I look up again, he doesn't seem offended.

"No twitching. Nice to meet you," he says as he extends his hand. "I'm Milo." This surprises me more than anything. I actually thought he was going to say something like Chase, or Chance, or something else, but definitely not Milo.

"I really should get going." He does let me push past him this time. I look back and see them laughing and passing around some kind of clear liquid in mason jars. Looks like I always leave just in time.

The next day, I promise myself I'm not going back. I make good on it until about midnight. I'm tossing and turning in my bed. Sleep has given me the slip again. I consider seeing what Hannah has in her stash. Being in the same room with her and all her medications is damn near impossible. I feel myself using very soon. I have to get out of here. If I left now, I would only have about an hour at Saloon Number 10 before they stop the show. Is it even worth it? Maybe I could sneak in without Milo or anyone else seeing me. I do talk myself out of it, so it's confusing when I find myself putting the key into the ignition of the snowmobile.

There's someone else on stage tonight. He's not as good, but I don't mind. I find myself getting lost in the crowd again and realize that I don't have the power not to come back. If they are going to keep having these parties, I'm going to keep coming. It's the only place I can escape to.

Back at camp, even seeing Brody reminds me that the world we live in is not kind. Watching him play should make me feel good and happy, but all I can do is picture him in danger and if I'm really honest, he confuses me. When I'm in Deadwood, it's like the Valium, only I'm not a zombie. I'm something else besides a sad, scattered girl. I never knew what music could do. Why did people give it up? Did it go away like the sports and schools, just another causality of our new lives?

I'm moving with my eyes closed and I'm feeling comforted by the usual swarm of bodies jumping to the beat when I feel one of them getting just a little too close. He's got his arms around me and is pressed in tight.

I open my eyes and turn around, ready for a fight. I should have known Milo was trouble.

"Bentley?"

"Is this where you go every night?" he asks as he looks around.

"So?"

"Let's go," he grabs my arm and I jerk it away.

Milo is watching from a few feet away and starts to walk over.

"Problem here?" Milo asks and I can feel Bentley's steam.

"No, we're leaving," I say and I stalk towards the door.

"Followed me?" I glare at Bentley as soon as we exit.

"Have you told anyone where you live?" he asks as he glances back in and then leads me away by the arm.

"Leave me alone! You're not in charge of me."

"Just get on your sled and get home."

He pulls away on his own snowmobile and leaves without checking to see if I'm following. I'm tempted to go back inside, but any good mood I had is over and I don't really feel like dealing with Milo. So I do the last thing I want to and follow Bentley home.

I pull into Tent City hoping to just slink into the cabin, but find Bentley starting a new fire. It's got to be 2:00 a.m. He must be expecting a late night chat session.

I sit down. Better to get it over with now.

"You know, I almost left you there," he says as he leans down to the fire and blows on it, hoping it catches.

"And?"

"You got something to prove?" He glares at me.

"It's harmless . . . I know what I'm doing." I'm kicking my feet around. I should have been more careful. Or really I should've known. Anything that fun was bound not to last.

"Oh yeah," he says with heavy sarcasm. "Do you even know who they are?" He sort of smiles now. It's not friendly, almost angry.

Silence.

"Your little buddy there, I can't be sure, but I think he runs with Rigby."

"What?" I let the information sink in a little. Part of me thinks Bentley is lying. It wouldn't be the first time and if I believe him, it would give me a good reason not to be able to go back. "How do you know?"

"I guess I don't for sure, but it makes sense. Think about it. Rigby's camp isn't too far from here. Who else would be so ballsy? No one in their right mind would try to pull that off . . . unless they're in bed with The Council. That saloon was practically lit up like a flare. Maybe we could send Callie in to find out. She'd be able to recognize them," he says as he considers this.

"That's about the dumbest thing I've ever heard." I'm standing and pacing now. I'm trying to picture all of the kids I've met with mud on their face. Rigby's gang likes to go full commando, mud and everything. I haven't seen them since the night they raided Tent City, unless you count all the times they intrude into my dreams.

"How else can we find out then, huh?"

"Isn't it obvious?" I say with a smirk. "I'm going back."

Chapter 23

"I don't like it," Bentley says as he tightens the elastic band at my waist and adjusts the leather strap my knife sits in.

"There. Leave it there," I say as he gets it to the sweet spot at my back. The only spot it can sit where I don't feel it gouging into me.

"Are you sure about this?" he asks again.

"Yeah." I smile with genuine warmth. I'm a mixture of excitement, and actually, a little bit of fear. "I'm surprised you're just letting me go."

"What else am I gonna do? Just remember everything I told you . . . first sign of trouble . . . get the hell out of there."

"Got it."

The entire ride into Deadwood, I'm a ball of nerves. The plan is to just keep doing what I'm doing, but don't be afraid to let Milo get close. "Engage him, get him to talk. Act like you care," Bentley says.

"Find out what you need and then get out of there, but don't be obvious. Any sign of Rigby, don't think twice, just get out." He tries to convince me to let him come along, but this is something I have to do myself. How am I supposed to get Milo to trust me if I have Bentley tagging along?

***

I exhale a sigh of relief and inhale a new sense of panic as I pull in. I've never been more afraid to enter Saloon

Number 10 than I am right now. I feel like the truth is plastered all over my face. But I've got my plan. Get in and find Milo. Talk. Get out.

I walk in and it happens again. I'm swept to the middle, maybe even pushed, but I don't fight it. I see Milo on the stage, but I ignore him for now. Right now, I just intend to enjoy myself. It could be my last time. I'll catch him at the end. No way to talk to him while he's going crazy on stage. Good crazy.

The floor is alive with vibrations. I close my eyes and get lost. When I open them, I'm surprised to see I've made my way to the front row. I'm only about a foot from the stage when Milo and I make eye contact. He gives me the smallest smile and starts a new song. I nearly jump out of my skin when I realize it's a Billy Idol song, "Rebel Yell." How appropriate.

Exhilaration sets every cell in my body on fire. I look up at Milo and give him my biggest smile . . . a sign of appreciation. He stops for a second and holds his hand up to his keyboard guy.

Milo walks to the front of the stage and reaches for me. What does he want? Does he want me to dance on stage? I've seen him do this before, but I know I could never do that. Too exposed.

"Know it?" he asks with his hand extended.

"Yes," I say breathless, "but I couldn't."

"Get her up here guys," he says almost laughing and some of the kids have hoisted me up on the stage.

How can he expect me to dance up here? He walks back to the side of the stage and picks up another mic. He's got to be kidding. He's smiling when he walks back over to me and the keyboard guy starts again. Then it's matched by the electric guitar. Is this really happening?

"Ready?" Milo asks with a wicked grin, but I have trouble finding it evil.

My heart is about to explode. I look out into the crowd and they're all looking at me, waiting.

I find myself moving with the beat when Milo screams out the first line, "Last night a little dancer came dancing to my door."

"Last night a little angel came pumping on the floor," I belt out, and every endorphin in my body explodes. He looks at me a little surprised.

I can't help myself and find we're doing this thing together. Never in a million years could I have imagined I would find myself in this situation. But I don't care. I wouldn't be able to stop myself, even if I tried.

Every lyric comes easily to me. It should. I've probably heard it a thousand times. He backs up and I feel a split second of panic, but he just smiles and I finish the song myself. The words come out raw and throaty, like they should for Billy Idol. My feet keep with the beat, dancing me around the stage and my hair whips around to its own beat, eager to keep up. I close my eyes just for a second. Everything is perfect. But before I know it, the song is over and I feel like floating away. I look over to Milo and all he does is laugh.

He puts his hand to my neck and says into the mic, "Let's give it up for Dani!" And because they will do whatever he says, the room explodes. Am I under his spell too?

I look across the crowd to the wall that has all the mirrors. I see myself above the crowd standing next to someone who was born to rock the stage. I look like a sweaty mess. My tank top has soaked through and is sticking to my skin. My hair is wild and crazy, but I also notice something else. I'm smiling. Not just regular smiling. It's like it was before. Before all the mess with the locusts. Before Drake died. I actually look happy.

I've completely forgotten what I'm supposed to be doing here. I'm trying to convince myself that what just happened only helps my cause. Gets him to trust me. One step forward. I jump off the stage and into the crowd and get lost for the rest of the set.

"Who knew you could sing?" Milo laughs from up on stage. The rest of the crowd has cleared and I'm standing around, unsure of what my next move is. "Are you going to stick around tonight?" he says as he stops winding the electrical cord and tosses it to the side.

Okay, here's my chance. I need to play it smart. I need to get him to trust me. Bentley wants me to get this done in one try, but I know once I have my answer, I won't be able to come back.

What now? I'm thinking of the clear liquid I saw them passing around in mason jars and I'm afraid of what I'm going to say if he offers it to me. I don't want to deal with it, but if I say no, will he see me as a kid, afraid to take risks?

He walks over to the jukebox and puts a quarter in it. "Only thing money's good for anymore." He smiles. He walks over to me and my heart skips. What's he planning? He extends his hand again. It's a country song and the twang drips from the box, but I don't mind.

"I can't." I smile sheepishly.

He doesn't care. He takes me by the hand and spins me around. "This is different," he whispers into my ear, which sends a shiver down my spine. I'm sort of afraid of him and I sort of like it. He takes me to him and then backs me away and then spins me again. It is awkward and jagged at first until I relax and let him lead. I think I've got it figured out as it just seems to be drawing close, backing away and then another spin. I let out a yelp as I find myself flying in the air into a complete circle before he drops me to the ground, my feet landing perfectly. He's flipped me in a 360 around his arm and I'm dizzy with the motion.

"Jitterbug. You done this before?"

"Never."

"Could've fooled me." He laughs and spins me again. We do this for an entire song and I'm kind of bummed when it's over.

"Let's sit. Leon," he calls, "grab me a drink—two actually." We take our seats at the bar. Now I'm nervous. This is the part I've been dreading, so it surprises me when Leon brings two sodas. Here's my in.

"Where do you get soda from? I haven't seen one in years," I lie. It's getting easier. No twitching.

"That's kind of personal, don't you think," he replies with almost a scowl before he starts laughing. "I'm only kidding. Who are you? Why haven't I seen you before?"

Most of the kids have cleared the bar and it's only Milo, me and the rest of his band. I'm rethinking the intelligence of coming here myself.

"Just a drifter," I say. "What about you? I've been through Deadwood before. I've never seen you here. Aren't you afraid The Council will find you . . . with all this racket you make?" I've scooted my chair back, giving us more space. He notices.

"Racket." He laughs. "I thought you enjoyed my music."

"You know what I mean." I look up and out the window. I think I see a shadow pass. Thinking of The Council has me on edge. It's like when you're little and you're home alone. It's totally fine until you start thinking about the boogeyman lurking outside. All brave at first, but once the thought sneaks in, there's no removing it. It's a little like that. Like thinking of them will bring them in. For all I know, I'm sitting with one of them, but he's too young to be The Council.

"Haven't you heard? Burke's dead. What's there to be afraid of now?" He looks like he's telling the truth.

"So we're free now?" Maybe we are. How else could he be getting away with this?

"I feel free." He looks into my eyes, and with some hesitation he does something I can't even believe is real. He has shoved the empty soda can off the bar without even touching it. I stand up out of my chair and back away. My heart feels skittish and not in a good way. There is weird techno music playing in the background and it's making me feel funny, this moment stranger. There's another can still standing on the bar. I look to him.

"Again?" He smirks.

"Can you?" Ping. The can slides off the bar without being touched. He's one of them. I've never seen this advancement before. Is this some kind of trick? I look around trying to figure it out. I pick up one of the cans and inspect it.

"It's real . . . if that's what you're wondering. Now you."

"I don't know what you are talking about."

"Is that so? One of the benefits of this thing . . . whatever it is, is that I can tell when someone else has one too."

Didn't Hannah say the same thing? She can feel them? I should be more shocked that he has an advancement, but more than that, I'm relieved. It means he's not part of The Council and that means I can come back whenever I want. If I have learned anything about these crazy advancements is that they happen to really good people.

"When did it happen for you?" I ask softly. I can finally relax. I sit back down and I'm almost giddy with relief.

"Not so fast," he says, matching me with his own soft smile. Are we toying with each other? "I've shown you mine, now you show me yours."

"Sorry," I say, and for the first time, I am. Bentley's so fast, he's blurry. Jack's so talented, he could heal the dead, but me, mine is boring and really nothing at all. I'm not even sure what it is. I guess I should be grateful, I don't have Hannah's, but I still feel . . . inadequate. Even if she will die young, she saves people. I do nothing, but alert people I have something . . . that is well, nothing. "I'm not really sure what mine is," I admit.

"Strange, I can feel it."

"What does it feel like?" I should have asked Hannah this before.

"I don't really know how to explain it; it's just a feeling more or less. Do you know anyone else?"

"No," I say almost too quickly. I force myself not to fidget. I've never been a good liar, but I'm certain he shouldn't have this information.

"I'll figure it out," he smiles. "Come back tomorrow?"

I say I will, but I'm not sure if I should. This is going to sound weird, but I liked coming here because it was an escape from the reality of Tent City and all the stuff that feels . . . well, supernatural. My home is the home to the Wonder Child, Superhealer, The Martyr, and The Great Flash himself. Saloon Number 10 was my home for the normal, and now that's not even normal. Why couldn't Milo have just been Milo?

Chapter 24

"So what did you find out?" Bentley's hovering over my bed and I'm not even sure it's light out yet. I turn over and tell him to go away.

"Come on," he says as he lifts the shades, "tell me all about it. I want to know how it went."

"Grrrr . . . go away." I've got my blanket pulled all the way over my head, but I can still feel him here and it's getting hard to breath. "Fine!" I whip the covers off and I'm surprised it's not dark at all; it's at least afternoon.

"Late night?" He smiles.

"You have no idea." My throat is dry and it feels like it's been days since I've had water. I get up and slam a bottle of water. "We can stop worrying about the saloon. It's not The Council."

"How do you know? Why is this like pulling teeth? What did you find out?"

"You know what it's like to pull teeth? This, I'd love to hear about."

"Come on, you know what I mean . . . why isn't it The Council?"

"Didn't you see it for yourself? I saw you outside the window."

"What are you talking about?" He does look genuinely confused, but I'm pretty sure that shadow I saw floating outside the window of the saloon was him after I thought about it some. I should've known better that he would actually trust me enough to let me go by myself.

"I know you were there. Did you see what Milo did at the bar?"

"Fine, I was there, but I only saw you in. Once you were safely in, I left. I didn't see anything. What was it?"

"That wasn't you outside the window?"

"No, just get on with it. What did Milo do?" He's bouncing around nervously, just keeping his weight on the balls of his feet.

"He's one of you." I'm studying him closely now. I'm still not certain he's not lying. He's not above it.

"What do you mean?" He does look sincere, but then again, he always did before.

"He has an advancement. He can move things. I saw it with my own eyes. I was sure you did too."

He sits in thought for a while. "Move things? Like telekinesis? Hmmm . . . wonder what it means?"

"It means we can stop worrying about him. Advancements only happen to good people."

"Fair enough. I still don't think you should go there anymore though." He walks towards the door and I can finally see good enough to notice Hannah is gone.

"Where's Hannah?"

"Out for a walk."

"With who? She's well enough to walk?" That seems impossible. She has been bedridden for days.

"The great healer has done it again," Bentley says sarcastically, "with the powers of breast milk." He fake gags as he walks out the door.

When I step outside the cabin door, the first thing I notice is that most of the snow has melted. How is that possible? Birds are chirping so loud, it almost drowns out the other sounds that should be obvious. Everyone is up and running around.

The guys have built a sort of a barricade around the cabins. I don't like it. I feel like it's closing in on me. The walls are piled high with dead pines. That's one thing the Mountain Pine Beetle is good for: killing trees.

I can't imagine that The Council would have much trouble getting past it, if they really wanted to. Maybe it makes my dad feel better. Why don't we just move? We've destroyed what's great about this place. The barricade has taken away Tent City's freedom. It feels like a prison, which gives me an idea. But Jonah stops me just before I get to Burke's door.

"Um, can I talk to you for a sec?" He's rubbing the sun exposed leathery skin on his forehead and he looks unsure, which is unusual for Jonah.

"Sure, what's up?" I walk a little ways from Burke's door. He probably thinks I've come here to kill Burke.

"Well . . . I'd like to ask your permission . . . to talk to Brody, if you don't mind." He looks around, almost as if he doesn't want to be heard.

"What do you mean?"

"Since it's out in the open and everything with . . . with who he is, I'd like to ask him some questions, if you don't mind."

"Why are you asking me? Why don't you ask my mom?" I've had a lot of bizarre conversations in my life, but this one is at the top of the list. What does he mean to ask him?

Does he want insight into the future? I think we all do, but the idea of asking Brody makes my stomach churn. Jonah is a good man though; he wouldn't do Brody any harm.

"She's not the one I need to ask," he states with his face hard as stone.

"What do you need to ask him? Never mind. Jonah, you don't need to ask me. You can say whatever you need to him. Just remember, he's only five."

He starts to walk away when I remember something that has been bothering me.

"Jonah, do you have a minute?"

"Sure, what can I do for you?" He says this so formally that it almost throws me off.

"You don't have to answer me, but . . . I was just wondering . . . why are you so sure?"

With all this God stuff and plague stuff, Jess and Jonah never seem to waver. Is it because they haven't lost anyone? They don't have pain to deal with? They can just believe in it like Santa Claus or the Tooth Fairy?

"Are we talking about what I think we're talking about?" He sighs as he takes a seat on the porch of the cabin, scraping off some of the dried mud that is caked on his boots.

"I suppose we are," I answer as I take a seat beside him. We don't talk much, but I feel close to Jonah, almost as if he's my big brother, so not even this conversation seems out of place, even if it should.

"Well, I never told you this before, but I used to be a bull rider. Back then, rodeos were about the only events left that were allowed. You know, when they shut down all the big sports events, music events, all that . . . because of the bombings and the shootings."

"Yeah, I remember— the stories at least."

"Anyway, around here in the Midwest, we never gave up our rodeos. This would have been around the time shortly before the plague of locusts swept through. I was young and Jess and I had just gotten married. It would make her crazy every time I got up on one of them mean bulls, but darn it, that woman loved me so much, she let me do it anyway." He smiles at the memory and is quiet for a minute before continuing.

"Well, I was gettin' pretty good. Almost no one around even compared, if I do say so myself," he says with some embarrassment. "There was this one bull that was dang near impossible to ride. He was called The Cowboy Killer and he earned his name. He had already killed one fella on the spot and put another in the hospital. That fella died a couple of weeks later. They were going to put the bull down, but I asked for a shot. Pretty dumb now that I think about it, but it was the big challenge you know? I could prove to everyone I was the best." He clears his throat and sits quietly for a while before continuing.

"Anyway, the morning I was to ride, I got a bad feeling in my gut, almost made myself sick over it. I tried to push it to the side, but it was there . . . a warning of some sort. It was almost like a voice telling me not to get on that bull. Jess could sense something. She begged me not to do it. Just this once, she pleaded. But I had to. Would've been a coward had I not. I was a bit of a wreck all morning, but then my time had come. I even got to the point where I was accepting that bull was going to kill me. So damn stupid of me. I had Jess and she didn't deserve that. But I was too stubborn."

I lean in closer. I had no idea that Jonah used to be a bull rider, but now that I think about it, it makes so much sense.

"So, my turn is up. The crowd is double its normal size. I suppose they all showed up to see a killin' and that's what they were gonna get. Most of us knew it. I knew it, but I was still gonna give it my best shot. I only had to last eight seconds. That feeling of dread was never stronger than right before I got on. I just knew. I got on that thing and you wouldn't believe it, when he shot out of the gate, he paused. The bastard was toying with me. He sat still for at least a full two seconds. Then before I knew it, he reared and no amount of hanging on was going to keep me put. No amount of training did any good with this beast. He was unstoppable. He tossed and flipped me and my foot got caught up in the stirrup. We had a rodeo clown in there and he'd done a pretty good job of ticking that bull off and I was certain that as soon as I got free, he'd go after that clown. I did finally get my foot free, even though it was all busted up. Then you know what happened?"

"What?" My heart is beating as if I'm at the rodeo and watching this unfold in front of me.

"He completely ignored that clown. He turned around and reared up on his hind legs and looked me straight in the eye. He was going to crush me right then and there. He was the Cowboy Killer and he was going to strike again. I did the only thing I could think of. But first you have to understand something," he says as he gets up and now starts pacing in front of me.

"I was no praying man. I thought all of it was hocus pocus. Fairy tales, told to keep kids in line. But I'll be darned if I didn't close my eyes and say some kind of prayer. I don't even know what I said at the time, but it was something like, 'spare me now and I'll change, I promise.' You know? The thing you might say when you're real desperate. All I could think about was that I was leaving my Jessica all alone, brand new bride all alone . . . I opened my eyes and he was still looking at me, that bull was, and you wouldn't believe it, he backed off. Maybe even went out of his way as he came back down on his feet to avoid me. Instead of crushing me, he actually just landed in a pile of bull, well, crap I guess." He shakes his head like he still can't believe it happened. "I should've been dead. A couple of weeks later the locusts happened. I couldn't deny it then. Everything changed that day."

After hearing this, I start to understand Jonah more and maybe even Jessica. In her mind, she thinks God saved her husband. But I have no bullshit story and I don't know where it leaves me. I get up to leave, but not before turning and looking at Jonah one more time.

"Remember, he's only five," I say with a smile.

"Yes, ma'am," he says as he nods and walks off, clearly with an agenda. I almost forget what I came for and head back to Burke's door. I try to shake the eerie feeling I have.

I open the door to find Burke sitting in almost the exact position I left him in.

"Feel like a walk?" I ask, but he is unresponsive.

Do we really have to do this again? I don't have the patience for it. I grab the keys and uncuff him. He still doesn't move. He doesn't even look at me. For a split second, I think he's dead, eyes open. I slap him across the face. Nothing. He feels warm though. Not dead, just sort of catatonic. Okay then.

I go outside to the water trough and check the water. Freezing cold. This ought to do just fine. I fill a bucket to the brim and walk back in. Some splashes on my jeans and the shock of the temperature almost has me reconsidering. I finally see him glance my way, but by then it's too late.

"Hey!!!" He's on his feet and finally looking alive. "What was that for?"

"We need to talk."

"Forget it! Lock me back up and get out of here." He's already removing the sheet he has on his bed and starts taking his soaked clothing off. "Get out!"

If he thinks he's going to shock me out of here just by removing some clothing, he's got another think coming. I see him watch me out of the corner of his eye as he unbuttons his shirt. He stops before he gets to his pants. I knew he didn't have it in him.

"Do you mind?"

"Not at all," I say with a smirk.

"Fine." He unbuttons his pants and from what I can tell, he might not be wearing underwear. He's got me. I leave, but not before he catches me blushing. Some preacher he is.

I sit out on the porch and give him a good five minutes before going back in. He's got the cuffs back on and now sits on a bed with no sheet. I don't know why, but that bugs me more than anything.

"You're not going away, are you?" He says without looking me in the eye.

"Do you need a sheet for that bed?"

"What difference does it make?"

"I see. Is this the part where you just sit around and feel sorry for yourself?"

"Is there something I can help you with?" He arranges himself on the sheetless mattress and the plastic squeaks, sounding not much different than nails on a chalk board.

Seeing him in his condition takes some of the fire out of me and I'm reminded of why I don't come in here more. He's wearing me down.

"I'm guessing you know who the Golden Child is," I finally say.

"I think I have a pretty good idea." Why are we playing around with this? I just want to get to it, but I can't come right out and say it because there is a chance he doesn't know. "Everyone here knows."

My heart is thudding in my chest. This is what happens to me every time I think of Brody being the Golden Child.

"Does Randy know?" This is really the only thing I NEED to know. Even if Randy isn't who Burke says he is, although I think he might be, if he knows about Brody, it's only a matter of time before he comes back looking for him.

"I think so."

"Why didn't he . . . um . . . get him when he had the chance? He was just here in South Dakota."

"I don't know."

"Does he think you're dead?"

"Well, I certainly hope so. Otherwise, I went to a lot of trouble for nothing."

"Why did you leave?" I don't really expect him to answer this one, but it has been on my mind. If he was part of the ruling of the country for so long, what made him suddenly want to leave?

"Bentley."

"Huh?"

"Well, you can believe me or not, but when Jack came back, it changed everything for me. I'd been chasing the wrong dream for so long . . ."

"What dream was that?"

"You're an impatient thing aren't you? Want me to tell you the story or not?" He shifts again. The plastic squeaking is going to drive me mad. He shivers and I'm glad for his discomfort.

"Okay," I say as I mock zip my lips shut and toss the key.

"What do most men chase? What are they after? What can take good men and turn them to dogs?"

"Fame?" Unzipped.

"Power . . . but I guess they are kind of the same. I could care less that my face was plastered all over the TV, but the power that came with it was . . . almost intoxicating."

"Couldn't care less. You mean, couldn't care less if you mean you didn't care about the fame."

"Huh?" he says as he replays the conversation. "You're really annoying, you know. Do ya mind?"

"Sorry." Not really.

"Anyway, if I really think about it, it might have even been why I became a minister in the first place. Instead of dreaming about how I could serve the Lord, I was probably dreaming about how I could control my own congregation. I wasn't striving to reach more people for their own salvation; I was imagining building the biggest church this country has ever seen . . . and Randy saw that. In his eyes, we were a perfect match." Squeak. Can he just stop moving around?

"Perfect match?"

"Yeah, it's genius if you think about it. He gets to move all the chess pieces, but hide behind the scenes in case it goes wrong. In the beginning, he was real nervous about it not working, but year after year, we got bigger and bigger. I think he even got off on running the country without anyone ever knowing, like his little secret."

"He had my parents last year. Was he really going to have them killed? If I hadn't made it back in time?"

"I've wondered about that. At the time, I didn't know your dad was his brother. He just told me Jack was there and I got on the first chopper. To be honest, at that point, I didn't care if they were killed or not. I was getting my son back."

"Monster."

"I know. I'm working on it."

"You know something that has always bugged me?"

"I'm sure you've got quite a list." Squeak. He's doing it on purpose now.

"Why did the president just step down after the locusts? How could he do that? How is that even legal?"

He starts laughing and the irritation is so high, I'm not sure I can stay in here anymore without slicing him up into pieces. I know my mind is getting darker and darker, but I don't care.

"Randy handpicked me and delivered me to the president. Said I had potential. Told him the people wanted a spiritual president and that I could help him achieve that. Randy told him it would make him one of the greats. The president became my biggest fan and one of my biggest contributors really. He gave my church millions. And then with the locusts, Randy convinced him to step down. Put the country in the hands of a spiritual leader, in light of the new times."

"Still not legal."

"You're too young to remember, but the country was spinning. They didn't know what to make of things. So when I took over, they more or less just accepted it. Those who might have resisted, well, they didn't last long."

I'm disgusted with everything. He's his natural self again. He almost seems proud. I get up to leave, but something's nagging at me. I don't want to ask, but I have to. "One more thing, was my brother really poisoned?"

"Are you sure you really want to go there?" His slight smile disappears. For the first time since he's been in Tent City, he looks nervous.

"I think I need to know."

He is quiet for a long time, his face anguished. He shakes his head slightly. Is this for real or is he messing with me?

He's so quiet, I feel like kicking him. I'm so close to the truth. I can feel it. "You're asking the wrong questions," he finally says.

"What do I need to ask?" I sit down on the chair and start to rock. In the movement, I can calm my speeding heart.

"Let me ask you one first," he begins.

"Anything." Yes, ask me anything. I'll tell you anything if you'll just tell me the truth. Tell me the truth so I can finally end this.

"You ever been to one of those butterfly houses?"

"Huh?"

"You know, they ship the butterflies in from all over the world? You go into the big butterfly sanctuary made of glass and hundreds of them fly around. After a couple of days, the butterflies die and they just order more?"

"Yeah, sure. What does that have to do with anything?" I'm losing patience.

"Do you think it was easy to order and ship butterflies to the United States?"

"I suppose so. Why?"

"Do you think it would be easy to order locusts?"

Chapter 25

As if I didn't have enough trouble sleeping as it is. I've gone in and out of light sleep and in and out of nightmares, but it's still pitch black out and I haven't gotten enough hours to catch the sunrise. When will it ever be morning? I'm not sure what time it is, but I go outside. I *should* make myself go back in and fall asleep. I'm again considering swiping something from Hannah's supplies. It wouldn't have to be an everyday thing and I'm desperate for sleep. Is it too late to go into Deadwood? Do I even belong there? In the little fits of sleep that I do have, I vaguely register that Milo shows up in my dreams, calling me to come back.

What time is it? Why is everyone outside by the campfire in the middle of the night? I even see Brody and Avery playing around. Has Mom lost her mind, or have I lost mine?

"What's going on here?" Maybe I'm still dreaming.

"Sun never came up." Avery giggles as she runs by me with an emergency glow stick. It flashes past me in a neon streak waving like a patriotic flag. Brody is chasing her with one of his own.

The darkness is so strange, I'm not completely sure it's not part of another extended nightmare. For all I know, I'm still in my bed, eyes closed, but this time I'm not waking up. I've sent the sun an invitation, but there's still no RSVP. How rude.

Three days go by in darkness. Supplies are running low and we're almost out of kerosene. We have enough wood to burn forever, but it's not enough light. The darkness does weird things to you. If I suspected I was crazy before, now I'm sure. Or does that make me not crazy, since crazy people don't know they're crazy?

I never knew how important the sun was until it was taken from me. Plague number nine, plague of darkness is here. There's only a couple of more before the one that has my name on it comes a calling. For I'm sure I won't die from lice and gnats, hail, or even pestilence. My death shall come in the form of death of firstborn. There's a little sense of peace in knowing which plague is mine, but not knowing how bothers me. I've come up with the idea that somehow I die in one of my nightmares and don't wake up. Maybe it's happening right now.

I'd love to know whether it's morning or night, but I'm so confused. I think it's night because Mom and Jessica are tucking the kids in and it's just the adults talking by the fire. I sit quietly on my porch swing, only half paying attention to what they are saying.

"Dani?" Dad calls for me to come over, but I don't move. "Dani, please."

"I'm not leaving," I call from the porch swing. He can tell I'm not moving so he walks to me.

"We need to get Brody to a more secure location. I'd like you and Kit to go too. Grant agrees with me. I don't trust anyone but you to watch over him."

"I don't believe you. I think you just want us both gone . . . Splitting up's a bad idea," I say as I finally sit up.

"Just for a while, until this thing blows over," he says and Jack approaches from behind him.

"It's where you're needed," Jack says.

"How do you know?" I scowl.

Jack looks away. I look to Bentley, but he says nothing.

"I'm not going anywhere," I say as I stand. If it takes all night, not that I would know if it was night or not, I'll convince them to let me stay. I'm irritated that they feel I need to be protected when I've gone through so much training. Maybe if it was a year ago and I was that weak little thing that didn't know left from right. But things are different now. Deep down, it feels like he's shipping me off again.

"Fine . . . for now," Dad finally says, "but when the time comes, you're outta here!" He actually looks upset and even in the dark night I see his REALLY mad face. The last time I saw it was when Kit and I stole the family van.

Bentley sits down beside me on the swing and gives it a little shove. He almost looks nervous. "I know it's pretty dark, but you still wanna do it?" he asks as he fiddles with the lantern. I look to the campfire and catch Callie staring at us. The guilt makes the darkness darker.

"Am I supposed to know what you are talking about?" I push the swing again, mentally exhausted.

"Want to go to the top?" he asks with a mischievous smile. I can see it as the flickers of lantern shadows dance on his face. "Harney Peak."

"Now?"

"We might not get another chance. Every time you say no is a time you don't get back."

"That's deep," I say with the beginnings of a sad smile. It feels dangerous in the dark. I decide it sounds perfect.

We pack up our stuff and before we leave camp, Callie makes sure to send me a message as she leaves the campfire and slams the door to her cabin. Dad almost seems relieved to see me leave. Happy about me going off in the middle of the night with a guy. Now I've seen everything.

It doesn't take long to get to the base of Harney Peak, but once we start climbing up, it gets harder to navigate. We don't talk for about the first mile. It's almost impossible to climb up Harney Peak with only the light of a couple lanterns, but with every step, I'm feeling more confident and I can almost feel the next step before I even see it.

"So how do you know?" I say. "How does everyone know there's going to be a big battle?" I ask again, even though somewhere deep inside I can feel something coming too. It feels evil and ominous, almost brought on by the dark.

"Whether there's a battle or not, Randy's coming. Tom said."

"So we're trusting him now?" Even the mention of his name has me almost stumbling and I fall forward a little. I look up to the moon, only to find it missing.

"I guess so. Jonah agrees . . . Plus, can't you kind of feel it?"

"Do you think it's really Randy?"

"Honestly, yeah, I've spent so much time thinking about everything he's told me and it makes sense. Back when he was helping us in Tent City, it was more of just a ploy. Sure, he'd give us good spots to raid and the attacks were on his own people, but he was getting information too. I can't believe how stupid I was. If I had never trusted him, maybe we could've beaten him. I could even respect him if it wasn't for that one thing."

"What thing?" It feels like I'm having as much trouble keeping up with his story as I am keeping up with him. He forgets he's so fast and leaves me steps behind. Almost as if he reads my mind, he reaches back and grabs my hand. There, this is so much easier. I don't even have to look down.

"Can you see in the dark?" I'm only half kidding, but it's like he's not even using his lantern.

"Yeah," he admits, almost embarrassed. "Can you trust me?"

"I guess so."

"Put that lantern down. We'll get it on the way down. We'll save the kerosene. Just keep a hold of my hand."

What a trip. This is freaking amazing. It takes me awhile to really fully trust him, but after he leads me around obvious boulders and downed trees, I decide he knows what he's doing. It's almost as if I'm climbing a mountain with my eyes closed, well maybe I kind of am.

"What thing?" I ask again, "What bothers you about Randy, well besides the obvious."

"Well, in war you have two sides and that's fine. That's what war is. But he was letting his own men get killed for his own gain. There's no honor in that. Makes me sick. Boulder to your left."

It takes hours to get to the top, at least what he tells me is the top. Every sore muscle hums in appreciation. The first thing I do when I get to the platform at the top is drop my bag and take off my jacket. My legs are trembling and I collapse. I almost forgot this feeling.

"We finally did it," he says and I can feel his grin.

"What can you see?" I ask as I force myself to stand again. Is this one of his powers or am I just handicapped?

"Everything. Weird though. It's like someone has been here. There's some new structures down below here. It's been a while. It definitely looks different, but it's gorgeous. You're gorgeous . . . even in the darkness," he says, and I can feel his eyes on me. I see nothing, but I feel his fingertips on my cheek.

"Close your eyes too," I tell him. So this is what it feels like to be blind. Knowing he can see everything and I see nothing has me feeling vulnerable, especially as I can feel him watching me.

"I don't know if I can."

"Why?"

"I'm enjoying the view too much," he says and I reach up to touch his face. His grin is wider.

"Do it." He does and I can feel his heartbeat in his cheek. It's like thunder and when his eyes close and I touch him, I can partially see. Everything is gray and silhouetted, but I can see outlines.

"How is this possible?" I ask and I back away. Darkness again. I move closer again and place my hands on his forearms. His pulse is still beating erratically and the shadowed vision returns.

"This is wild," he says, his smile now nervous. "I can see you the way you see me . . . Come closer." Now *my* heart beats like thunder.

I breathe in as far as I can and then let the breath go. “I don’t know if I can.” Even with my hands steady on his forearms, they are trembling. I’ve known this was coming for so long. Why do it now? Images of Jack and Callie flash through my mind and I push them away, for fear he can see that too.

“It’s okay,” he says, “get it over with. I’m ready.” He sounds steady, but there’s a slight tremble in his voice at the end. “It won’t change anything okay? Just don’t let me go. I can take it. It’s oka—”

“Shhhhh . . .” I can do this.

“Dani, please just don’t cut me out of your lif—”

“Seriously, just stop.” This is it. I’ve been dreading it for so long. It has me so panicked and scared that I do about the most inappropriate thing I could do—I cry. Messy, embarrassing sobs.

I try to talk, but my breath catches. Can I really let him go? I’ve tried to back up, but he hangs on.

“It’s Jack,” I sob, “I choose Jack.”

I open my eyes so I can’t see him, but he brushes his fingertips over my eyelids and they close again. He’s more beautiful in this moment than I’ve ever seen him. He leans in, but I don’t back away. I can feel his breath at my neck as he starts there. I wasn’t expecting that and it sends a shiver up my spine. He lingers for just a second before pausing at my ear. The slight breath in my ear has my skin exploding in goose bumps. The thought occurs to me that he’s teasing me with what I’m not going to have. By the time, he gets to my lips, I’m almost sick with anticipation. He brushes his thumb over my lips and the soft skin at my chin and lets out a small groan. It doesn’t scare me. Finally, his lips touch mine and I find myself leaning in further. If this lasted forever, it wouldn't be long enough. How can I let him go?

He backs up and releases me. "I won't do that again until you ask."

As if the outside is feeling how I'm feeling on the inside, thunder booms in a loud crack and I let out a shriek. Another boom. It's so loud, my ears are ringing. Then the sky lights up a huge rod of lightening and I'm seeing the landscape for what it is for the first time in days. We're up too high.

"We need to get down now!"

"Everything's going to be fine," he says and his face is all business. "I have an idea. Are you up for it?"

"Does it involve near death?" I'm trying to joke, but the thunder has me spooked and my body is actually shaking.

"Most certainly. Follow me," he says with a smile. He's in his element again and for a second, I am too.

We get to another platform on the top of Harney Peak and I can't believe he's considering this in a lightning storm.

"Zipline?"

"It's the fastest way down. It used to be an old emergency line. If they had an injury up here, it was the quickest way to get down, although I think they used a basket." He considers. "We'll improvise." I see the first glimmer of unease cross his face. He's contemplating something.

"I'll go first." He kicks a locked metal box open and a couple of huge carabineers spill out. He checks the line and it feels taught and intact. "When I'm halfway, take off. I'll catch you at the end."

I can't help but worry there is some equipment missing. Like maybe that basket. Sliding down the mountain for a couple of miles on just a large hook seems ridiculous. Another blast of lightening. Now I'm wondering who will get cooked first.

I don't have much time to think about it. He clicks his clip into place and turns to give me one last look. "See you at the bottom." I realize when he lets go that I don't have a choice. Without his sight, I can't get down any other way. If I don't go, he'll have to come back up to get me and we'll waste more time. Why didn't I talk him out of it before he left? Within seconds, he's already out of my sight.

I take a deep breath. Click and jump. Don't think about it. The first second is the most terrifying—actually forcing myself to jump. I close my eyes, but that is even scarier. I open them and my arms are tight and trembling as I slide down. I'll never last the whole way like this so I straighten them out and just hang. I can feel the hook heat up as I pick up speed. I forget to breath and when I let out a breath it's heavy and trembling, but I'm flying.

I'm really flying. It's a shame there are no superpowers for flying because I'd like to have this one. If I ever felt free and alive on the Valium, or even in the midst of blaring music and sway of sounds and bodies, it still doesn't compete with this. If we get to come back as something else, I choose a bird. I'm not even scared anymore. I am smiling as the wind dries my teeth and I grin like a lunatic. I even let out a scream of freedom. I almost forget that something terrible is about to happen. The storm tells me so.

I come barreling in so fast that I knock us both over when Bentley catches me at the bottom. He meant well, but he managed to land on me when we finally stop and it has knocked the wind out of me. I've got some road rash from my wrists to my elbows, but mostly I'm fine.

It doesn't take long to get back to Tent City. I don't know why we thought the battle was happening now. That's definitely not what is going on. I'm not even sure how to process it, but as we roll into camp, the sun is FINALLY rising and I can't be sure, but it looks like Milo is there. Jonah has his rifle pointed at him and is telling him to leave. Jack is exiting Hannah's cabin to see what's happening.

"Hey, there's a familiar face!" Milo shouts to me as I come jogging in. My eyes are adjusting to the sun and I try to remember if it's always been that bright.

"What are you doing here?" I ask and I'm genuinely happy to see him.

"Not so fast," Bentley says. "Jack, clear out that other cabin."

"Sure," Jack says almost quietly. He must be as curious as I am.

"In there! Now!" Bentley shouts at Milo.

"Hey, what's the big idea, man? I'm not here to hurt anyone. If it's going to be like this, I'd rather just be on my way," Milo says. Obviously, this isn't what he was expecting.

"We'll see," Bentley says to Milo and Jack comes back with Bentley's pistol. Bentley points it right at Milo's face. He means business. "Now."

Bentley ushers Milo into the cabin and I try to give Milo a look to say I'm sorry, but he's gone too fast. Jack stays behind as Jonah and Bentley follow Milo into the cabin. Another prisoner, I think as I see Jonah grab the rope.

"What's he going to do?" I ask Jack.

"Did you tell him to come here?" he asks back. "That's the guy right? The guy you've been hanging out with down at the bar in Deadwood?"

"You know about that?" My face heats up and I wonder if I'll ever have anything to myself. "Why does everyone need to know about everything I do?"

"You look exhausted," he says as he looks me over. "What did you do to your arm?"

"Shark bite."

He smiles and suppresses a laugh.

"Sit down," he says. I sit in the chair by the fire, but it's almost too hot as the sun beats down and the heat of the fire bites at my skin.

Doctor Jack gets out his medical kit and starts cleaning my road rash. I wince as he wipes gravel from the wounds and stare absently at the cabin door that has Milo and Bentley behind it. This is starting to become a regular prison camp.

"How's Hannah?"

"Better, but she's sleeping now. How about you? You doing okay?"

"No, not really," I admit and by saying it out loud, I feel myself start to unravel. Everything is out of control. I don't even know how anyone copes. Death is just a matter of time. Only a few plagues left to finish us off and supposedly my beloved uncle is the one who will finish us off if the plagues don't.

"Wanna talk about it?" He looks over the bandages he has wrapped around my wounds and seeming satisfied, lets my arm go. I try not to look him in the eyes as I can feel my chin already quivering. Seconds away from crying, I bite the inside of my cheek to keep it at bay.

Before I can tell him to stop, he pulls me in for a hug that should be comforting, but it makes my skin itch. I hold it for a few seconds, thinking by pulling away he'll think I'm rude or ask more questions. I finally back up and when I glance up, I see the worst thing I could have: Bentley's eyes on me as he exits his cabin. His face drops for just a second and then he leaves.

Chapter 26

Bentley avoids me. I would too. I try to convince him that Milo is safe, but he won't hear of it. I busy myself with Hannah duties and it seems like the combination of helping with her and Bentley's distance brings Jack in closer. This is what I wanted right?

"You ready for some fresh air?" I ask Hannah as I help her get dressed.

"More like a bath I think. What's been going on? I feel like I've missed so much," she says as she slides her boots on. "What's going on with you? Something seems off."

"Oh, I don't know, the usual. Waiting for the next plague, Bentley's got another prisoner. My brother's going to be the next king, and my best friend is dying. You know, the usual." I gulp at my impetuous ranting, but she doesn't seem to mind.

"Let's get out of here," she says. "Some fresh air would do us both some good."

We walk outside the cabin to see Bentley taking Milo out. Hannah doesn't seem to notice and I'm glad. She would be upset by prisoner treatment. She thinks everyone is good. Milo is tied up by the hands and Bentley is shoving him towards the trees. What is he planning? Letting him go? He won't speak to me and I can't blame him, but I feel terrible for Milo. What has he gotten himself into?

"What's going on?" Hannah asks as she squints towards Bentley and Milo.

"The prisoner."

"Poor fellow."

***

I've been shy to seek out Bentley, but something has to be done about Milo. It's been a couple of days and they still have him locked up. I go to the cabin where Milo is being kept, and I ask Bentley to let him go, but he refuses.

"He stays until we can figure this out," Bentley answers, arms folded, clearly not backing down.

"What? You can't be serious?" Milo says, almost in a rage, as he tries to stand, but gets tugged back by the cuffs hooking him to the bedpost.

"What happened to his rope?" I ask as I see it lying on the ground by his feet.

"Slippery fellow," Bentley says in disgust. "Where'd you learn that trick? Rigby teach you?" he asks, not really expecting an answer. "That's why we have to use cuffs on this one," he says to me.

"You have to let me go," Milo pleads, "I haven't done anything wrong."

"Hey, you're our guest here. Our rules, we decide what happens," Bentley tells Milo.

"Guest!" I shout, "You can't just keep him locked up in here. It's not right. Let him choose. He's obviously not with Rigby."

"No," Bentley says. "We don't know the whole story yet." Bentley has his arms folded across his chest and face bent in a scowl. I'm going to have to pull out the big guns.

"Bentley, please. Trust me on this one. You have to let him go. Give him a fighting chance." Here it goes. "I trust him completely. Don't ask me how, I just do."

I don't want to tell him that I dream of him almost every night. I don't know if it's false trust—because I see him in my dreams—but when I wake up, sometimes I feel like I really know Milo, like he's someone who's been around all my life. It's probably some trick of the mind, but I'm trying to learn how to trust my instincts and besides, Milo hasn't done anything wrong, except maybe come looking for me.

"Fine," Bentley says with his shoulders slumped, looking exhausted. "Have it your way." He looks at me as if I have betrayed him and then looks back at Milo. "I don't want to see you around here again . . . ever."

Chapter 27

That night, even though I know I shouldn't, I go to Deadwood. It might be guilt about the way Milo was treated or the unsettling of my soul. Either way, I'm here. I'm surprised and more than a little disappointed when I hear nothing coming out of Saloon Number 10.

I creep in just to make sure no one's here and that's when I hear it. It's most definitely an acoustic guitar and it's most definitely Milo, but he sounds alone. I lose all my fear and almost skip in, eager to hear more.

He sees me come in and only smiles. I motion a question of "can I sit down?" He nods and I just sit back and enjoy the show. In some ways, this is better than an entire crowd of screaming, sweaty kids. I can really hear the lyrics now. This song seems to be something he created himself, but how would I really know? The extent of my music knowledge is limited to Billy Idol and Roxette, the only relics I have left for my Walkman. He could sing, "It Must Have Been Love" and I could sing right along with him.

He finishes the song and then says, "What are we doing here?"

"What do you mean?" I prop my feet up on a barstool and ask him to play me something else.

"Aren't you going to get into trouble with your boyfriend?"

"He's not my boyfriend." I want to scowl at him, but it's Milo, so I don't.

"Does he know that?"

"Can we not talk about it? I don't know what this is. I just like being here. Can we just keep it like this? This is the only place I know of where the world isn't falling apart."

"Fair enough," he says as he begins to strum again. I close my eyes and let myself get taken away.

Just like before, I keep going back. I don't ask where all the others went and he doesn't offer the information. I know my family notices when I leave, but no one presses me about where I'm going, not even Hannah. I park my four-wheeler at the back and go back in, ready to leave plagues, death, and the Golden Child out of my mind for a while.

Milo gets out his guitar and instead of playing throaty rock and roll songs like he used to, he plays soft melodies and I find myself able to fall asleep. My very own sleeping medication.

I don't really see any reason not to trust Milo. He seems like he tells the truth in everything he says. No twitching. I guess the group he was running with was Rigby's group, but Milo claims he didn't know Rigby worked for Randy. All he knew is that they worked against Burke. I've told him everything I know. All this time, he thought he was fighting for the good guys, only to find out the truth. I think it's been hard on him. He's been asking a lot about Brody. He's never actually met him, but he says he's drawn to him.

He tunes his guitar, probably mostly out of habit, as it already sounds fine. "When can I meet him?" he asks.

"I don't think we're there yet."

"Who makes the call? You?" He doesn't say it in a malicious way, more curious.

"No," I say with a smile, "my parents, of course."

"Well, I can't wait." He coughs. Another one of his rituals. He is warming up his voice. "I can feel him here for some reason. You know what I showed you at the bar?"

"With the cans?" I say as I scoot my chair closer to the stage.

"Yeah, well, when you're around, it gets stronger. I think that's how we all are. I mean, I wouldn't know, I've only really hung out with you, but I think you amplify it." He looks over at me, as if studying me, but then starts to play and I'm lost in the moment.

"I have an idea," he says with a mischievous smile. This can't be good. "Stand up," he demands.

I was just reaching the point where I could be lulled into sleep and I'm irritated that he is talking about stuff I am trying to avoid, but he does so much for me that I feel compelled to humor him.

He puts the cans back up on the bar and easily flips them off with a wave of his hand.

"Can you do it with more than just pop cans?" I ask.

"Yeah, especially when you're here. Watch this." He grins like a child and moves a speaker away from him. It scrapes against the floor and I still can't help but look for wires that might be helping it along. "So if mine is stronger with you around, why don't you try yours."

"I told you, I don't have one. Not anything cool anyway."

"Speaker, try to push it away further."

"All right." I close my eyes and hold my hands out in some kind of motion to make it move, but it doesn't budge.

"Maybe something easier," he says as he places the empty pop cans back up on the bar. "Try this."

I close my eyes again and hold my hands out and I'm startled when I hear the can drop at my feet.

"Interesting," he says with his hands to his chin, deep in thought. "Try it again."

Another pop can drops at my feet. "Weird. When you do it, does it ever come to you or just away?"

"Just away. Try to push it away from you."

I do, but it just falls at my feet again. What does this mean? Why does his go away and mine comes close? Maybe our powers are mimicking each other's.

"Try it again," he says. "This time, don't try to push it away from you, try to pull it in."

I close my eyes and do what he says, but open them right before I see the can whiz by me with such force it has flown all the way through the hall and into the next room.

"Amazing." He smiles. "Put your hand up."

"No!" I don't know why this scares me.

"Just do it." I do.

Our hands are an inch apart from touching, but there's a pull or more like an anti-pull, like a magnet. The hands don't want to touch. He pushes his forward and there's a slight sting.

"Ow!"

"That's crazy." He laughs. "I wonder what it means."

"Whatever it means, don't do it again." I give him a smile too. I finally have something and it's taken Milo to bring it out. We both sit there and think about what it means.

"What does it feel like?" I ask after the silence becomes uncomfortable.

"Come here," he says as he takes me by the hand and leads me to the stage. He plugs in the speaker and messes with some dials. "Check this out," he says as he places my hand on the speaker. "Do you feel it?" he asks.

"Yes," I say as I feel the quiet hum vibrate.

"This is me when you're not around."

"Okay." I'm still watching him, waiting for his next move.

He turns the dial up. My hand is vibrating so much, it starts to tingle.

"This is what it feels like when you are around. See the difference?"

"Yes, but why doesn't it happen for me?"

He backs up and turns the stereo up. "I don't know, but maybe it's because you don't really believe."

"I never said I didn't," I respond, but it has my mind spinning. What do I have to believe? All of it? Or just that I can do it? Is it as simple as that? Click my ruby red slippers together and say, "there's no place like home?" I don't like how it's making me feel. I feel defective . . . like a fraud.

"Don't worry about it for now, it'll come," he says as if reading the anxiety on my face. "Sit, I'll play you another song."

"Milo?"

"Yes?"

"What did you want to be before all this happened . . . the locusts and stuff?" I'm expecting him to say musician, because it'd be a shame if he said anything else, so it surprises me when he tells me he wanted to work in TV.

"Yeah, cheesy huh? My dad was in the reality TV biz. Me and my sister used to go and watch him all the time. The way it works is like a big orchestra with all the different pieces and players. It's just amazing when it all comes together at the end."

"What about music?"

"Oh, I'll always love music. It's more of a hobby. Not that I'm going into television . . . not much call for it these days."

"So you would have been a director or something?"

"In the world of 'what ifs?" He considers for a moment. "Nah, I was thinking more like cameraman, the one who sees it all first and watches the magic unfold," he says and then he looks back at me, gauging my reaction. "Stupid?"

"No, not at all. It suits you."

"Promise you won't laugh?"

"Well, you hafta tell me first." I smile. I don't know why, but getting to know Milo on a real level is just as satisfying as hearing him sing. I've forgotten that people are just people. All they really want is connection, knowing that we matter. I want Milo to know he matters. He gets up to leave and comes back with a small gadget that I can't even begin to figure out, but as soon as I see the lens, it becomes clear.

"My very first camera," he says as his face lights up in a smile so wide it could only be described as beaming.

"Let's make a movie," I suggest, getting lost in the moment. He raises his eyebrows.

"Not like that!" I blush.

"You'll be the star." He laughs.

I wasn't sure that was what I had in mind, but it's making him deliriously happy so we do. It's not much of a film, but we document Saloon Number 10 and I perform as a news reporter, letting the world know about all the wild parties we've had and the upcoming talent of Milo, the musician.

"I have an idea," I say as Milo is telling me good-bye for the night. "Come with me. Come back to Tent City with me."

"Oh, no. No way. I'm not going near that place."

"I can't say that I blame you," I say as I touch his arm to help my plea. "You're meant to be there. You're meant to be with me." I hold up my hand, encouraging him to put his hand to mine, to remind him of the shock that only happens when we are near each other.

"How can you explain that?" I ask as he places his hand up to mine and it practically crackles.

"I know that." He looks down. "I just don't feel like dealing with your boyfriend. Can you blame me? He had me locked up the last time I walked into camp."

"Can you trust me?"

"You know I can."

"Then let me worry about Bentley."

He looks around Saloon Number 10 awhile before he gives me an answer. "This is probably the dumbest thing I'll ever do, but if it'll make you happy," he says and I almost squeal with delight. I don't know why, but I know Milo is supposed to be with us. He belongs with us. I just know it.

We sneak back in the middle of the night and camp is quiet. I slip him into the empty cabin and his eyes flutter as his head hits the pillow. It's been a long night.

"Don't come out until I come to get you. I want to talk to Bentley before he sees you," I say as I tuck him in. I realize that it probably looks ridiculous, me tucking in a grown man, but it doesn't *feel* ridiculous.

"I won't," he says, his voice heavy with sleep. "Come and get me when it's over."

I throw another log on the fire at the middle of camp and settle in for the night. I don't know why, but I actually feel kind of happy. I don't know what I'm supposed to do with this new friendship with Milo, but I'll take it. I make my bed outside in a lounge chair, propping my feet on a big log and tuck my blanket in tight. I want to catch Bentley first thing in the morning. I haven't sleepwalked in weeks. It should be safe enough. The fire crackles and I've settled in just right. Exhaustion sets in and I'm out. I don't know that I've ever fallen asleep so deep or so fast.

I'm startled when I realize that I've slept outside all night. The fire smolders in dirty smoke and the sun barely rising, fresh and pink, tells me it's still early. I see I have the perfect opportunity. I'm about to walk over to Burke's cabin when Brody pokes his head outside of his cabin. I hear a rustling on the other side of camp to see Callie exit her cabin. Her face seems to be healing, as the bruises are no longer purple, but yellow and fading.

"Hey buddy, did you sleep well?" I ask Brody, as I focus my attention back to him.

"I have to poop," he says as he rubs his eyes.

I laugh. Our future leader says he has to poop. "Do you want me to go with you?"

"No. I'm almost six, you know. Where's the toilet paper? I couldn't find it."

"We're out. Can you use leaves, or do you want me to find you something?"

"I'll be fine," he says as he scampers off into the woods.

"Don't go far, Bro," I call after him. I look back to Callie and she looks around nervously. Does she want to have another talk?

"What are you doing out here?" she asks me.

"Waiting for Bentley to get up."

"Oh," she says as her face drops. I don't have time for this now. I glance back up to see where Brody's gone.

"Why are you watching me?" Brody yells and goes out further in defiance. I shake my head, distracted by what I was planning. Now I can't go into Burke's cabin with Callie watching. As if she sees I want to be alone she says, "Want me to look after him?"

"Thanks," I say in appreciation, "Just don't let him know you're there." I smile. She nods and follows Brody into the forest.

I should have enough time for a quick chat. I want to know more about the man-made locust invasion, if that's even the truth.

Since no one trusts me, Burke's cabin is usually heavily watched and I haven't had a chance to talk to him again since his big revelation. I'm relieved to know today when I visit him, I don't burn with malice, but I do still have more questions. I scan around and everyone seems to be sleeping. All I can hear are the early morning chirps of ambitious birds.

I walk over to the cabin and my skin pricks. His door is partially open. He's done it. He's finally escaped. But why now? He claims he's waiting to mend things with Bentley, but he slips out now? As far as I know, Bentley doesn't speak to him. But Bentley doesn't really speak to me anymore either. Maybe they reconciled last night and he took off before anyone could stop him. But then I see it. Footprints. Muddy footprints leading out the door and off the porch. If he's not allowed outside, how is it that he was able to walk in and out with mud on his boots?

Maybe I'm overreacting. The prints are probably Jack's. He probably forgot to shut the door and Burke's probably still cuffed to the bed. The idea that I get to irritate him so early in the morning doesn't bring me quite as much joy as usual.

I'm at the door about to open it when a bad feeling washes through me. I feel like I should go get my dad before I go in. He could be waiting to jump me inside. I remove my knife from my back sheath and hold it up. I'm ready. This could be good. If he comes at me, I'll have no choice and I can finally end it.

I open the door and drop my knife. I walk back out and collapse down to my knees. There's a knife in Burke's chest and that knife belongs to my dad.

Chapter 28

I sit for a while, trying to figure out what to do. Why would he just leave the knife there? Is he trying to get caught? I look around camp nervously and it's still quiet. I have time. I can do this.

I walk back into the cabin and hesitate. Burke's eyes are open and empty. Without thinking, I close them. My breathing is becoming erratic and I'm aware that I'm probably making about 100 mistakes right now. I'm going to get caught for sure. I put my hand on the ivory handle of the knife that is unmistakably Dad's and swallow hard before trying to tug on it. It catches on tissue before it releases with a sludgy pop. Blood drains out, which means this was recent. How could this have happened while I was just outside, only feet away? I wipe the knife on Burke's shirt and shove it in my back pocket.

I scurry outside and toss the knife into a rain barrel that catches the overflow from the cabin. Another one of Jack's improvements. Why did I do that? Now it taints the water. I fish it out, getting my clothes soaked and I shove the knife behind a huge wood pile. I can get to it later. I'm shaking with guilt or fear, maybe both. I feel like I'm going to faint. I crouch down by the cabin where Burke lies inside dead. The whole world seems silent again.

"Dani!" My arms are being shook and I look up to find Jack with what looks to be confusion and terror. "What have you done?" He grabs me by the arm and lifts me up. He's dragging me aggressively and it becomes clear to me what I have to do. I say nothing.

He's still dragging me out to the center of camp and I look around to see most everyone has exited their cabins. I see Bentley and I look down in shame, for what I'm not sure.

"What are you doing?" he shouts at Jack.

"She's finally done it! Are you happy now? Trust her, you say? Now she's the murderer! How could you let this happen?" He finally shakes me loose in disgust, as if touching me will infect him.

"You can't be serious? If you *ever* touch her like that again, I'll kill you," Bentley says, his voice a bubbling rage. He seems to calm himself down, but then begins pacing.

"What's going on around here," Dad asks. I can see his alarm bells are going off and he steps in between Jack and Bentley. "Can someone tell me what's going on?"

"Why don't you ask her?" Jack practically spits out. "Look at her, she's got blood all over her clothes and then she tried to wash it off. Dani, who *are* you?"

Mom walks up to Dad and touches him on the arm. She looks white as a sheet, back when sheets were white. "John, we're leaving."

This is good. Yes, Mom, leave. Get out of this crazy mess. Leave with Dad. Get him as far away from here as possible. She's doing exactly what she needs to. God, I love that woman.

"Dani, pack your stuff," Dad says.

I look up to notice everyone staring at me. Are they wondering if I have done it or do they already assume? I would if I were them.

"Wait just a minute," Bentley starts, "I would bet my life on it. She didn't do it. Hasn't anyone thought to ask her? Where's Milo? He's aware of the camp and I just bet you he'd like to have a crack at the old man. He's been chomping at the bit. Anyone thought to ask him?" Bentley says as he looks around. "Dani, tell em', " he insists.

Oh . . . my . . . God, Milo. Even if he hasn't done it, he'll be framed for sure. It dawns on me what a fool I've been. What do I mean if he hasn't done it? The night I bring him into camp, Burke winds up dead? How could I have been so stupid?

"How do you know that about Milo?" I ask Bentley. Milo hasn't said anything to me about Burke. I knew he was unhappy about us keeping him prisoner, but he really didn't say anything . . . that I can remember.

"How do you think I know? I interrogated him. He wanted him dead even more than you, Dani. I know you've been going to see him. How do you know he didn't follow you back here? Finish him off when you weren't watching? How do you know?" Bentley's wavering a bit as he looks at the blood stains on my clothing.

I don't say anything. I'm hoping I can hold off until Mom and Dad leave. Hannah comes out of her cabin and looks confused. I glance at Milo's cabin. Any second he's going to come walking out. Unless, he did do it. If he did, he should be long gone.

Mom comes out with her bags. "Dani, get your stuff."

"I'm not going." Everyone looks to me now, as if this is the first time I've spoken.

"Leave her be," Dad says.

So he must think I've done it too. Am I wrong about him? He isn't even pushing me to go. I can't even imagine the disappointment he's feeling. The very thing he warned me of, he thinks I've done. So, this is it. This is when I leave my parents. I couldn't have imagined that it would end up like this, but it's what needs to be done. I've thought for a long time that we needed to split up. They can keep Brody safe now.

Brody!

"Dad." My voice comes out shaky. "Brody's out in the forest. He went to the bathroom. He's not back."

"They took him, John!" Mom screams, "Whoever did this took him!" She is in hysterics and all I do is just stand there and stare. So familiar. Why is this happening again? I'm certain this isn't a game of hide and seek and I'm even more certain I can't just go out into the woods and find him sleeping next to a wolf.

Avery has come out and is starting to put things together. She doesn't seem too alarmed yet.

"It's okay. Brody just had to poop. He said he would be right back." I feel a glimmer of hope. Maybe it's a game of hide and seek after all. Everyone ignores the fact that we have a dead body in one of the cabins and we begin our search for Brody.

"Do you know where he might have gone?" I ask Avery as I pack up my binoculars and secure my knife.

"I don't know," her lip quivers as she finally starts to panic a little. "I never go with him for that." She pinches her nose.

Before I leave, I have to check. If he's gone, I'll have my answer. If he's still in there, I still won't have my answer, but it will be something. I can't figure out if I want him to be in there or not. I walk slowly, afraid of what I'll find.

I try to peek first in the window, but the curtains are closed and I resign myself to the fact that I'm going to have to open the door.

"Dani, where are you going?" Bentley calls to me. I look up to him.

"Can you trust me on something?" I can't even believe what I'm asking him. I don't even trust me right now.

"You don't have to say anything," he says back, "we'll figure this out."

"Do you trust me?"

"You know I do." I believe him. I take his hand and lead him over to Milo's cabin. I'm almost certain he's gone. And then it will be my fault Burke was murdered. I invited Milo here, gave him the opportunity.

Bentley looks at me, squeezes my hand and I open the door. Milo's not there.

He's not in his bed; he's sitting straight up in the chair across the room. His hands are crossed, thumbs nervously twisting in his lap.

"I know what you think," Milo begins. I feel Bentley practically jump out of his skin. He looks to me.

"How could you?" He looks at me, betrayed and snatches his hand back. I look to the doorway to see Hannah and it looks like she's seen a ghost. Everything feels like it's in slow motion.

"Milo?"

"Hannah?" he asks and shoots up out of his chair. "What's happened to you? What did they do to you? I'll kill them!" he roars, looking back to me and Bentley before rushing to her and taking her in his arms.

I look at her confused and she peals herself away. "Dani, meet my brother Milo." She smiles. "I can't believe you found him." She looks close to tears, but she's happy, really happy.

"All the way from California?" I smile with a lame and totally inappropriate half joke. I'm looking for words to say, knowing nothing will work for this situation.

I can feel Bentley simmering beside me and I take his hand again. "Milo, we only need to ask this once and we'll believe you. I guess you're one of us now. Did you do it?"

"I don't know exactly what you're talking about, but from what I've heard though the door, either someone's been kidnapped or killed, either of which, I had nothing to do with, I swear."

"I believe him," Hannah says.

"So do I." I look to Bentley, praying this will be enough for him.

"Fine, we've got work to do."

***

We search until nightfall. Mom's a wreck and actually Dad's not holding it together so well either. Jonah tries to comfort them and tell them if whoever wanted him dead would have just killed him. Jonah's theory is that whoever took him probably just wants to keep him and control him. This will give us time.

Bentley and Grant are both highly trained trackers and they've been searching for hours, but there's no sign of Brody or Callie. The few leads we had lead us nowhere. I also haven't spotted Waite. Maybe he's with Brody.

I'm so exhausted when I finally get back, I'm not even sure which cabin I pass out in. I wake up startled when I see Bentley sitting in the chair beside the bed.

"Welcome back, Sleeping Beauty." Bentley half smiles.

"I thought we established that I like Bonnie better," I say with irritated sarcasm.

"I thought you'd never wake up."

"What time is it! I need to get back out there. Have you found him? Why are you just sitting here?"

"I have to tell you something."

"No. Don't say it. Don't even say it. I'll never forgive you if you say it." I put my face into my hands. Why is this happening again? I can't seem to get a break. What good is it to have your brother be the Golden Child if it's always going to be like this?

"Dani, stop. Listen to me, this is going to sound crazy, but you need to hear me out."

I look up at him and he looks confident, almost peaceful. What could he possibly have to tell me?

"Brody's fine. I can feel it."

"That's all you have to say? You can feel it?" I get up, tired of this and start rummaging around, looking for my hiking gear. I'm going into the caves by Harney Peak today.

"Sit down," he says, not so gently now. "Sometimes your stubbornness is cute, but not right now." I sit, even though I don't want to.

"Close your eyes." I do, but just for a second.

"Can you feel that?" he asks.

"No."

"Look harder, search for Brody. Can you feel him? He's still alive. You can feel it if you look hard enough." I stay silent for a few minutes because I want what he's offering. I see him, but where I see him it's hot.

"What's happening? Why's it so hot?"

"I don't see that part, but I see him. He's there." He puts his hand to my chest and it's beating so hard I can feel it through his hand when I put mine on top of his. He moves it and blushes a little.

"Sorry, I just wanted you to see."

"Where are my parents?" I should be with them.

"They're out looking with Jessica and Jonah. They left early this morning." I bow my head. It feels as though they've abandoned me again. It confirms to me that they think I've killed Burke. They don't trust me. I look up and there's no distrust in Bentley's eyes, only kindness.

"I saw what you saw. Now what do we do? We still don't know where Brody actually is. We have to find him before he gets too far away."

"I've got a plan," he says, with a cocky smile.

***

I still can't believe what I'm seeing. Yesterday, Milo and Bentley were at each other's throats and now they're working together.

"Stand here," he instructs me as he places me beside Milo. "Hannah and Jack across from each other. We're missing Brody, but we'll have to make it work."

We're placed in a circle and something is starting to happen. Even the wind picks up and rustles the leaves in the forest.

"Okay, join hands," Bentley says.

We do and I feel it. Something's definitely happening, but something's also missing and we all sense it.

"So what's this going to do?" I'm irritated that we are not out looking for Brody. It feels like we're wasting time.

"This can help us find him. Everyone close your eyes. Visualize him. Find him."

I close my eyes and I feel like a fraud again. I can't get the picture of him burning out of my head.

"How is this going help?" I'm dangerously close to tears. "We're wasting time."

"Kit," Bentley calls to her, as if this is something they have talked about.

She stands up and it's like I'm seeing her for the first time. She looks like herself again, only her mid section seems to have changed.

"Kit," I breathe out.

"I didn't lose it." She smiles. "Brody helped me. I don't know how he did it, but I was spared," she says, her voice so steady, it's hard to believe this is the same girl I saw who wouldn't leave her room only a few weeks ago. Her face even looks like her face again, only traces of tiny little scars you would only see if you were looking for them.

"I'm really happy for you, Kit, but what does that have to do with what's happening right now. I can't even think straight."

"Brody didn't help me and save my baby just so he could die at the hands of some psycho. Can't you see? There's a bigger picture here. Everyone else sees it except for you. They need you. It's you. You're the reason everyone's here. Brody needs you."

I hold up my hand. I don't need to hear anymore. I look down for a minute and I can feel everyone's expectation. I look back up and look them all in the eyes, one by one before I smile and say, “How do we get started?”

I’m in a hurry to reach Brody, but for some reason I also know we have to do this. Bentley sets up stations and we all get short training sessions. I start with Grant.

He refreshes me on all the moves he taught me before and even slips in a few new ones. I only hope I can remember them all.

Next is Bentley who shows me how to shoot a gun. I only get off a few rounds, but I feel comfortable enough. Hannah watches quietly from the side. She takes a special interest in Milo, who is currently letting Bentley show him how to toss some knives. He’s actually not half bad.

The sun is setting and Bentley wants to use the last of our time for me to work on my advancement. I knew he was going to do it and I’ve been dreading it. Everyone takes a seat around the fire and all eyes are on me.

“You ready?”

“I’ll try.”

Bentley backs up and places a small log in front of me.

“Okay, so can you move this?”

“I think so.”

“Give it a try.”

I close my eyes and hold my hand out. I hear a slight rustle, but when I open my eyes again, it couldn’t have moved much more than two inches.” I growl in frustration.

“I don’t see why I’m going to have to move a log,” I say to Bentley, but he ignores me.

“Milo, up here,” Bentley commands. “Stand beside her.” I study him to see if it bothers him to have Milo so close to me. It doesn’t seem to. He’s starting to trust him.

"Can you feel it?" Milo turns to ask me.

"No," I answer back.

"Stand closer," Bentley says, but his voice catches the tiniest bit. "Take her hand."

Bam! There it is. Only it's not like it was before. The shock has traveled up my entire arm.

"Oww! I don't think that is supposed to happen."

"It's fine," Milo says as he rubs his arm. "Put it there again." I do and instead of a shock, it's a steady flow of electricity.

"I don't understand what this is for." I sigh. I want to believe in all of this. I really do. I just don't see what the point is of Milo getting shocked by me.

"You're the magnets: north and south." Bentley says, almost tenderly. "You might not use that, but that's certainly what you are. Think about it. Why do we always want to be where you are? Milo, all those kids in Saloon Number 10, how did they end up there?"

Milo looks to Bentley and considers this, "I don't know, just good friends I suppose."

"Well, I know Milo," Bentley says as he gives Milo's shoulder a little squeeze. They were there for you. Just like with Dani. When this thing is over, the people will come for you and stay for Brody."

"How do you know that?" I ask, even though for some reason, it seems true.

"Brody told me."

Chapter 29

Milo wakes me early in the morning. He's had the same dream I had, only this time we were all there. We're both certain where Brody is. I'm chomping at the bit to get moving to the top of the mountain now, but Milo convinces me to come with him. He says he can't do it without me.

"We have a plan. We'll be fine. I'll explain it all later," I shout to Bentley as I mount the four-wheeler with Milo. Milo revs the engine and waits for my go ahead.

"Why can't I come with you?" Bentley asks as he jogs up to me. "I need to be there. I'm worried. Something's off. We have to stay together."

"They need you here. You need to get them ready. Get Kit somewhere safe. It's time. You know it, and I know it. Please, I'll be fine. Just let me go. I'll be back before you know it."

"You had the dream too, didn't you?" he asks me.

"Yes." I smile. "So you know where to meet if I can't find you."

He shakes his head. "If anything happens, never give up. I'll find you. Whatever happens, I'll find you." The look on his face makes me want to bring him in close to kiss him somewhere on his face, maybe his mouth, but I look back to see Jack watching us. I turn around and tell Milo to go.

As we're riding the four-wheeler into Deadwood, I can't help but feel excited. I don't know why, but I feel like we are going to get Brody back today and maybe end this once and for all. If we can get back in time, I'll have time to tell Bentley all about this genius plan of ours.

Milo walks into the back of the club and starts rummaging around in his stuff. I feel peaceful as I walk through the saloon and remember all the good times I've had, but I'm also a little on edge. This has to work. It's for all the marbles. If even one part of this plan doesn't work, we'll fail and The Council will continue on.

"Milo?" I haven't seen him for at least a minute and something feels off. It's too quiet.

I should have known something was wrong by the silence. Milo can never keep quiet. If he's not talking, he's at least whistling. I get one glance back at him before my world goes dark. He's standing by Rigby and before I can even register the full betrayal, I feel a blinding pain at the back of my head and my world goes black.

***

I almost feel like I'm having another nightmare, but I've never been in this much physical pain in a dream before, so I register that this is real. Only it's not real. All I can see in the darkness is gravel and dirt moving in blurs and feel my face squished up against what feels like a . . . horse. I'm hogtied . . . to a horse. I try to look around, but there's a piercing pain at the back of my head that's producing a blinding light. I crack open one eye and try to look ahead of me. I'm on a horse that appears to be going up Harney Peak. So it's really happening.

Milo. How could he do this to me? Advancements are only for the good. He only brought me to Deadwood to split us up. How could I be so stupid? It occurs to me that with me missing, Bentley might stop searching for Brody and come looking for me.

It goes blurry again and the next time I wake, I'm tied to a metal hand railing that's just below the top of Harney Peak. And it's hot. Really hot. I look down and almost slip off the edge. If it hadn't been for me being tied to the railing, I'm not sure I'd still be here. Below me is the biggest bonfire I've ever seen built into a huge cavern at the top of the mountain. When you have a regular fire, you have chopped up pieces of lumber all stacked up. It's a lot like that except for the fire is built out of entire trees. I've never seen anything like it. I look up to see Randy coming down the stairs that lead to the top. It's strange that a tourist attraction is housing such an evil deed.

"You're up. Good. I've been worried about you," Randy says and I try to entertain the thought that this is all a ruse and he's really good; he's biding time to evade The Council.

"Can I get you something to drink?" he asks as if we are home on the farm, and I am sitting in the living room, not tied to a pole in front of what looks like a huge sacrificial fire.

"How about untying this," I say as I struggle with the rope against the railing. Hey, it's worth a try.

"There's time for that."

"Where's my brother?"

"He's safe, for now. Whether he stays safe, is up to you."

I've lost all fight in me. I know in this moment I will do whatever he asks. "What do you want?"

"You, of course."

"What?" He's lost his mind. If all he wants is me, then fine. Let's do this.

"Well, the both of you. I figure if I got you, Brody may want to come with me and make my job simpler."

"Why are you doing this?" I'm starting to sweat now and I'm even considering taking him up on his offer for water. I must be losing sweat by the gallons. I'll be dehydrated soon and I won't be any good then. "He's your nephew. How can you be doing this? What do you want?"

Thoughts race through my mind of all the theories about what Randy would want with the Golden Child—first and foremost to destroy him. I search the sky and my heart sinks when I see the moon looks full. Thoughts of that baby are almost my undoing. He can't really believe he could take Brody's powers. But I also remember the theory where he might just want control of him.

"You can have us both. We'll come back with you, to the capital. Is that what you want?"

"Such a bright girl, Dani. You are making this a lot easier on me than I thought. I knew we had a special relationship." He puts a water bottle to my lips and it's as if he is testing me. I drink it.

"Good girl, there's just a few things we have to take care of first and then we'll be on our way."

The heat is almost toxic to me and I push out violent coughs every so often, but Randy doesn't seem to care. He sits with me in silence for a while before he makes his way back up to the top of what looks like a platform and that's when I really see him. He's got Brody dangerously close to the fire. If I'm hot where I'm at, Brody must be roasting. I jerk at the rope, in hopes it will budge. Nothing. I'm burning with hatred again. I understand that in this moment I want to kill Randy more than I've wanted anything in my life, more than I ever wanted to kill Burke. It's distracting me from what else is around.

I look further down in the gassy haze and see men with suits on. The Council. I can't think of any other idiots that would wear suits to a bonfire: a human bonfire. This is the last sacrifice. But why is Randy teasing me? How could he possibly benefit?

I look further up and I have my answer. He's got us all. He's planning on burning us all. He believes the moon theory. He wants all our powers. We're even in a weird sacrificial circle now that I really look around. I'm at the bottom of it. Above me are Jack and Hannah. Above Hannah towards the peak is Milo. Milo?

Hannah and Milo look like they are trying to talk to each other. On the other side is Bentley. They've got Bentley. He looks bloody and his face is puffy. He obviously put up a fight. They were smart to put him down. He's the most dangerous. How did this happen so fast? They must have come into Tent City right when I left. So Milo has not betrayed me. He's one of us. The six of us make a perfect circle. Brody is where he belongs, in the center.

I look towards The Council again. They are lined up on a bench, almost as if they are at a show. Rigby must have done the dirty work and then disappeared. No one else is around, except when I strain, I can see Callie far behind them. So, they've got her too. I look further and my heart sinks. She is in no way, shape, or form tied against her will. She sits there among them. How could she? I search further to see if my parents have been captured. They are nowhere to be found.

"Bring her up!" I hear Randy yell to one of his Council members.

The Council member comes down, almost unsure of himself. I'm betting he doesn't get his hands dirty very often. Well, he's about to.

"You don't have to do this, you know," I start on him. Right now, I just want to get a gauge on him, see where he stands. He says nothing. I consider trying to overtake him, but he's big and if it goes wrong, we both go into the fire. He brings me to the top and I obey, still weighing my options.

"Good girl," Randy says, as he reties my rope to the top of what I guess is the altar. I finally get a good look at Brody. He doesn't look good. The smoke must be getting to him because his head is bowed down and he looks like he is seconds away from passing out. He looks up briefly and makes eye contact with me and I almost break down. He's looking at me with confusion and hurt. He doesn't understand what's happening.

"You have to move him," I say in an even voice. "He's no good to you dead." My tears are threatening to expose me as they form in heavy drops at the edge of my eyes.

"You're right, let's get moving on this, so we can get him out of here. A deal's a deal."

"What deal? What do you want?"

He laughs a little, almost giddy from the power as he stands at the top of the altar. I've never seen him like this before. I need time. I need to buy myself some more time.

"Can you please move him? I'll do whatever you want. Please just move him."

He looks back to me and looks as if he is going to deny me, but then motions another Council member. He unties Brody and I fight every urge to lunge at him. He moves him back, but Brody is still trapped, hidden behind Randy now and I have no access to him. If I find a way to push Randy in the fire, will this be over or will I have to deal with The Council? He tries to let him sit, but Brody doesn't move. He lays there, motionless. Stay calm. You're going to have to think your way out of this, I coach myself.

"Okay, what do you want?"

"I'm glad you brought that up actually," he says as he pulls at his collar. He removes his shirt and laughs. "Getting hot up here, isn't it?"

I look again to the other five. Bentley is still passed out, but the others look at me, wondering what we are going to do. We're trapped. Milo and Hannah are still whispering to each other.

"I'll let you and Brody live, Dani, but it comes at a price. Your lives for theirs," Randy says as he motions to the other four. He wants them dead. He wants the circle dead. Brody's circle.

"Why not me?"

"Family's family right?" He's serious now. "Besides, I need you to keep the kid in line."

"What are you going to do with him?"

"Oh, that's the best part, darlin'. I'm going to teach him. We'll be the best team this world has ever seen," he says with a gleam in his eyes. He used up Burke and now he's moving on to my brother. He's truly crazy.

"And if I say no?"

"Then I kill you all. I really don't need Brody, you see. I can continue doing what I'm doing and I won't have anything to worry about. No coming prophet. No kids with powers. I can just keep on doing what I'm doing. I've earned it."

"You don't actually think you'll get our powers, do you?" I choke out.

He considers this for a moment. "I'm not sure about that, but it could always be worth a try." He smiles as he glances up at the moon, flashing all of his boxy, white teeth. How could I have ever thought so much of him?

That sick feeling is coming to my stomach again. I'm not sure if it's the smoke, but I can't handle it much longer. I'm either going to pass out or just as likely . . . die.

"I know about the locusts," I say as I take a quick peek at Milo, hoping to buy just another minute so I can figure out what to do. Milo looks like he is about ready to pounce and I notice he's slipped out of his rope. I shake my head slightly to him and hope he understands.

Randy's face lights up. "Pretty ingenious, huh?"

"So it was your idea?"

"Well, not entirely. I had a couple of friends from the United Nations help out a little. They were sick of the United States having the best of everything, and well, I was just sick of the United States."

"So you decided to create your own plagues?"

"Just the first one, girl. You all have earned the rest of them. Those locusts were the best thing to happen to this country. Taught you all a lesson. Did you know they have entire task forces dedicated to keeping locusts populations in check? I kind of came to look at my little locusts much like a beekeeper might look at his bees. With a little help, I had huge colonies and with no one to stop me, the possibilities were endless. It did go a little further than I wanted though, I must admit I got a little carried away. It was supposed to just be a sign from God. I had no idea they would decimate the food supply the way they did. Hard little workers, those Desert Locusts, my personal pick," he says with a creepy grin.

"Is this about Joshua?" I ask and his face crumples in surprise.

"You leave my son out of this!" he roars at me.

"No, that has to be it right? After the shooting, you must have been sick with grief. Well, you know what? We all were. We lost him too. And all the other parents, they lost their children too."

"Exactly. Something needed to be done and I did it. This country was corrupt, evil, run by Satan."

"What about the poison?"

"I don't want to talk about that," he responds, and for the first time, he looks a little uncomfortable.

"I deserve to know!"

"What makes you so special?" he spits out.

"Because Drake was my brother."

"Fine. You'll figure it out eventually anyway . . . if you live that long."

I can feel vomit rising up my throat, but I don't say anything. I need to hear him say it.

"I poisoned the water and you were all too stupid to notice."

"Why is killing millions okay? After losing Joshua, you should know how that feels. How terrible it is to take someone's loved one away. How could you? What about Drake? Was he evil? What about Jack and Bentley's mom? Was she evil?"

He steps back a bit, surprised. "What do you know about her?"

"That she found out what you were doing and you had her killed, is that right?"

"Never. I would never . . . I loved her." His eyes actually glisten a little, probably from the smoke.

"Drake?"

"Collateral damage. After the locusts, I had to do something about the population. There was never going to be enough food for everyone. I did what I had to."

"And what was that?" Strangely, I'm keeping my cool . . . despite this heat. It's going to be the death of me.

"Why do you care so much!" He's starting to unravel. I can feel my opportunity coming soon. I need to keep him there.

"There's nothing to prove it," he says lowering his voice. He's starting to pull himself together. "I did you all a favor. If they hadn't died, you all would have starved. The millions that perished died from something they consume every day: plain old fluoride. Put in our water to keep our teeth from rotting, but in large doses, lethal. You were lucky because you drank from the wells. You should be thankful for that."

He finally sits down, as if this is exhausting. I can feel him thinking about Joshua. Joshua was one of the victims in the shooting that involved almost 50 preschoolers. I remember Dad telling me the story. Randy and Dad had argued about Joshua being put in preschool. Dad told Randy to keep Joshua home with a nanny where it was safe, but Randy insisted that he be sent to preschool. He said he wasn't going to let fear run his life. And then it happened. Joshua and his classmates were gunned down, robbed of life, never to graduate high school, get married, or have children of their own. Just thinking about it again makes me crazy and I realize I'm living in the same hatred Randy is.

I'm defeated. This is over. There's nothing I can do. My head drops and the tears are mixing with the drops of sweat as they splash onto the rope. How does this work? Jonah said he just said a prayer, but I don't know if I'm even qualified to do that. I don't even know what to call him. God? Lord? The Big Guy? This all feels so wrong. I look back to Bentley and Brody, just feet from each other, almost gone.

My head drops again, "Chief?" I say quietly. "Are you there? If you are, this is the time. If you can't do this for me, can you do it for him? There's nothing more pure in this world than Brody. Please."

I open my eyes again and that's when it hits me. I'm sweating buckets. The heat is making me sweat even more than usual. I give a little tug. I try to quiet my heart, as I realize I'm going to be able to slip out. The rope has gotten slippery. I feel like Billy the Kid about to be hung, just waiting to give them the slip. Only he was running for his own life. I've got to stick around, for at least Brody. I'm sick to admit it, but he has to come first, before them all.

I almost laugh when I look down to the rope that will not hold me much longer. Using rope was Randy's first mistake.

"So what's it going to be, Dani?" Randy asks as he gets up, seemingly recovered.

"Why do you want them all dead?"

"We've been over this," he says, irritated. "Do we have a deal or not?"

"What about Bentley?" I need to make him believe me.

"Callie! I see you back there, you coward! How could you?" I scream, hoping it sounds good.

It must work because it brings a chuckle to Randy. "Oh, her? Amazing what a scorned lover is capable of."

"What are you talking about?" I ask in the most sincere voice I can muster.

"Come here," he commands Callie, and it looks like she wants to crawl in a hole. I want to see if she will admit what I figured out minutes ago.

"Why don't you let her know how she wronged you," Randy says as he nudges her.

She's crying now and suddenly I don't want this. "Forget about it," I tell Randy. "It doesn't matter."

"No, I think you should hear this." He pushes her again, her feet teetering dangerously close to the edge.

"You promised me," Callie says, only making eye contact with me for a second, letting her eyes rest on Bentley lying on the ground. She's sobbing now.

"Oh, jeeze girl, go sit back down," Randy says, almost irritated by the delay. "Somehow this girl thinks you promised her you'd leave her lover here alone, but once you broke your promise, she came running to me and brought me Brody. Revenge is a very powerful motivator."

I look back to her and she cries out, "I'm sorry." I want to hate her for what she's done, but I can't. All I can think about is Brody and getting him out of here. Randy seems irritated again and before I can stop him, he shoves Callie into the fire. She claws and grasps at the sides, but it's too late. She's gone.

"I never wanted that . . . you monster!" I scream at him. Oh God, he's serious. He means business. Every move I make is going to matter. I have to be careful.

"She was annoying. Good riddance. Now where were we? As you can see, there are real consequences here. What's it going to be? Should we start with him?" Randy says as he motions towards Bentley. "Remember, it's them or Brody. Seems like an obvious choice."

I have to get this right. My heart is ready to explode. I steady my hands. I feel something come over me. I'm good here. It's now or never. It either ends well, or it just ends, either way, I need this to be over.

"You can't have him," I say as I finally slip out and crouch. There's no way I should have been able to do it. The rope was tight, too tight, but the shear amount of sweat has given me just the right leverage to slip out. Is this why I'm like this? Is it for this moment? I pop up and it gives me just a little momentum, as Randy registers the shock of me setting myself free.

His body comes alive with rage and he's about to take it out on my brother. I can see what he's going to do. He's going to yank Brody free and toss him in, teach me a lesson. He might even be happy it turned out this way. Take out the risk of the Golden Child. But he doesn't know what I do, and he doesn't know he's about to make his second and last mistake.

"Waite!" I call.

"Change of heart?" he asks as he has Brody by the shoulder. My baby brother is slumped over, not even able to hold his own weight. Please, just a few more seconds.

I can see him creeping up behind Randy. His yellow eyes glow menacingly. I have seen him like this once before. My heart is beating furiously. This has to work.

"I'd let him go if I were you," I warn Randy.

"What are you going to do about it?" Randy sort of laughs, but he's looking around. He's sees Milo who is untied and advancing towards us.

"Milo wait!" I shout, but it's too late.

Randy's movement is so fast I don't have time to stop him. He shoves Brody into the fire before even Waite can stop him.

"Brody!" I reach down but it's already happened. I can hear Waite snarling and snapping so I look up. Waite is tearing Randy apart and there's blood everywhere.

I'm bawling and searching around for a stick or a rope, anything I can find to get Brody out, even though I know it's too late. I watched him go over the edge. He's gone.

I look up again and The Council has disappeared, but the other four are moving quickly, almost as if working together. Jack has woken Bentley. Hannah looks sick, but she's here, and now Jack is helping her find a seat. They nod to each other and then Jack moves to where Milo is.

Milo has his arms stretched out and he's holding something. He's holding something! I look back down into the fire pit and through the gassy haze I see Brody, but he's all blistered and just hanging there, against the rock wall of the fire pit. I'm not going to be this lucky. This isn't going to work. He's dead. I shove my face into my hands and sob. Bentley comes to my side and I try to push him away.

"Don't you do that," he whispers into my ear.

"He's gone. He's gone. He's gone."

"Don't you dare give up. Look around you." He lifts my chin and the first person I see is Milo. He's standing with his arms still reaching towards the pit. He has a fierce, determined look on his face. Jack is there too, part of our circle. Hannah stands by his side. She nods with a small smile. I don't dare give myself the option of hope. I look down.

Brody's still there. He doesn't look good. There is a fresh trail of blood dripping down his face, but he's there. He has not been swallowed by the fire. Milo has caught him and suspended him to the wall. The flames tease and taunt by his feet. Brody's skin almost looks as if it's melting off.

"Get him out of there!" I'm on my feet.

"I can't," Milo shouts back. "I can only hold him. You have to do the rest. Get on the other side."

Of course. The magnet. I go to position myself, but I can hear that little whisper again. I'm not good enough for this. I'm bad. I'll never be one of these people. I'm only lucky enough to know them. I'll never be as good. I have too much doubt, too much hate. The bad has trapped me and I'm as bound as I ever was by the rope.

I reach my hand down and close my eyes. Please, Brody, come to me. I got you. Just come to me. I open my eyes and he has not moved. The fire seems to be getting closer to him and I can't stop sobbing long enough to concentrate. Center. I need my center. A flash of Jonah's bull comes floating in my mind and I crash to my knees. Okay, this is it. I should feel silly for what I'm about to do, but I don't.

I look towards the sky and see the stars blinking at me once again. "Okay! You win! You win. I give up. I can't do this myself. Please, just save him. Help me save him."

And here's the weird part. I'm not even sure I believe it myself, but something happens to me in that moment. The even weirder part is I know that if I drop him, it will be okay, but yet somehow I'm not going to. But that's not the point. The point is that if I did drop him and he was lost, something would be okay about that. It would be okay if I fell in and was never found. I can't explain it, but whatever happens, it's going to be okay. I look up and everyone is staring at me with hopeful smiles.

"She's got it," I hear Bentley say.

"Easy," Hannah adds.

"Ready?" Jack asks.

"Let's do this," Milo says as his hands tremble. "A little help here?" he asks with a smirky smile.

And then I do it. I don't even really have to think about it. I just follow Milo's lead and point my arms down the fiery hole. And instead of the force of being pushed against the rock, I am sliding Brody to me. It's actually working and at this point, I'm not even a little surprised. I use all my concentration to get him up as quickly as I can. He is scraping the wall, but that is the least of my concerns. As happy as I am that I'm getting him out, the closer he gets to me, the more obvious it is that he's dead. No one could survive this.

I pull him up, but he's not moving. I squeeze him hard into my arms and I never want to let go. Jack forces me to set him back to the ground.

No heartbeat. No breathing. He's dead. "It's all for nothing!" I scream up at the sky. "All this? For what?" It was stupid to hope, foolish.

I'm pounding my fists bloody into the rock when Bentley pulls me away.

I see Jack and Hannah walk up hand in hand. He looks at her. "You ready?" Oh. Why am I always two steps behind?

"Yup. Let me see him."

She leans down to Brody, but then looks back up at Milo. "I'm glad you found me. At least I had that." I'm watching them in awe. All this time we had Hannah in Tent City, Milo was only miles away in Deadwood. I wish we could go back and give them more time.

"Did you get it?" she asks Milo.

"Every second," he smiles.

"You get that out as soon as you can. Take them down, Milo. Do it for me." She leans back down to Brody.

"Are you sure?" I ask her before she starts.

"This is meant to be. Can't you feel it? It was always to be him."

"Yes," I say only for her sake. I know after this she will be gone.

"Hannah?" I'm sobbing again. I don't want to lose her, but I can't lose Brody either. It's always been about him. I think that's how we all feel.

"Yes?"

"I'm going to miss you." I bawl as I take her into my arms. There's not much to her, but she's the one steadying me.

"Me too." She finally cries. "You've been a good friend to me. Don't ever forget that. And take care of my brother . . . Now go, I have to do this before it's too late."

Milo walks off. I can't blame him for not wanting to watch his sister die. It occurs to me that the six we have here are all related. Brody and I are tied as siblings, Jack and Bentley obviously are brothers, and now we have Hannah and Milo. Our six has finally been completed, but we are about to lose one.

I want to stay for Hannah, but I can't. I walk away too. At least she has Jack and Bentley. They are brave enough to see her through this. Milo walks away because he doesn't have the heart to see his sister succeed, and I walk away because I don't have the heart to watch her not. As much as I love her, Brody's the one I can't lose.

I come back a few minutes later and she's gone. In her face, there's no sparkle. She lies there on the ground with dead eyes staring at the sky. But I don't look at her for long. He has all my attention. He is still badly burned, but even before my eyes I can see his chest heaving breaths in and out and the skin is repairing itself right before my eyes. Hannah is truly magical.

Milo comes in and doesn't say anything. He just picks Hannah up and looks to Bentley, "You got this?"

"Of course, see you down there," Bentley says as he picks Brody up.

"Don't you want the horse?" Bentley calls to Milo as he begins to carry his dead sister down the mountain.

“No, this is something I have to do myself,” he answers as he begins his descent. Before he turns to leave, I see his shoulders shake in silent sobs as he bows his head down into Hannah’s hair.

“Jack?” Bentley asks.

“Got it,” Jack replies and takes Brody from Bentley and begins his journey back down. I’m sure he’s itching to get Brody back to begin treatment. I’m itching for that too. Hannah’s life can’t be for nothing. I know he’s going to be okay.

Chapter 30

Jack places the last handful of dirt onto Burke's grave and says a silent goodbye.

He turns to me. "I lost you when I died, didn't I?"

"You haven't lost me Ja—"

"You know what I mean. You fell in love with Bentley when he was there for you and I wasn't. I left you. And then with the fake helicopter crash. That was it, wasn't it? When I died . . . You let me go."

"Let's not do this now. It's a weird time for everyone. Do you want to go for a walk? Just talk about normal stuff?"

"Thanks, but I've got things to do . . . but, it's okay, Dani. I understand. I'll be all right," he says and turns to leave before I have a chance to say anything else. He walks away, withdrawn and sullen. I don't have the heart to tell him he's right.

Tent City's residents have spread out and I find Bentley sitting on an old tree stump behind the cabins. His head is buried in his hands and I consider turning back. I should leave him be, but there's something he needs to know.

"You know, he told me the only reason he came back here was for you."

"Who?" He looks out into the forest and won't make eye contact with me.

"Your dad."

Bentley kind of chokes out a cough for his response, but actually says, "You believe that?"

“Coming back got him killed.” I swallow. “And he wasn’t exactly having the time of his life here. You know, his last days were actually kind of miserable. And then to die like that.”

“You sound like you feel sorry for him.”

“I do, sort of. And every day I knew him, it was harder to hate him. I could see you in his face and hear Jack in his voice . . . a little unnerving, a man you think you hate reminding you so much of someone you lo— well, you know.”

He gets up to walk back to the center of camp, still not looking at me.

We walk back in silence. I don’t know if he even wants me to be around, but it feels lame to leave him.

“Where are the others?” I ask Brody as he tosses wood chips into the fire.

“Jack’s with Hannah. He’s hoping to discover the next great cure for the world. He’s testing her blood right now,” he says with a giggle. “She hates that.”

We walk back over to the front of my cabin and I spot Hannah coming out of her cabin. Jack is trailing after her, begging her to just give him a few more minutes.

Although, I can’t say for sure if it’s Hannah though, because this girl is healthy. I mean really healthy. Hannah’s never looked like this. This girl is bouncing and smiling and jabbing playfully at Milo’s side.

“Hannah?”

“I love you all! I love the air. I love the trees. I love the wind. I love the sun. I love you all!” the crazy girl I thought was Hannah says.

“Don’t mind her.” Milo chuckles. “She’s high on life.”

"What's going on? I don't understand."

"She's not sick anymore."

"How is this possible?"

The so-called Hannah leans down to Brody and pinches him in the cheeks. "If I would have known saving the Golden Child would have healed *me*, I would have saved you a long time ago." She winks and when she looks me in the eye, I see it's her.

"Oh, Hannah." I grab her and squeeze her and almost think again it's not her because I'm not hugging a bag of bones. She has a real body, all filled out and her hair is back. Towards the end, there were only wisps left.

"He's really real."

"I guess so," Hannah says, but you probably always knew that, didn't you? Where's Bentley going? I saw him leave with a bag."

"I don't know. He just said he's leaving," I say, trying to hide the hurt. After all his claims he would never leave me, he finally has, not that I can blame him.

"Are you okay with that?"

"What am I supposed to do about it?"

"Oh, I don't know." She rolls her eyes. "Maybe tell him how you really feel?"

"I'll be sure to do that as soon as I figure it out." I put my arm around her and we make our way to find Brody. He's got a big day ahead of him.

Chapter 31

"Happy Birthday, Brody," I say for about the tenth time today and lean down and kiss his cherub cheek. He swats me away and gives me the "I'm too old for that" look.

I turn the battery-powered TV off. It looks like he's watching the news footage again. I don't like him watching it, but it's not like he wasn't there. Milo was right. He got every second. The Council was brought down as soon as the tape was released. Milo's love for reality TV actually came in handy. Going back to Deadwood and being captured was worth it after all. Milo secured his camera and somehow managed to capture Randy and The Council up on Harney Peak exposing them for who they were. Four have been captured and are awaiting trial. Two more are in hiding, but it's only a matter of time.

"Are you sure you are ready for this? You don't have to, you know," I ask Brody as I fix his newly cut hair. As sad as I was to see the curly locks go, he has insisted he look proper for his big day.

"Yes."

"Do you know what you're going to say? Do you want to practice your speech or anything?"

"No, I've got it. Jonah helped me. How many people will there be?" he asks, with the first sign of nervousness.

"I don't know. They're coming in by the hundreds now. They all want to meet the new king."

Waite is whining at the door, so I get up to let him out and I see him trot towards the forest. He must not be a fan of crowds.

Jack and Bentley have set up what would be a podium for Brody where he will go out and make his first speech as the new king. That still sounds weird, even in my head. I look for my parents out in the crowd, but only see Mom. I haven't seen Dad since they took him.

I shut the front door of the cabin and turn to Brody, "Can I talk to you?"

"Sure."

"What will happen to him?"

"Who?"

"Dad. What will happen to him now?"

"He broke the law."

"Can't you do something about it?" As soon as I ask it, my stomach turns in knots. I have basically asked my little brother to bend the rules to help spring my dad, our dad.

He looks to the floor and doesn't respond. I fidget with my shirt, unsure what to say. "Sorry, Brody, I shouldn't have said that."

"How about an easier one," I start again. "Can you tell me about your dreams? What do we all have to do with this? Why are we here? What are we supposed to be doing?"

"You call that an easier one?" He laughs and then tries to punch me in the arm, but he's still too short. "Sit down, this is a good one," he says as his body shivers in excitement and he grins so large, every one of his little chiclet teeth are exposed.

"Okay . . ." he begins. "There are six of us right?" he asks, and I nod. I can tell he thinks this is going to be good. "So, there are six of us and three sets of siblings." That much I figured out already. "We each have a counterpart." Counterpart? I didn't even know Brody knew what that word meant. He raises his finger as if to interrupt my internal dialogue. "My counterpart is Bentley."

"Bentley?" I raise my eyebrow. They seem to be the least likely to be paired. I might have guessed Jack.

"Are you going to let me tell you the story or not?" he says, practically biting on his lip.

"Sorry."

"Yeah, he represents physical strength and I guess you could say I represent spiritual strength. We both need each other. Our jobs are to teach strength. Next are Hannah and Jack. Theirs are obvious. They are healers. They will be gifted at healing sickness, but more importantly, they will teach us how to heal the inside. They will teach us about forgiveness. And finally, you and Milo. You said something about magnets and that's exactly right. You guys are here to keep us together and bring in the new ones. That's why you dream about Milo."

"You know about that?" I blush.

"Of course, he dreams about you too, and Jack and Hannah dream about each other. You get the point."

"So you and Bentley are best buddies now?"

"Sort of, but he's hurting."

"Brody, are you really only six?"

"You can find him you know. Make him feel better."

"Where? Where can I find him?"

"I think you know." He sort of winks, but he's not real good at it yet, so he kind of just screws his face up in order to get the one eye to wink.

"What about the plagues?"

"Done."

"Are you sure?" I ask and he only nods.

"Were they real?"

"I can't answer that. Only you can figure that out."

Jonah pops his head in and asks Brody if he is ready to go. Brody nods, but then adds, "One more thing, Dani."

"Yeah,"

"Kit needs you too. Don't forget about her. She's going to have a baby now and she will need your help."

"I will, I promise." I sit still contemplating whether or not I have the guts to ask my next question. I've been wanting to know for so long and the only person who can tell me is Brody. But I'm afraid of the answer. I want to know, but I don't. In the end, I have to ask. Because if I don't, it will always be there, nagging.

"Can I ask one more thing?" The coward speaks.

"What?" He looks at me as if he will tell me anything. I'm having trouble figuring out exactly what the look is . . . It's trust. I have to ask him. I squeeze my hands at my side to keep them from shaking.

"Drake?"

He's quiet so long; it seems as if he isn't going to answer me. He bounces on the edge of the bed, contemplating whether or not to answer. "You'll see him again, just not the way you remember. You can let him go."

"How will I see him?"

"You don't need to know all that. Just know that he's okay."

I can't get over this kid. "Thanks," I whisper because I'm not real sure what to say. I watch him leave and still can't believe he's my little brother.

Chapter 32

It takes me the usual hour to get to the place I know for sure I belong. I have decided to skip Brody's little speech. Hey, I'm comfortable with him being the Golden Child and everything, but for now, I do have my limits. I'm taking this one day at a time.

I get there and it's exactly as it should be. I'm trying to deny that I'm a little crushed Bentley isn't here. Brody must have meant I could find Bentley somewhere else. I should have known. Brody doesn't know about the waterfall. The water crashes in a deafening roar and I start to strip. You would think with all the new people coming in to meet Brody, someone would have discovered this place by now. I wonder if Jonah secretly leads the newcomers away from this place, to save it for me.

I'm down to my bra and underwear when I hear a rustling in the trees. For the first time in days, I feel panicked again. I've been discovered.

"Bonnie?"

I slowly turn my head and can't help but smile.

"Yes, Clyde?"

"So you finally made it," he says as he walks towards me.

"Stay there. I don't have any clothes on."

He keeps walking up to me, but to his credit he keeps his eyes on mine as I put my t-shirt and shorts back on.

"I should have known this is where you'd pick to live."

"I should have given you a few more minutes," he says with a guilty laugh.

"You wouldn't."

"I shouldn't."

I sit down and watch the water crash. It's deafening and silent at the same time. When I'm this close to the falls, all the other unnecessary noise of life gets muted and I can concentrate on anything.

"You know, I was thinkin'," Bentley says as he sits down beside me. "I could build a tree house up over there. Be plenty of room for the both of us. You could get away when you wanted. This is probably going to get pretty crazy with all the new people coming in. You're going to need a place to get away to."

"I just came for a swim." I don't know why I'm shy and embarrassed. I think I know that however this conversation goes, my life is going to take a turn, in one way or another.

"You mean you didn't come here looking for me?" His joyful face disappears and now he looks guarded, hesitant.

I go quiet. I can't get the truth out of my head. It will never work. There will always be a big ugly history between us that no amount of time will erase.

"I just need to know one thing," he says as if reading my mind.

"Anything."

"Did you mean it?"

"Mean what?"

"I think you know what I'm talking about. And it's okay. Just tell me the truth, so I can move on. You're all I think about. If you tell me it really is Jack, I'll leave you alone. Of course, I'll always be around for Brody . . . but."

"I only said that to get rid of you."

"Why?"

"It's a long story, but mostly for your own good."

We sit in silence for so long, I think the conversation is over.

"Why don't you let me decide what's good for me. But I need something from you. I'll only ask this once because it makes me feel like kind of a jerk, but if it really was me you loved, why? If you can tell me why, then I can believe you," he says as he fidgets with the corner of my shirt. I hadn't even noticed that he had scooted closer to me.

"You want to know when I knew?"

"Yeah, I guess so."

"Well," I start to say as I look off into the background, but I decide that if I'm going to do this, I'm going to do it right and I look him in the eyes. I put my hands together to keep them from trembling. I take a deep breath.

"Every time I'm with you, I feel alive. You bring something out in me that, I don't know, feels real. It's not always good. Sometimes you make me feel like punching something, but sometimes you make me feel like I'm flying. You make me feel capable. I'd like to say that when I'm with you, I'm me, but actually it's more than that. I'm a better version of me. I actually like the girl I am when I'm with you. Does that sound cheesy?" I ask.

"No," he says quietly.

"Plus, you're kinda cute," I add to lighten the mood. "But if I'm really being honest, I knew because of Jack."

He looks away at the mention of his name and I turn his face so he has to look at me again.

"I'm embarrassed to even admit this, but every time you were with Callie or talked about Callie, I had this sick feeling in the pit of my stomach. I didn't like it. I guess you'd call it jealousy." His face drops as we both think of Callie.

"What does that have to do with Jack?"

"Ever notice how much time he spends with Hannah?"

"I guess."

"Doesn't bother me—even a little," I say with a half smile. "I kind of even wish they would give it a go. It'd make things a lot easier."

"Are you sure? I mean, really sure?" he asks and I nod. He pulls me to my feet and says, "Well, are you gonna?"

"Gonna what?"

"Ask. I made you a promise. I told you I wouldn't do this again until you asked. Are you gonna ask or what?"

"Okay . . . I'm askin'," I say, almost giggling. Something is coming over me and I can't say that I mind. He doesn't waste another second and his lips are on mine. He lifts me up into his arms and I dig my fingers into his hair and squeeze around his neck. It feels like I've waited an eternity for this. I'm actually feeling foolish for not seeing it earlier. It was always Bentley I was meant for. He knew it. Why didn't I?

"You know it will never work," I say as I try to slip out of his arms, but he's not letting go.

"Why not?"

"Don't be coy."

He looks down, almost disappointed, and releases me. "I'm not. Just tell me. If you're willing, we can get through any of this. Just let me help you."

"Are you saying that you can really get over the fact that it was my dad that killed your dad? That's not dysfunctional or anything."

"Oh . . . that."

"You'll never forgive me."

"Because there's nothing to forgive. You had nothing to do with that and I know why he did it."

"Why? I don't even know. It's so unlike him. He preached to me my whole life about consequences and now he's the one in prison for murder."

"He did it so you wouldn't."

I can actually feel the color drain from my face. I wouldn't have. How can he think that?

"Don't put this on yourself. I don't think you would have done it either, but you were like a caged bull. He did it out of love. He did it to protect you." I sit down. I'm so sick of feeling this way. Every time I feel like I'm getting it together, something new pops up to drive me insane. I'll go crazy with all of it.

"Then don't. Let it go," he says.

"How do you know what I was thinking?"

"Just a guess. But it's true. It's all any of us can do. If I've learned anything from Brody, it's to forgive and move on."

We sit in a comfortable silence for quite awhile as I think about everything that has happened. Can I really just move on? Is it possible to be happy again? I already feel lighter after telling Bentley how I feel. And I believe him when he says he forgives me. And although I don't know exactly what Brody meant when he was talking about Drake, something feels different, hopeful.

"Come on, race you to the top!" Bentley yells as he takes off, bounding over huge boulders. I'll never get used to that.

I've decided to pretend I'm happy as I climb to the top. I stay there for a minute and take in the breeze. It floats through my hair and I look up to the sky. Right now, here with Bentley, knowing Brody is safe and Hannah is alive, maybe I am happy. I look to Bentley and he gives me his hand. I choose to believe. I'm going to give it a shot. What do I have to lose? In this moment, I will believe . . . anything's possible.

"Look," he says as he points down to a clearing in some of the trees. It looks like Waite is exiting a cave and not far behind him is Duke.

"So that's where she went." I can't help but grin. So Waite's got a girlfriend.

"There's more." Bentley laughs.

"Whoa, is that even possible? Or more end of the world craziness?"

"No, it's possible. Happens all the time," he says, face still full of astonishment and mine must be the same. We stare in silence as we watch Duke and Waite tramp around the forest, with four little pups close behind. New life for a new world.

He smiles and gives my hand a little squeeze. "On the count of three. One, two," he says slowly.

I take a look up once more and I smile at that Chief in the sky. I don't wait for three and we leap off the boulders. In this moment, I am free.

The End

The Music of Red River

As always, anything I create can only be done with music flowing through the headphones and me being transported to a different world. Without it, the paper would continue to be blank. I'd like to share some of the music that inspired Red River.

Of course, I couldn't write Dani's story without Imagine Dragons. I worried that they might wear out their welcome after two novels, but nope, they just keep getting better and better. One new song that made it to the playlist while writing Red River is 30 Lives. Sometimes I would listen to it right before I fell asleep and from there, I got some of my greatest ideas. I could almost feel Dani sitting on the front porch of her cabin, thinking about the mess she was in and what she was going to get out of it.

NEEDTOBREATH was also huge in this book. I found them after my husband recommended them and I never turned back. I listened to the album "The Reckoning" so much; there are actually parts of the novel that I can tell were shaped by the album. Listen to track #9 and you will see what I mean. I smile just thinking about it.

I also used the album My Head is an Animal from Of Monsters and Men. It has a mystical feel to it. Dystopia and mystical belong together.

Music continued…

There's also a song by Eric Hutchinson called "Watching You Watch Him" that I can't listen to without thinking of Bentley in the corner somewhere watching, wondering how deep the connection is between Dani and Jack.

Billy Idol. If you, the reader, have finished the novel and are now reading the back, you know why Billy Idol was instrumental in Red River. He tends to bring out Dani's wild and free side.

Roxette has a special place in my heart. It's while listening to her that Dani let me know who she was in love with and who she wanted to end up with in the end. That was a surreal moment.

Acknowledgements

For my sister, Courtney. If everyone had a Courtney in their life, all people would chase their dreams. You give me the strength and the confidence to keep moving forward. You also do all the things I can't wrap my brain around and for that, I will be forever grateful.

For my children who are walking works of art, Mason, Hayden, Grayer and Ryder. They inspire me and help make the characters in my stories legitimate. They don't know it, but sometimes when they think I am staring lovingly at them in fond adoration, I'm actually studying them. Shhh . . . don't tell.

Dad, I'm not sure if you realize it, but you affect pretty much every aspect of my life, even my writing. Pay attention, you're always there.

To my new friend and edit-savvy beta reader Jennifer, we met at the Book Review Depot and have been friends ever since. Thanks for taking the time to make Red River cleaner. To everyone else at the Depot, thanks for all the great information and helping with every crazy question I had. It's nice to have such an amazing support group. Removing "salty sun" may be the best move yet. Seriously, what was I thinking?

Acknowledgements Continued…

Laura, for being responsible for my favorite part of a book, the cover. Without your creativity and expertise, I couldn't get excited about the finished product. Thank you.

To my beta readers, Red River changed dramatically because of your input. You remind me what it's like to be a reader, full of wonder and innocence at the journey of a story. That's more valuable than anything.

My aunt Shirley, you have a real eye for catching something that's out of place. Thank you.

Renee, oh, Renee. Just when I think I'm done you find even more stuff for me to fix. I didn't realize you were also of the eagle eye kind. Thank you.

Cheer, thank you for your input. I value your opinion more than you know. Somehow you have become my intended reader and I'm better for it.

Kiara, since I'm barely capable of turning a computer on, I'm incredibly grateful to have your help with all you do on the technical side.

Michael, what would the blurb be without you? Probably still not done. Thank you.

For Hailey, I'm always hoping you'll come back to me.

Author's Note

Red River is a self-published novel. If you enjoyed the read (and even if you didn't,) please consider leaving a review on Amazon or Goodreads. The most valuable asset for an Indie author is their reviews. It helps connect us to our readers and lets other readers know your opinion. Writing is our passion and seeing your thoughts (good or bad) is the best feeling in the world. It lets us know we are not alone. Thanks for all your support!

Contact Kelly Van Hull

Goodreads:
www.goodreads.com/author/show/7000882.Kelly_Van_Hull

Website:
www.kellyvanhull.com/